AGAIN

FOX HOLLOW ZODIAC NOVEL 2

MORGAN BRICE

ebook ISBN: 978-1-64795-029-3
Print ISBN: 978-1-64795-030-9

AGAIN
FOX HOLLOW ZODIAC NOVEL 2

By Morgan Brice

1

DREW

THREE MONTHS AGO

"YOU WERE THERE, at the cabin when the fight happened. I saw you." The young man glanced up and then looked down again before Drew could meet his gaze. The almost stranger lay in a hospital bed, still pale from his recent ordeal.

Drew nodded. "I was outside, but I was there. My brother, Russ, was the wolf who helped stop the Huntsman. And his boyfriend, Liam, was the fox. I'm Drew Lowe, and I'm a wolf shifter too. You're Noah Wilson, right?"

"Yeah," the man in the hospital bed replied. I think you sat with me in the car on the way back. Sorry—I'm kind of out of it right now."

Drew smiled. "Understandable. You've been through a lot. Since you and the other shifters who were captured need time to recover, they assigned each of you a buddy. I'm yours—and I'm glad to help out with anything you need."

Noah returned a shaky smile and held out his hand. "Thank you. It's nice to know someone here. I'm a long way from home."

Drew shook Noah's hand. A frisson of energy surged through the contact that left them staring at each other in surprise for an awkward moment before Drew dropped their clasped hands and looked away.

Yesterday, Russ, Drew, and their Fox Hollow friends stopped a hired Huntsman who had been capturing shifters and selling them to the highest bidder. They had turned the Huntsman over to the Tribunal authorities. The traumatized captives were admitted to the local hospital, which was customized for the needs of residents with supernatural abilities—like shifting into animal forms.

Since the doctors wanted the former prisoners to have time to recuperate from their mental and physical injuries, that meant staying in Fox Hollow for several weeks until they were well enough to go home. Hence the buddy system so that they didn't feel alone.

He's cute. I shouldn't be thinking that. I'm here to be his friend, not to ask him out, Drew scolded himself.

That doesn't change his looks. He's handsome. And he smells good—even if he is a cat. Drew's wolf eyed the stranger with interest.

He's a lynx. Behave, Drew reprimanded his other half.

It's not a crime to look. Did you feel that shiver when we touched? He's our mate. His wolf sounded certain.

Drew felt a little queasy at the sudden revelation.

I don't know what I felt, and neither of us need adding something like that right now. If we're fated mates, we'll have time to deal with it. One emergency at a time, okay? Drew was definitely not up to exploring that possibility and felt sure that Noah was probably even less in the mood for romance right now.

"Is there anything I can get for you?" Drew asked, clearing his throat. If Noah had felt surprised at the surge of energy when they touched, he covered it well.

Floofy, Drew's wolf said, teasing about the lynx's thick fur.

Noah had at least managed a shower and a shave since he and the other kidnap victims had been brought to the hospital last night. His long hair looked blonder, and without the full beard, he looked younger—close to Drew's age.

"What's going to happen to the Huntsman?" Noah glanced at the door like his kidnapper might show up at any moment. He looked vulnerable and scared, which broke Drew's heart a little.

"Okay if I sit down?" Drew asked with a gesture toward the chair beside the bed. At Noah's nod, he scooted a little closer so they could more comfortably have a conversation. "You don't have to worry about him—the sheriff turned him over to the Tribunal. They deal with crimes involving the supernatural community," Drew added because he wasn't sure how much Noah knew about the paranormal world, even though he was a shifter.

"Can they keep him in jail forever? Is he going to get out?" The slight tremor in Noah's voice warred with the resolve in his gaze.

"I don't think he's going to be a danger to anyone, ever again." From what Drew had overheard, it sounded like the Tribunal's verdict could be *final*—and fatal.

Noah swallowed hard and nodded. "Sorry. I'm not usually this off my game."

"Nothing to apologize for," Drew reassured. "You've been through a lot. Russ said the hospital was lining up counselors for everyone as well as making sure all your physical injuries are seen to. And while you're here in Fox Hollow, after you leave the hospital, you can stay at our house with Russ, Liam, and me."

"Liam was so brave," Noah said quietly. "He figured out how to open the cages. And then he gave the Huntsman a real run for his money. When it looked like Russ might get shot, Liam practically bit the guy's face off. He saved us."

Buried inside Noah's admiration, Drew could hear a kernel of guilt. *Is it weird that I feel like I've known him forever, and we've barely met?*

"Don't blame yourself—for getting caught or not doing more. You survived. That was your main job," Drew replied. Noah met his gaze, and Drew thought he saw a hunger for reassurance in the man's beautiful eyes.

"I tell myself that, but I'm not sure I believe me," Noah said ruefully. "Maybe that'll get better with time."

"I know you haven't had the best introduction to Fox Hollow, but it's a great town," Drew answered, changing the topic. "I don't know what you're used to, but almost everyone here is either a shifter or has some other paranormal ability. The few who don't have abilities are family to those who are. We get some tourists in the summer who aren't in on the secret, but otherwise this is a very supernatural-friendly place."

"Good to know," Noah replied. "I live in Ottawa. Shifters definitely aren't the norm."

Drew knew a little about Noah from Sheriff Armel. Noah was a wildlife photographer and an independent television producer who created documentaries and nature shows. He was thirty, single, Canadian, and his other half was a lynx.

I like him. I think we could really get along well.

Mate, his wolf corrected.

Too soon, Drew protested. *Let the poor guy recover.* Normally shifting accelerated the healing process, but the Huntsman had drugged his victims with something that kept them trapped in their animal form. Now that he was human again, Noah probably wasn't ready to change back right away.

"Is there anyone you need me to contact? Family, friends, work?" Drew offered, unsure whether in all the chaos the sheriff's department had already done that.

"Just Rob—he's my best friend. No family. And I'm self-employed. My film project sponsors won't notice anything unless I miss a deadline."

"I can call Rob right now for you—what's his number?"

Noah groaned. "Shit. I don't have it memorized, and the Huntsman stole my phone. But he's the manager of Tents and Treks, an outdoors equipment shop, and you should be able to look up the store."

It didn't take Drew long to find the number, and the person who picked up the call hurried to bring Rob to the phone. Drew handed it over to Noah and got up to excuse himself.

"I'll go get some coffee while you talk," he said, knowing Noah and Rob's peace of mind would be well worth the international calling charge. "Do you want me to bring some back?"

"You don't have to leave," Noah said, looking a little freaked out. "Please—stay?"

"Sure." Drew couldn't fault Noah for not wanting to be alone in a strange place. It didn't escape him that his protective instincts were going into overdrive about a man he barely knew.

I told you—mate, his wolf said, smug.

We'll see, Drew argued silently, although he feared it was a losing battle.

Even without putting it on speakerphone, Drew could hear Rob.

"Noah! Where are you? Are you okay? We've been scared to death."

Since Noah had been missing for a week, Drew didn't doubt that. Rob sounded genuinely upset, and Drew was glad Noah had someone who cared.

Are they more than friends? He doesn't know I'm gay. For that matter, I have no idea whether Noah plays for my team. What if he's my mate—and he's straight?

I don't think that's a problem, his wolf assured him. *He smells like mate.*

"It's a long story," Noah said, fending off Rob's questions with answers that avoided the paranormal issues. "I got attacked by a guy who tried to rob me when I was hiking, and then I ran away and got lost in the woods, and now I'm in the hospital. Exposure, dehydration, but no broken bones," he added with a wry chuckle. "Docs want me to stick around here for a couple of weeks. All my videos are in the Cloud, so if my computer didn't get stolen out of my SUV, I can work from here."

Drew made a mental note to find a computer for Noah to use that could handle video editing if his own was damaged or stolen. He knew it had to be difficult for Noah to stick to the script the sheriff had suggested without lying to Rob. Having a Canadian shifter involved complicated the story, because they couldn't afford to have international *human* law enforcement poking around.

The official story was that someone had tried to rob the victims, but they had escaped by running into the woods and gotten lost, only to be found by locals. The robber was apprehended and would be facing charges. The victims could go home after they were released from the hospital and given their testimony. The two who needed additional treatment would be cared for by the community until they were well enough to leave.

Sheriff Armel's version skirted any reference to the paranormal, avoided the need to explain about the Tribunal, and gave a plausible explanation for the elapsed time. Fortunately, other than Noah and Liam, the Huntsman only had one other prisoner—an ocelot shifter who was spending his recuperation time with Ty.

"Mugged? Lost in the woods? Hospital? My God, Noah! I can take off work and come get you."

Noah looked a little panicked. "No! I mean, thank you, but I'm okay for now. Thanks, man. I appreciate the offer."

"Your Tahoe is at the police impound. The cops called when they found it and couldn't reach you—I'm your emergency contact, remember?" Rob said. "They said it didn't look damaged and hadn't been broken into. So don't worry about that. Are you sure you want to stay there?"

Drew respected Rob's skepticism and felt grateful that Noah had such a good friend, although in a corner of his mind, he felt a wiggle of jealousy. *What if he's more than a friend? What if I've met Noah too late and —mate or not—his heart already belongs to someone else?*

"Yeah. The people here are really nice, and I need to get untangled a bit over what happened. Besides," Noah teased, "I know you've probably got a hot date lined up with your boy."

Drew's jealousy eased, and his wolf gloated. *See. I told you.*

"Okay—but call if you change your mind or need anything," Rob said. "Did you lose any camera equipment? If so, I can find out what you need to do to file an insurance claim."

"I'm honestly not sure yet what happened to the cameras I was carrying. If I need to file a claim, I'll take you up on your offer. Thank you," Noah said, and Drew thought that he had lost some of the tension in his body.

"Are you alone? Do you know anyone there?" Rob sounded worried.

"Actually, I do." Noah glanced at Drew with a big smile. Drew felt his heart melt a little.

Crushing on Noah is a bad idea. But I don't think I can stop, even if I wanted to.

I told you—mates, his wolf whispered.

Drew ignored him to pay attention to Noah.

"The rescue squad matched me up with a sponsor. So I've got

someone to show me around and put me up. They're taking good care of me."

"A guy, right? Is he cute?" Rob teased. "Please tell me they're not wasting some girl's time."

"It's not a dating service." Noah blushed, and his answer was a little sharper than necessary. Drew wondered if maybe, just maybe, Noah had noticed him too.

"So…yes?" Rob was clearly fishing for details.

"I'll be okay," Noah repeated. "And I'll stay in touch. Thank you for worrying about me."

"It would be a lot of work to find a new best friend," Rob said with an exaggerated tone of resignation. "And I'm lazy."

"Can you please clean out my fridge and take out my trash before it stinks up the place?"

"I'm ahead of you," Rob said with a chuckle. "Did that already. I owe you grocery money—I took what was still good and pitched the rest. Figured you wouldn't mind."

"I owe you a month of pizza," Noah said.

"Just come back safe," Rob replied, mollified but still clearly worried. "And don't make me chase you down for news."

"I promise. Now I'd better rest before Drew takes his phone back." Noah said goodbye and handed off the phone.

"He sounds like a good friend," Drew said.

Noah smiled. "He's the best. We met at a diner not long after I moved to Ottawa—kept showing up at the same time. Turned out that he lived in the building across from mine. We liked all the same movies and games, had a lot in common."

He glanced quickly at Drew as if concerned he had misspoken. "For all that, he and I never even considered dating. Not my type for that, I guess."

Drew smiled back. "I'm glad Rob's there for you. Now let me take care of you while you're here." *And longer, if my wolf is right about us. How can I feel so attracted to someone so quickly?*

His wolf opened his mouth to speak. Drew glared at him. *Don't say it.*

Don't say what? Mates? Nope. Not saying it at all. His wolf gloated. *Can you tell? I think he feels it too.*

No need to rush. Let him get better.

So he can go back to Canada? Great plan you've got. Mate him and bite him. Make him ours—even if he is a cat.

He's "floofy." You like that.

Bite me. His wolf sauntered off, leaving Drew and Noah alone for now.

Drew left when visiting hours ended, promising to return the next day. Noah seemed to be in better spirits than when he first woke, and Drew found himself hoping that the attraction between them played a part in that.

He refused to dwell on the logistical problems that could be obstacles to being fated mates and focused on getting to know Noah while he was in Fox Hollow. *If we're really fated mates, we'll figure out how to be together. And if we're not, we can be good friends while he's here.*

"I HOPE THEY FIT." Drew placed a bag on the bottom of Noah's bed when he came back the next morning. "I guessed at the sizes."

Noah looked at him, puzzled. "What's that?"

"Clothing. You didn't have any except the emergency stuff out of the lost and found from the sheriff's office—and the chic little backless outfit the hospital gave you," Drew replied with a smirk. "They're still processing the evidence in the Huntsman's cabin, but when the cops release your keys and the SUV, Russ and I will bring it to the cabin, and you can check the rest of your stuff."

Noah took in the size of the bag, which was big enough to hold several changes of shirts, jeans, underwear, and socks, as well as a pair of sneakers. "I don't have my wallet. I can't pay you back."

Drew shook his head. "I bought them, but the sheriff's emergency fund paid for everything. I hope I got the sizes right. And don't worry —there's a stipend from the fund as well, so you don't get behind on your bills while you recover."

Noah just looked at Drew, shocked. "Why? We're not from Fox Hollow. Why is everyone being so nice?"

"Because Fox Hollow takes care of its own," Drew replied, not even needing to think about his answer.

"Thank you. I'll find a way to make it up, pay it back—"

"Don't you dare." Drew's abruptly serious voice startled Noah. "Everyone here feels awful that the whole Huntsman thing got as far as it did. We should have known. Should have realized there was a danger. And we should have moved faster. So let us do right by you."

Noah looked away, adorably shy. "Your town saved me. I'm not going to quibble about who might have done something differently."

"When you're discharged, I'd like to show you around town," Drew said, surprised at the butterflies in his stomach. In his mind, he was asking Noah out on a date, even though it might not seem like that. Drew also knew he needed to not abuse his role as sponsor to pressure Noah into anything beyond friendship, and he didn't intend to.

It's just that every time he saw Noah, the pull between them felt stronger, and Drew had no idea how to deal with it. Normally, he would ask his big brother for advice, but Russ was busy dealing with Liam's post-traumatic stress from being captured. As badass as Liam could be, Drew suspected that some of the courage was bravado and that Liam took things to heart much more than he liked to let people know.

Which left Drew on his own to navigate an unusual situation.

"I know you didn't get to see much before they brought you to the hospital, but for its size, Fox Hollow is a special little town." Drew figured he might as well give Noah the travelogue since they hadn't connected yet on other topics.

"The nearest cities are still pretty far away, so the town takes pride in making sure that residents can get everything they need right here," Drew said. "Might not have every brand or color, but you won't have to drive to a larger place to get the necessities. Internet service is surprisingly good. And between you and me, this town knows how to have a good time."

"Yeah?"

Drew wondered if it was his imagination that Noah seemed to be paying more attention to him than to what he was saying.

"The library and the Fox Institute work with the town to have all kinds of cool events. There's a big Summer Arts Festival, a classic film fest at the theater, dances, street parties, snowmobile rallies, and community barbecues," Drew added, chagrined when his stomach growled from thinking about the food.

"And then there's the county fair and the holiday lights and book clubs. People here are good at coming up with ways to be together and have fun." He paused, suddenly worried he came off like a bumpkin. "I guess that's not very exciting compared to Ottawa."

Noah reached out and took Drew's hand, giving a reassuring squeeze before he let go. Drew had to stop himself from chasing that hand and capturing it once more.

"Ottawa's fun, but it's impersonal. All those events you mentioned —your neighbors came up with them to make the people around you happy. People you know and call by name. Ottawa isn't like that," Noah said.

"Who knows? By the time you're healed, Fox Hollow might be your new favorite place." *And maybe if I'm lucky, you'll decide you never want to leave.*

TWO DAYS LATER, Drew and Noah pulled up in front of the cabin. "Here we are. Home, sweet home," Drew said with a flash of pride. In the years since he and his brother Russ bought the place from their grandfather's friend, they had tweaked and improved it to make the cabin modern and more comfortable and suitable for a year-round permanent dwelling.

"Thank you again for letting me stay with you," Noah said as he got out of the car, still favoring his left leg after the encounter with the Huntsman. He carried a new duffel bag filled with a couple of changes of clothing, toiletries, some paperback books, and a temporary phone.

"Happy to help," Drew said and meant it. "Sheriff Armel says we should be able to get your Tahoe and everything in it in another day or so."

"Good," Noah replied. "My clothes and gear should be in the SUV. I wanted to catch the light, so I didn't check into a hotel before I went into the woods. I only intended to take an hour or so," he added ruefully.

His inconvenient crush aside, Drew had come to like Noah a lot from their long conversations in the hospital. So far, they hadn't run out of things to say, and the overlap in what they liked was a little spooky. Drew, suspicious Capricorn that he was, even discovered Noah's sign. Cancer—the most compatible with Drew's own.

I'm screwed. I'm going to fall for him even more over these next few weeks, and then he'll go back to Canada, and I'll be drowning my sorrows.

He's our mate. He's not going anywhere...not for long, Drew's wolf reassured him.

"Wow—this is really nice." Noah looked around at the cabin's big main room, fireplace, and oversized furnishings. "I bet it stays warm in the winter too."

"Definitely," Drew agreed. "While my wolf doesn't mind being outside in the cold, I prefer some creature comforts."

"My lynx is the same way," Noah confided.

Drew showed Noah around, pointing out where everything was located. He felt nervous as he opened the bedroom door.

"It's a two-bedroom cabin, but I added an air mattress, so I'll sleep on it, and you can have the bed." Drew looked everywhere except at Noah.

"I'm not going to kick you out of your bed," Noah protested.

I'd rather share it with you, but that's not likely to happen.

"You're recuperating," Drew countered. "And the air mattress is comfy. I insist."

Noah looked like he meant to argue, but he let out a long breath. "Okay. Thanks. That's really nice of you."

Drew wasn't sure whether it was his imagination that Noah also looked a bit red in the face and didn't make eye contact.

Two gay guys sharing a bedroom...thoughts are going to go there. But that doesn't mean we will. He and Rob might not be together, but there still could be someone back in Ottawa, Drew warned his heart. *Be his friend first, help him heal, and don't do anything stupid.*

Drew felt sure it was already too late for that.

During the next two weeks, Drew and Noah were together most of the time except when Drew was needed in the auto body shop that he and Russ ran. Noah spent that time going to counseling, doing physical therapy, or wading through the near-endless paperwork to replace the camera equipment he'd had with him that the Huntsman jumped him and the driver's license and credit cards his captor apparently burned. Noah holed up at the library during the day, and Liam helped him fill out the forms.

Drew did his best to push down his attraction to Noah, but he'd never felt anything this strong before. He didn't want to put Noah in an awkward position or have him feel he owed Drew anything. Sometimes, he thought Noah suspected his interest, especially when he caught Drew watching.

At other times, Drew could almost convince himself that Noah was watching *him.* That made him happy until his skeptical Capricorn sensibilities made him doubt.

He's our mate. Claim him, Drew's wolf insisted.

That's not how humans do things.

Amazing they haven't died out by now, his wolf snarked. *You've got to make your move before he goes away.*

Drew didn't disagree—he just had yet to come up with a way to approach Noah while making it clear that the choice was up to him.

We still have time. What if I take the chance and he isn't interested? That's going to make it very awkward for the rest of the days we have left. But if I don't even try, how will I live with not knowing?

None of Drew's previous boyfriends had been so easy and natural to be around. He and Noah never ran out of things to talk about, and the silent times together were just as comfortable as when they were joking around. The more Drew got to know Noah and heard him speak passionately about his video photography and love of nature, the deeper Drew fell for him.

Yes, he's sexy and pushes all my buttons. But I want more than just getting him into bed. I want him. *I'm happier when I'm with Noah than I've*

ever been. I feel more settled, less restless. Wolfie's right—I need to man up
and make a move. I can't risk losing him.

Bedtime was the most difficult. Drew and Noah moved around
each other in the close quarters like a dance, hyperaware and
pretending otherwise. The glimpses Drew got of Noah without his
shirt or just in his boxer briefs only made it harder to push his feelings
away.

He hurried to get under the covers before he sported an embar-
rassing hard-on. Drew also noticed that Noah kept himself angled
away so that Drew didn't get a full-frontal view of his sleep pants.

Once Noah settled into bed, he turned out the light. "Are you
asleep?"

"Still winding down," Drew replied.

"I was just thinking about my favorite restaurant in Ottawa—
Ricky's Diner—and wishing I could take you there," Noah said. In the
dark, their conversation had a confessional feel, like they could say
anything. "It's not fancy, but everything they make is good. My
favorite is the meatloaf—and the poutine. Amazing."

Drew had tried the Canadian version of what Americans called
"garbage fries"—French fries with all kinds of toppings. He'd been
surprised at how good they were.

"I found the diner when I first moved to the city from the little
town where I grew up. I didn't know anyone, and I worked for myself,
so I wasn't going to meet people in the office. Ricky's was family-
owned, and they kind of adopted me," Noah said with a chuckle.

"I was just learning how to cook for myself, so at first I ate there for
all three meals, every day. It was better than my early cooking experi-
ments or microwave dinners—or eating alone. Bonnie, the owner, took
me under her wing. She even taught me how to cook a little, so I could
look after myself."

Noah smiled in the dim light, remembering. "I got to be close
friends with the whole family, even spent my first Christmas in Ottawa
with them. And that's how I met Rob."

"Yeah?"

"I got to know the regulars, and then they were like an extended
family. Rob always came in on Wednesday and Friday nights, around

seven. I started to eat later, so we'd run into each other, and we got on well."

Noah gave a hurried glance toward Drew. "I just liked him as a friend. You'd understand if you met him—something about Rob draws people in. So we started to eat together on those nights, and things just went from there."

Talking in the dark before bedtime had become one of Drew's favorite times of the day because he got to hear about Noah's life.

"How'd you decide to move to Ottawa if you didn't know anyone and it wasn't for a job?"

"I left because my family wasn't okay with me being me."

Drew understood. "That's how Russ and I ended up in Fox Hollow. I'm sorry you had to go through that." Their family hadn't approved of Russ coming out as gay. Drew chose to leave with Russ out of loyalty to his big brother and because although he hadn't yet revealed that he was gay, he had no illusions that his announcement would go over any better.

"Don't be. It sucked, and they were wrong to be like that, but it pushed me to throw myself into photography. Maybe I wouldn't have done as much if I'd been happy and comfortable."

"You made something good out of a bad situation."

"Damn right. And I'm proud of everything I've accomplished," Noah said with conviction.

"You should be."

"Seems like you and Russ made a go of things too."

Drew chuckled. "It took a while, but yeah—we've done okay."

Noah was quiet, but Drew had the feeling he was working up to something, not falling asleep. "I'm sorry for taking up so much of your time. I'm keeping you away from your friends—and your boyfriend."

"I don't have a boyfriend," Drew answered, too quickly to be cool. "Hasn't been anyone for a while. Just...haven't clicked with anyone." *Until you.*

"Same here. No one's really fit right." He fell silent, and Drew found himself holding his breath, hoping Noah would go on.

"I really like you, Drew. I mean—I'm grateful for everything you and Russ and Liam have done for me. But this is different. I *like* you.

And I don't think it's because of all the things you've done to help me, although I appreciate them. I'm not saying this right, but you make me feel things I haven't felt with anyone. It's like we already know each other so well or spent our whole lives together. Fuck—I'm messing this up."

"I feel the same way." Drew's heart pounded, but he knew he had to take the leap. "I'm comfortable and excited all at the same time. I'm happy when we're together, even if we aren't doing anything. When we aren't with each other, I feel like I'm missing part of myself."

"My lynx thinks we're fated mates," Noah said, so softly Drew almost couldn't hear.

"That's what my wolf says too."

Noah had been lying on his back, staring at the ceiling. Now he rolled over so he faced Drew, and there was just enough light for them to see each other's faces.

"Do you want to give this a try?" Noah asked, and Drew caught his breath. "I think we both feel it, and I could swear I've caught you looking at me—when I wasn't looking at you, first. I have to go back to Canada. We'd be long-distance, but it's not far to visit, and if things work out, we can figure out what to do. So—do you wanna?"

Drew felt so happy and surprised that he didn't realize he'd stayed silent.

"Drew?" Noah's voice sounded worried.

"Yes! Oh God, yes. Sorry—I was just a little overwhelmed. I think I started falling for you that first day, but you were hurt and upset, and it wasn't the right time—"

"I'm pretty sure it was love at first sight, but I told myself it might be a concussion. Everything was topsy-turvy, and there was so much going on, but you were the anchor in the storm," Noah admitted.

"I'm glad I could help."

"You've helped a lot. But I think that what I feel for you isn't just because of that. This attraction, it feels like it's meant to be. It's not just fated, it's like we've always been together. I can't explain it, and when I say things like that out loud, they sound silly—"

"No, they don't. Because I feel the same way."

Noah smiled and held the covers open. "Then why are you all the way over there?"

Drew didn't need to be asked twice. He slid into the bed beside Noah, lying on his side so they were face to face. He caught Noah's scent: sweat, shampoo, toothpaste—and arousal. Drew didn't feel as self-conscious about his own achingly hard cock once he realized that Noah was just as turned on.

"Can I kiss you?" Drew asked.

Noah reached out and traced his fingertips down Drew's cheek. "I'd like that."

Drew leaned in, Noah met him halfway, and their lips brushed together—lightly at first and then with intent. The frisson of energy when skin met skin sent heat right to his groin. Drew let his hand slide down Noah's arm, his side, then across his chest, making sure to brush against dusky nipples. Noah caught his breath, and his body jerked toward Drew.

"Like that?" Drew teased.

Noah kissed him, insistent and hungry, giving Drew his answer. He pulled Drew closer and ran his hand down Drew's back, then cupped his ass and squeezed.

Drew bit back a moan, reminding himself at the last moment that Russ and Liam would hear if they were noisy. He let his hands roam across Noah's shoulders, down to his hipbone, and then to his ass and pulled them together.

Noah's moan set Drew's blood afire. He grabbed both of Noah's hips and pushed one thigh between his partner's legs so they could feel each other's erections through the thin fabric of their underwear.

"This okay?" Drew asked, breathless.

"Fuck, yeah."

They wriggled out of their briefs. Drew started to buck and grind against Noah, and every movement brought their oh-so-sensitive hard cocks into delicious contact. Noah's hands slid down to pull on Drew's ass so their bodies were skin-to-skin from lips to toes.

Noah let his head fall back, and Drew licked and kissed his way down from jaw to throat to the place where neck and shoulder met— where a mating bite would go. Noah shivered when Drew licked the flat of his tongue over that spot, and Drew thought he might shoot his load right then.

"God, Drew—what you do to me," Noah gasped.

"Not going to last," Drew apologized in a desperate whisper. "Wanted you since I saw you, and it's been too long since—"

"Me too."

Drew kissed Noah hard and felt the scrape of teeth. He rutted against Noah's leaking cock as they held each other tight and ground against each other. Noah rode Drew's thigh, chasing his release. Drew aligned himself just right so that every movement rubbed their dicks together until he felt Noah tense, head back, arching into the friction as his orgasm slammed through him.

Drew came seconds later, hips jerking frantically, sucking a hickey into the spot where a bite would go without breaking the skin, raising a blood mark to claim his mate with spit and spunk.

When their climaxes eased, they lay in a sweat-soaked tangle. Drew felt the rapid thud of Noah's heart, and he knew his lover—mate—could feel his own heart rabbiting in his chest.

He combed his fingers through Noah's hair and then leaned in for a slow, gentle kiss. "That was...amazing," he murmured when they came up for air.

Noah's eyes gleamed in the near-darkness. "So were you." He followed up with a searing kiss. "Sleep here, with me, from now on."

Drew nodded. "Let me get something to wipe us off, or we'll be stuck together by morning." He rolled to the edge and grabbed a discarded T-shirt, then cleaned them both.

Noah welcomed Drew into his arms, and in a love-drunk, sex-fogged afterglow, they settled down with careful touches and lazy kisses.

"Mate," Noah said, pressing the flat of his hand against Drew's bare chest over his heart.

"Mate," Drew replied, doing the same. Together in the near-dark, the words felt like a vow.

2

DREW

Current day

"Best two out of three?" Drew's adrenaline was still high from the fight. They'd been playing *Zombies: Urban Warfare* for hours, but Drew wasn't ready to quit yet.

"Dude, it's after midnight," Noah protested.

"That's not late." Drew finished off his beer and decided to reach for a bottle of water instead of another brew because it *was* almost one in the morning.

"Gotta work tomorrow," Noah replied, but Drew could hear the regret in his voice.

"Maybe I just don't want to let you go." Drew looked away, but he felt his cheeks color at the admission.

"Just until tomorrow night. We'll do video again," Noah promised.

"It's not the same as being with you." Drew knew he was pouting.

Noah snickered. "That's not what you said when I got you off last night."

Drew moaned. "Fuck, that was hot. Watching you watching me and listening to that dirty mouth of yours…getting hard again just thinking about it."

"Mmmm…tempting. But I've got to be out with the photo shoot just after dawn." Noah's regret was clear in his voice. "Raincheck? How about if I promise you a best two out of three in a *different* kind of game?"

"Not helping with the hard-on," Drew replied. "But I'll take you up on that offer. Which shoot are you doing?"

"The Hidden Byways channel hired me to do a series of wildlife video and photo shoots for their website. The money's good, and they gave me a lot of creative leeway. I plan to get the first few done here and then swing your way for a working vacation…if you'd be up for that."

"Oh, I'm totally *up* for it." Drew couldn't resist angling the camera to give Noah a good look at the bulge in his jeans. "And yes, you're welcome to stay with us."

Stay forever, he wanted to say, although it was much too early in their relationship to blurt out something like that. Except that with Noah, it felt like they'd been together forever even though they'd only known each other for less than four months.

That's because we met under extreme circumstances. Proof of life and that sort of thing.

"I was hoping you'd say that," Noah replied. He had a muscular build like his animal, with legs that were a little long for his torso, and stood a few inches shorter than Drew's height of a shade taller than six feet. Noah was a good foil for Drew, who looked like his wolf with dark brown hair, green eyes, and a notable five o'clock shadow.

And to top it all off, Drew was a Capricorn, and Noah was a Cancer —perfect match Zodiac signs.

He's cute—for a cat, Drew's wolf commented in his mind, something he felt compelled to mention frequently. *I guess he'll do since he's our mate.*

And our soon-to-be brother-in-law is a fox. Your point is?

Do you think he'd get stoned on catnip? his wolf mused. Drew ignored him.

"How long do you think it'll be before you can come back? I can think of all kinds of games that'll be more fun in person." Drew had never considered himself good at flirting, but he felt so comfortable with Noah that it seemed like second nature.

"It's going to depend on how the video shoots go," Noah replied. "I want to get a couple of episodes finished, so we have a little more 'us' time. It also depends on the animals cooperating."

"I'm still chuckling about a shifter being a wildlife photographer," Drew teased.

"Humans are people photographers," Noah said with a shrug. "Not so weird."

"Did I tell you how much I loved that video you posted with your outtakes? I laughed so hard I snorted my beer."

"Then my secret agenda was accomplished." Noah grinned, and the word that came to Drew's mind was *smitten. Do I look that love-struck? I hope so.*

"I really do need to get some sleep." Noah yawned. "I'll text you while I'm at the shoot—there's a lot of sitting around in silence waiting for something to show up. Although my Wi-Fi at the site is iffy. And I promise to make good on that raincheck," he added with a sexy smile.

"Be careful out there," Drew warned. "I know you're a big scary lynx, but bears don't care."

"Nah, you're the big, bad wolf," Noah joked. "I'm the luscious, lusty lynx."

Drew growled, a fair approximation of his wolf. "I'm totally okay with that."

Noah put his palm against the screen, and Drew did the same, fitting their hands together. "I care about you, Wolfie," Noah said. "Don't forget about me. I'll be there as soon as I can."

"I care about you too, Catman," Drew replied. "And I won't forget. You rock my world."

Noah ended the call, and Drew set his laptop aside, then fell back onto his bed, arms flung wide. *I swear it gets harder to say goodbye every time we talk. And speaking of hard...*

Drew reached for the lube on the nightstand from when they'd jacked off together earlier in the call. Although they hadn't had much time in person to explore the physical side of their budding relationship, they had done everything they could to push the limits of phone sex, sexting, and video calls in ways that would put OnlyFans to shame.

Never thought I'd be a cam boy. Just for him. And damn, he works it like a pro.

Drew was still hard from their conversation, so he didn't expect it to take long—especially after the intense climax he'd enjoyed near the beginning of their "date." In person, they'd only traded some blowjobs and hand jobs, along with a few frot sessions that would forever grace Drew's mental spank bank.

From the start, they hadn't been awkward together like Drew recalled being with his previous boyfriends. He and Noah had been in sync since the first kiss, and while everything was new, Drew felt comfortable enough that it was like they had been learning each other for years.

Drew slicked his hand and tightened his grip around his cock, as drops of pre-come added to the slide. He closed his eyes and remembered the feel of Noah's solid body against his, recalling his musky scent. Noah had kissed and touched him with confidence as if they were long-time lovers. Drew had tasted and nipped Noah with shameless abandon. The foreplay had been excruciatingly perfect, and the climaxes mind-blowing.

Drew came with a muffled cry as his release flowed over his fist. He lay still for a moment when the aftershocks subsided, tipsy with endorphins.

A cooling pool of jizz on his stomach brought Drew back to the moment. He tried to remember whose turn it was to do laundry, figured he didn't care, and wiped himself up with his discarded T-shirt.

He glanced at the darkened computer screen and sighed. It got harder to say goodbye every time, but Drew wouldn't give up their stolen long-distance moments for the world.

"Be safe, and hurry back to me," he whispered, looking at the selfie of the two of them that he had printed and framed.

He cleaned up for bed, changed into sleep pants, and brushed his teeth. *Russ and Liam must have already turned in,* he thought when his brother wasn't in the living room, and no light came from under the door to the bedroom he shared with his mate. The three of them shared a generously-sized cabin that once belonged to their grandfather's friend. A few strategic renovations had made it more comfortable and modern in the ways that mattered.

Once Russ and Liam get married—I'm sure they're thinking about it—will they want to build a new place? Should I offer to move out and look for somewhere Noah and I can be together?

In the few weeks after freeing the Huntsman's prisoners, the four of them had shared the cabin while Liam and Noah recovered. It had been a little tight but cozy, and Drew suspected their shifter need for pack outweighed more human desires for personal space.

Figuring out how to live together is a good problem to have. He got under the covers and pulled out the flannel shirt Noah had left for him. Drew had given Noah one of his shirts as well. Maybe it was a shifter thing, but Noah's scent made Drew immediately relax.

That's because we're mates, his wolf told him.

We already figured that out. We're trying to take it slow. Drew struggled to explain human insecurities to an apex predator.

You desire one another. And we would hunt well together, given the way you take cues from each other. What is the purpose of delay? Sometimes his wolf could be a jerk with a twisted sense of humor, but Drew sensed his other half's honest confusion.

There's more to it than just sex. Deciding to combine lives is complicated.

Only if you make it so.

Could it really be that simple? Drew didn't doubt that he and Noah were mates, and he knew that his boyfriend felt the same bond. Before he'd seen Russ and Liam together, Drew had wondered if fated mates were real. What he had seen of their connection convinced him and made him long to find something similar for himself.

I want it so much that it scares me. I'm afraid of screwing it up or going too fast, or finding out the whole thing is wishful thinking. Maybe I'm just afraid that every good thing comes with a bad thing. Until recently, our luck hasn't been so good.

Ten years ago, when Russ came out to their parents, he'd been disowned by his family and the pack. Drew chose to go with him since the two had always been inseparable. They had left home taking only what they could carry and gotten a room at the cheapest motel they could find that first night, heartsick and unsure of the future.

When their grandfather's friend heard what happened, he tracked them down and offered them the cabin. He told them that his fishing days were over and that the house was theirs if they wanted, but it needed some fixing up. They just had to get to Fox Hollow.

Wolves don't believe in luck. If you see something you want, run it to ground and seize it with your teeth.

Wolf logic.

What other kind is there?

Drew started his playlist of Noah's videos. It was long enough to get him through most of the night listening to his boyfriend's voice narrating the nature movies. His wolf sauntered to the recesses of his mind, and Drew curled up with a pillow draped with Noah's shirt. As he drifted off, he found himself hoping with all his heart that his wolf was correct.

"LATE NIGHT?" Russ seemed to delight in giving Drew a hard time about his new-found romance.

"Jealous, old man? We're still young and virile."

"Which is why you look like something the cat dragged in? Oh wait, it did!" Russ joked. He socked Drew playfully in the arm.

"Funny—the first time. Now, not so much." Drew dodged the well-telegraphed punch. *Once brothers, always brothers.*

"Better suit up—we've got a full schedule," Russ warned him. The two of them had built Lowe's Automotive Care from the ground up, taking over an old service station and creating a one-stop repair/towing service that met the needs of tourists and Fox Hollow residents year-round—and did its share of snowmobile and boat engine repairs as well.

Drew had originally worried that living and working together might strain their relationship, but they had always been close, and the stress of starting over had pushed them even closer. Now, there was nowhere Drew would rather be.

So what does that mean for Noah? He's Canadian. Will he be willing to move to Fox Hollow? Can I ask that of him?

Drew pushed his worries from his mind. He stopped in the break room for another cup of coffee and looked up as Liam swanned in with his usual panache.

"Donuts!" Liam announced, dropping a box on the table with a resounding *thwack*. "Jack has outdone himself. There are three new varieties—strawberry-margarita, peach-mango, and coconut-banana. I might have had to wait in line for an hour if I didn't call in a favor and meet him at the back door."

Russ walked in and grinned when he saw his mate. He grabbed Liam and pulled him into a hug. "Couldn't resist stopping at Bear Necessities again, huh? You brought some for us so we'd share in the guilt."

"I admit nothing," Liam announced. Even in human form, it wasn't difficult to glimpse his fox. Almond eyes with a hint of natural kohl, red hair, a lithe build, and a natural swagger proclaimed his other side. All that drama presented a perfect counterpoint to Russ's steady nature.

Russ and Drew bore a strong family resemblance, but Russ's brown hair had been flecked with gray since his twenties, close to the shade of his wolf, with gray-green eyes. Drew's coloring was nearer to the russet tones of his wolf, but the eyes made it clear he and Russ were related.

"Drew, how's that sexy lynx of yours? When are you going to bring him home for good?" Liam demanded after he'd greeted Russ with a kiss.

"Soon," Drew promised, grinning. "He said to say 'hi' to everyone, by the way."

"I've caught some of his videos," Liam said as he scarfed a peach-mango donut and washed it down with a sip of his take-out cup from the café. "He's got a lot of talent."

"I suspect that one advantage for wildlife photography is being wildlife yourself," Drew replied, snagging a strawberry-margarita donut. Their friend Jack, a possum-shifter, was the night baker at Bear Necessities, and his inventive donut flavors had become a local obsession.

"Tell your boy that the library would love to do some kind of film festival of his work for the Spring Fling," Liam said over a mouthful of pastry. "His videos have won awards in Montreal and Toronto, but he hasn't made the big time until he's headlined a Fox Hollow festival," he added with a broad wink.

My boy. I like the sound of that.

"He's planning to visit soon. Maybe you two can knock some ideas around. I'm sure he'd be interested." Drew's wolf bristled at the idea of sharing any of Noah's time with someone else.

Down, boy.

Noah is ours.

And Liam is Russ's mate. There's no threat. Stand down.

His wolf growled and gave Liam the side-eye, then stalked off.

Liam kissed Russ goodbye and headed for the library.

Russ and Drew changed into their garage coveralls, and by the time they came out of the locker room, Jimmy and Steve, the other mechanics, had arrived.

"Liam brought donuts," Russ announced as he headed to the front desk. "I'm going to check the day's schedule and take Kerrie coffee and a donut so she takes pity on booking us."

"You'll need the sugar," Drew heard Kerrie, their office manager, tell Russ as she handed over a clipboard with the list of repairs and appointments for the day. "Busy roster. Also reminding you that set-up for the Fire Department fundraiser starts at five."

"Okay," Russ replied, "I'm officially reminded." His tone never changed, but Drew knew his brother well enough to see the stress in his shoulders. He was probably figuring out how to get it all done.

"Let's play it by ear," Drew suggested. "I volunteered for clean up, but if you're still busy at five, we can swap."

"Thanks," Russ said, and the gratitude in his smile made Drew happy.

Russ took his role as the older brother seriously—sometimes too much so, at least in Drew's opinion. Add to that the wolf dynamic of protecting their little pack—which in Russ's view extended beyond Liam and Drew to include their closest friends and the shop crew— and Drew's big brother could be a bit much at times.

Drew knew Russ's behavior came from the best intentions, and he appreciated all the hard work and sacrifices it took to build up the garage business and create a life for them here in Fox Hollow. He loved his brother dearly. They'd been through a lot together, spent years relying largely on each other. It had been difficult at first to allow friends into an inner circle. Untangling themselves to allow room for partners was a new challenge for both of them.

How will Russ take it if Noah moves in? Even though he has Liam, how well will he "share" me with Noah?

Drew shimmied underneath the first car of the day. His thoughts careened from wondering what Noah was doing, to thinking about where to take him on dates when he came to town, to considering how to handle living arrangements when he and Russ finally settled down with their partners.

In between cars, Drew checked his phone, happy at the texts he saw from Noah. Some were photos or video snippets from his current shoot. Others bemoaned snags in setting up his cameras or shared funny memes. Noah made naughty suggestions and assured Drew that he had plenty of ideas on how they could get reacquainted. Drew raised the stakes and outlined a few of his fantasies, which left him hard and aching.

Russ jostled Drew's shoulder accidentally-on-purpose in the break room, and Drew hurriedly tilted the phone to hide the screen.

"I don't care how many eggplant emojis he sends you, no 'alone time' in the garage bathroom," Russ said under his breath.

"Screw you."

By the time five o'clock rolled around, Drew had already figured out that Russ wouldn't be done with his repair on time.

"I'm sorry." Russ slid out from under the car he was fixing. "Can you cover for me at the firehouse? You'll get to go home early since I'll handle the clean-up."

"I don't mind," Drew assured him. "And I'm okay with helping afterward if you need me."

"Thanks, bro. You're the best." Russ's tired smile made Drew glad he had offered.

Drew changed out of his coveralls, and headed down the street toward the combined firehouse, police station, and sheriff's office, where he and Russ both volunteered as firefighters. He got a quick shower, which sluiced away the grime and grease of the day.

Fox Hollow was a small town with a big secret. Misfit shifters who didn't fit with their own kind founded it as a haven. Later, outcast psychics found their way to the town and made a place for themselves at the Fox Institute, a center for studying parapsychology. Both groups coexisted in peace, and so did different kinds of shifters—predators and prey. If the town had one central rule, it was "don't eat your neighbor."

"So you're the 'new' Russ?" Brandon Davis joked when Drew showed up. "Big surprise. Covering for your big bro?"

"Yep. Surprised?" Drew asked. Brandon was one of Russ's best friends and part of their regular poker group. The tall, gangly man was a moose shifter, just as adorably awkward as his human counterpart.

"Russ is finishing a transmission. We swapped start and finish duties," Drew added.

"Pay up!" Justin Miller, another poker buddy—and the only non-shifter in their friend group—elbowed Brandon. "I told you Russ wouldn't get here on time."

He still walked with a slight limp after a building collapse during a fire several months ago damaged his knee but was healing well. Justin wasn't a shifter, but his weather-witch talents came in handy with his seaplane business. He was back to flying but wasn't ready to resume his fire department duties just yet.

"You bet on us?" Drew rolled his eyes, not surprised.

"We just know your brother," Justin said. He glanced across the firehall to where Tyler Williams was setting up a drink station. "Don't we, Tyler?"

"Whatever, Justin. Get your ass over here and help me with the tables," Tyler replied. "Drew and Brandon—as we get the tables set up, put out the bake sale and craft items with the price cards. We've only got a little over an hour—so move your asses!"

Drew heard some of the other firefighters bantering in the kitchen as they prepped the corn dogs, French fries, and fried cheese curds that were part of the fundraiser.

Fox Hollow's fire department covered a broad territory, both the town and the areas surrounding it. Here in the Adirondacks, cities were few and far between. Fire remained a constant risk in a huge forest, and medical emergencies required towns to be self-sufficient.

That put a heavy burden on the firefighters to act as first responders for all kinds of incidents, especially during the worst of the winter months when Fox Hollow could be cut off from the outside world for days or weeks at a time.

Fundraisers helped cover expenses that weren't part of the budget, which could range from replacement parts for the truck to repairs to the firehouse. They also brought the community together and served as a fun gathering to liven up long, dark nights.

"Man, these cookies look amazing. Do you think anyone would notice if I—" Brandon eyed the chocolate chip plate longingly.

"Yes. They would. Unless you want to pay for it," Drew replied. Brandon sighed and Drew understood. The cookies not only looked fantastic, but he bet their baker friend, Jack, made them and that they tasted just as good as they looked.

"That's the problem with bake sales. I end up giving a chunk of my paycheck back to the firehouse because I've never met a dessert I didn't like," Brandon admitted.

"Occupational hazard," Drew agreed. "You know I'll be buying the corn dogs."

Tyler was the youngest of their group of friends, still in his late twenties. The rest ranged within the two-year difference between the brothers, ranging from thirty-three to thirty-five. Justin flew seaplanes, Brandon was a guide, and Tyler—a bobcat shifter—helped his parents manage their motel on the shore of Fox Lake.

After the tables were set up and the sale items laid out, Drew and the others hung banners and decorations and did their best to give the utilitarian all-purpose room a party atmosphere.

"I think it looks pretty damn good." Drew stood back after they had finished the last few swags of crepe paper streamers.

"Fuck yeah," Tyler replied. "We should be event planners and bring in the big bucks."

Drew's phone buzzed, and he stepped away to read the messages he'd missed. When he got a call, he walked to the storage room to answer.

"Hey, what's up? And just to let you know, I'm at the fire department fundraiser, so keep it G-rated—for now," he warned Noah.

"I just wanted to hear your voice," Noah replied.

"Everything okay?" Drew thought Noah sounded sad.

"Yeah—except for being a couple of hundred miles away from you. The shoot's going well, but there's a lot I don't control because the wildlife is...wild." Noah sounded tired. "There's also not much to do except the shoot. The nearest town has one diner, one grocer, and a general store. Cellular is spotty and the hotel Wi-Fi sucks. I brought books to read when I'm not prepping for the next shoot, but...it leaves me a lot of time to think about what I want to do when we're together."

"Go to better restaurants? See a movie? I know—midnight bowling!" Drew teased.

"Fuck you," Noah responded. "No, wait, that *is* what I want to do..."

Usually at this point in the conversation, their shared fantasies got descriptive. Drew didn't want to spend the next two hours with a hard-on. "Save those thoughts for later. Even if I stay to help clean up, I shouldn't be home much later than ten. I'll need you to *lift* my spirits."

"Oh, I'll give you a *rise*," Noah promised. "Go do your thing. Talk to you later."

While Noah had no close relatives, he never questioned Drew's deep loyalty to his brother and their group of friends. *Compatible signs,* Drew thought, remembering that both Capricorn and Cancer placed a big emphasis on family.

When the doors opened at seven, plenty of their friends and neighbors crowded into the fire hall. Tyler had rigged a sound system and took requests for a dollar a song. Liam brought a tableful of used library books and sold them to benefit the firehouse.

Brandon did a brisk business selling the donated crafts and baked goods, while the guys in the kitchen could barely keep up with orders.

Drew sold raffle tickets for the prizes donated by local merchants. Familiar voices called out greetings, and people waved over the heads of the crowd since it felt like the entire town had shown up.

"Great turnout." Rich Jeffries handed over five dollars for a string of tickets.

"This time of year, people love an excuse to have some fun," Drew replied. Late fall brought cold rain, early nights, and the certainty that winter was just around the corner.

"Can't blame them for that. And for its size, Fox Hollow serves up plenty of options. Our fall classes are full, and signups have been better than usual for the Paranormal History lecture series." Dr. Jeffries was the director of the Fox Institute and a psychic in his own right.

He'd been one of Liam's college professors in Ithaca back in the day, which was how Liam found the town. Jeffries was in his mid-forties and looked like a teacher, with dark hair graying at the temples and light blue eyes.

Drew hadn't had much reason to connect with the Fox Institute folks, but he remembered how much the psychics and witches had helped when some of their friends had been in big trouble. He didn't doubt their abilities; he just hoped he never had reason to ask for their aid.

Russ walked in during the last fifteen minutes of the fundraiser. His hair was wet from a shower, and he looked clean and presentable after scrubbing away the motor oil and dirt of the day.

"Wow—they cleaned us out." He stepped up to help Drew sell tickets to the remaining people waving bills at them. Drew looked at the ticket roll that was a third of the size of the massive wheel he'd started with and glanced around for the first time in an hour.

The baked goods were gone, and only a few craft items remained. As he watched, Liam sold the last book on his table with a broad grin and a big "thank you" to the buyer. A hand-printed sign explained that the kitchen was out of food. Tyler still accepted song requests, but time was running out to play them, and the donation jar was full.

"We have the best neighbors in the whole world." Drew felt a little overcome at the turnout and the generosity of the community.

"You've got that right." Liam sauntered over and greeted Russ with a kiss. "You missed the party." He managed to flirt and gently chide at the same time. "I don't know what I'm going to do with you."

"I have suggestions," Russ replied with a smirk.

"TMI!" Drew protested in mock horror.

"Why don't you go home and call your lynx?" Liam told Drew. "I'll help Russ with the cleanup."

Drew glanced to Russ, who made a shooing gesture. "Go. You've had a long day. Just keep the volume down on your phone call, or I'll have to bleach my brain—again."

The cold night air cleared Drew's head as he walked back to the garage to get his car. Usually he and Russ drove together, but with the fundraiser, they brought two cars. The winter wind swept away the adrenaline crash after the event ended, cooling him after the hours spent in the packed, too-warm firehall.

Just thinking about talking with Noah gave him a semi. *I've got it bad.*

Once he got home, Drew stuffed his work clothes in the washing machine, set his clean coveralls out for the morning, and checked the fridge to make sure they had food handy since he knew Russ hadn't eaten. He glanced at the time and then made a ham and cheese sandwich for his brother. He put the plastic-wrapped plate in the fridge, left a note on the counter, and headed for his room with time to spare.

Weeks of separation from Noah between visits meant Drew had lost his self-consciousness about phone sex or sexy video calls. As the time went by, he paid more attention to his room as a backdrop, making his bed, tidying the area seen by the camera, and even bringing in candles to set the mood.

If Russ noticed the candles, he was either too stunned or appalled to tease him.

Drew locked the door, reached for the lube, and stripped. While he waited, he got comfortable, propping himself up on pillows to be half-reclined, which provided a good view if they ended up using video. He tucked in his earbuds, spread his legs, and ran his hands down his chest, rolling his nipples between thumb and forefinger until they hardened into nubs.

He squirted some lube into his palm, warming it before giving his half-hard cock a couple of strokes that sent his blood rushing south. Drew kept a lazy rhythm with light friction, just enough to keep him hard but not sufficient to get him close to climax.

His phone rang right on time. "Sorry—the hotel's Wi-Fi is really slow tonight, so video's out tonight. You'll just have to be *satisfied* with my sexy voice and my very naughty ideas." Noah dropped his voice into a lower register that sent a shiver down Drew's spine.

"I think that will *take care of things* very nicely." Drew hoped he sounded half as sexy.

"What are you doing?" Noah asked, practically purring.

"I'm on my bed, with the lights low, touching myself. How about you?"

"Mmm...I like the sound of that. I've got my legs spread, one hand on my dick, and I'm on my knees opening myself up with two fingers, thinking about taking that pretty cock of yours as deep as it'll go."

"Oh my God," Drew gasped, thinking he might come right then at the mental image. "I wish I could see you. And you know I'd like to switch."

"Oh, I know. Gonna do things every which way once we're together," Noah murmured. He moaned and Drew guessed Noah had brushed against his sweet spot.

"Are you hard? Because I'm hard just thinking about us together." Drew ignored the blush that came to his cheeks. He'd had a couple of boyfriends and lost his virginity in high school, but while he'd been fond of some prior lovers, he'd never been in love. Not the way he felt about Noah.

"Not just hard, I'm practically blue I want you so bad," Noah panted. "Tell me what you're thinking."

Drew smiled. "Once I get you alone, I want to give you the best blowjob you've ever had. Gonna peel your pants off, push those briefs down, and deep throat you. I don't have much gag reflex if you remember."

"Oh, I definitely remember. Fuck, Drew—that sounds so good."

"Gonna lick you and suck you and tease my tongue up the vein, give you a little scrape of teeth along the way, and run the tip through your slit—"

Noah's moan made it clear that Drew's words had pushed him over the top, which brought Drew's climax seconds later.

"That was—" Noah sounded fucked out, and Drew wished he could see his face.

"Yeah, it definitely was," Drew agreed. "Give me a sec to clean up. These nightly calls are great, but I'm going to be permanently stuck on laundry duty."

"Worth it?"

"Definitely." Drew wiped up with his T-shirt, pulled on sleep pants, and got back into bed, feeling boneless and sated.

"Everything go okay at the fundraiser?" Noah sounded equally blissful.

"It was a big success. That's Fox Hollow for you." Drew told him all about it since they'd found that even the trivia of each other's days was fascinating after so much time spent apart.

"I'm glad it worked out. I got the video shots I wanted today, although the light could have been better, and the wind was the devil's own. I would have shifted to my lynx if the scent wouldn't have scared off the animals I was trying to film."

Noah talked about camera angles and remotely triggered video and editing, details that would otherwise make Drew's eyes glaze over but now seemed fascinating.

"Do you have anything new posted? I've watched everything that's up—several times." Drew hadn't admitted to listening to the episodes as he fell asleep each night. That seemed a bit over the top, even for his love-addled state.

"Not yet, sorry," Noah replied. "Like I said, the hotel's Wi-Fi signal sucks, but this is where I needed to be for the shoot. It's a pretty place, but the hotel is old and the plumbing creaks. At least the heat works."

"Are you still on schedule?" Drew didn't want to push, but the weeks until they could visit stretched out like an eternity. A very horny, frustrating eternity.

"For the most part. That's the thing with wildlife—you can track their paths and look for footprints, but just because they went that way yesterday doesn't mean they will today. Animals are fucking fickle."

"Says the lynx."

"Laugh it up, wolf boy," Noah joked back.

"If you came to Fox Hollow, I could get our friend, the moose shifter, to help with your video. You could explain it to him, and he'd remember when he shifts."

"That's cheating," Noah protested.

"He's a real moose. Just…trainable." Drew yawned despite his best efforts not to. "I'm falling asleep—wish you were here."

"I was dead on my feet *before* the mind-blowing orgasm. Now I'm boneless."

"Mind-blowing, huh?" Drew teased.

"Definitely. Just remember—there's more where that came from." Noah sounded groggy. Drew pictured him warm beneath the covers, still smelling of sweat and spunk.

"You're going to have so many rain checks you'll never leave Fox Hollow," Drew said, realizing after the words were out that he'd said more than he intended, although he didn't regret it.

"I might take you up on that, and then what would you do?" Noah's voice was a low rumble, and Drew wondered if whiskey roughened its edges. He'd poured a shot for himself that was on the nightstand, a way to blunt the loneliness that always came when he and Noah ended their calls.

"Enjoy every minute," Drew told him and meant it.

"Me too. Maybe…" Noah might have drifted off then. "I need to… get some sleep. Good night, Drew."

"G'night, Noah. Dream about me, okay?"

"Every night," Noah confessed. "Talk to you tomorrow. Take care."

"You too," Drew replied and meant *I think I've fallen in love with you.*

Drew set his laptop to the side and pulled up the playlist of Noah's videos. He sipped his shot of whiskey, relishing the burn. Usually, he was more of a beer fan, but loneliness and longing made the bite of whiskey a pleasure.

I'm so far gone for him; I don't know what I'll do if he doesn't feel the same.

But deep in his heart, Drew felt more certain than he'd ever been. *We're mates. Fated. And maybe more...*

He drifted off to the sound of Noah's soothing voice and soon found himself lost in dreams. Since Noah had gone north, Drew's dreams had changed, gradually growing more detailed and vivid.

At first, Drew hadn't remembered what he'd seen as he slept, with the memory growing hazy come morning. As time went on, he recalled more and more and started making notes so he could share the strange stories with Noah. Tonight's dream was no different.

Drew's right hand combed through soft dark hair while his left pulled his lover closer. Their kiss deepened, shifted until he ached with longing. The man in his arms returned the kiss with passion, holding onto Drew like he was drowning, his erection hard against Drew's thigh through their trousers.

"Want you," Drew murmured, knowing they had to be quiet, that they didn't dare be found out.

"Want you just as much," his lover whispered. "Tonight, come up the back way after the lights are out. Can you find your way in the dark?"

Drew nodded, though part of him wondered at the need to hide. Gentle fingers combed through his hair and stroked down his cheek.

"Be careful. It's a risk—" his lover said.

"It always is. But you're worth it."

Their arms slipped around one another, and over his lover's shoulder, Drew caught a glimpse of them in a mirror on the wall.

What the hell? Drew didn't recognize the eyes that stared back at him, in a face not his own. The man in his embrace was a stranger and yet known in his marrow. They were dressed in a style that made Drew think of the 1920s— shirt and trousers, suspenders, and starched collars.

Drew woke with a start, heart pounding, cock hard as steel. The lingering grief he felt over the two lovers in his dream ached like a new wound.

They had to hide what they felt for each other, who they were to one another. If they'd been found, they would have been jailed—or worse. But they didn't give up. They hung on. What happened to them? They couldn't marry, but did they remain together? Did they make a way to have their love? Were they happy?

Something about the long-ago lovers reminded Drew of him and

Noah, though they looked nothing alike and more than a century separated them.

Who were they? Were they real? And why do I care so much?

Questions circled in his mind until he finally fell asleep clinging to Noah's soothing voice, and this time he did not dream.

3

NOAH

"I WISH YOU COULD SEE THIS VIEW IN PERSON—EXCEPT FOR HOW COLD IT is." Noah snapped a photo that didn't do the colors of dawn justice, and sent it with his text to Drew.

He waited for a reply and realized Drew probably wasn't awake yet. *No one in their right mind is up at this hour.*

He'd made the best of the cramped hotel room, knowing from experience to bring an extra blanket, good pillow, books, and power strips. Hotels never had enough outlets to charge his cameras. Fortunately, travel wasn't a constant, but staying overnight to get the right light or have time to set up cameras happened fairly often.

Will that be a problem with Drew? Will he resent my photography? It's a demanding job.

Noah cleaned his lenses and checked his batteries as he packed his day bag. Travel made it easy to find overnight company without entanglement, and he'd long ago grown tired of waking up alone. He'd had a serious relationship back in film school, which fizzled after graduation. There were a few boyfriends who lasted more than a month or two, but his irregular hours always ended up being more than anyone wanted to deal with for long.

Can it be different with Drew? We felt such an immediate bond—I've never had a connection like that with anyone. It's like we've known each other forever.

"Of course. We're fated mates," his lynx reminded him, as if Noah could forget.

He smiled, thinking of their conversation that ended only a few hours ago. It wasn't just the sex—although that was combustible in a way Noah had never experienced before. Everything took on a different light when it involved Drew. Talking about the trivial activities of the day wasn't boring. Sharing a movie or even reading the same book and talking about their reactions now felt satisfying and fun.

I'm a Cancer—we're protective and defend our family. Except I don't really have any.

Noah didn't have many living relatives. His father had vanished when he was young, and his mother died two years ago from a bad heart. He had a brother and sister, but they drifted apart, and Noah hadn't heard from them in years. He wasn't sure he even had valid addresses for them.

Drew is my mate. He's my family now. And he has Russ and Liam and their friends. A pack. Someday, they'll be my pack.

Clowder, his lynx sniffed. *Lynxes have a clowder, not a pack.*

Sounds like soup.

Clowder is not chowder, silly human. But we could vote to let Drew be an honorary lynx and join.

Vote? Who—you and me?

We are the only ones in our clowder now. It would be nice to add our mate —even if he is a dog.

Wolf.

Canine.

I've fallen hard. And it should scare me. But it doesn't. When I worry that he might not feel the same, I can't breathe.

Noah felt certain that Drew cared for him, but was it love? Would it survive their separation? And what happened when his upcoming visit came to an end? How many times could he come and go before Drew had enough?

Noah realized he had stopped packing, lost in his thoughts. He thought he finally understood the term "besotted."

Would I move to Fox Hollow to be with Drew? That's assuming I could get a visa, work out the details. I can't ask him to leave his brother and friends and be a vagabond like me.

Noah had a comfortable apartment on the outskirts of Ottawa, where he spent his time when he wasn't on a shoot. That gave him access to the film industry based in the nation's capital, as well as universities that paid well for guest lecturers with solid resumes. Montreal wasn't far, with all that city had to offer. Both cities were gay-friendly, and he enjoyed the nightlife.

Rural New York? It wouldn't be the same. But Fox Hollow is different. Special. I felt it just in the time I was there recovering. If this works out between us, if Drew wants a commitment, could I be happy there? I know I could do my work—but would I miss everything I'd be leaving behind?

He didn't have the answers, and it scared him because his heart had taken off without waiting for his head. *Heart and soul*, he thought. *And, okay, my dick's involved too.*

And there's that crazy Cancer streak again—pessimistic. I feel too much, and I want security. Blame it on the stars.

"Gotta get moving," he reminded himself. Once he stowed the last of his gear and packed enough food for the whole day plus a huge Thermos of coffee, he got ready to head out.

Dressing for the weather wasn't just a matter of comfort—it meant life or death in the extreme temperatures in the far north. That required layers and plenty of them. Wool clothing and waterproof, insulated outerwear. Gloves that let him manipulate electronics and camera controls and a hat that wouldn't fight with his headset. A ski mask and long scarf to protect his face and a snorkel parka rated for the lowest temperatures. Even with all his gear, Noah knew he'd be miserably cold before the shoot was over.

That's because we aren't in our fur. I'm almost never cold, his lynx pointed out.

Hard to use the cameras with paws and claws. We've tried.

Pfft. I can catch us dinner, keep us warm, and find a den for the night. So what if I can't use the picture box? His lynx actually sounded miffed.

You're a totally badass kitty-cat. Except for the camera part.

The flick of his lynx's tail said his animal side wasn't completely mollified.

He'd barely suited up when his phone rang, and he fished the waterproof case out of a zippered pocket.

"Are you on location yet?" Rob Girard, his best friend, sounded like he'd already had a few cups of coffee.

"Just heading out. What's up?" Drew made a last check of his supplies and equipment. He connected his earbuds and put the phone back in his pocket as he loaded his Chevy Tahoe.

"I'm checking in. When you get back, let's get dinner. There's a good band playing all week at The Buck Stops Here."

"Sounds fun," Noah agreed. "Buck's" as the bar was called by regulars, had good food, Molson on tap, and a huge collection of antlers that were used in all of its decor. "Things okay at the store?"

"Yeah. All the snow lately has been good for business. Except I've been working extra shifts, so I haven't been out on the slopes myself."

Rob worked for a large local outdoor outfitter. When time permitted—which wasn't often enough—he and Noah loved to go snowboarding.

I wonder if I can get Drew into boarding. Do wolves like that sort of thing? Noah's cat reflexes were perfect for the physical demands of the sport. Rob was human—and clueless about the existence of shifters and supernatural creatures—so his snowboarding skills came from practice and talent.

"You're on—if I don't freeze my nuts off."

Rob chuckled. "Your boyfriend wouldn't like that. Better keep the crown jewels and the royal scepter warm and cozy."

"Funny. You're hilarious."

"I think so."

The call ended, and Noah looked at his phone background, a selfie of him and Drew together. *Soon.*

"Fuck winter," Noah muttered as his breath formed ice crystals on the knitted wool of his ski mask. The Tahoe warmed up while he brushed several inches of snow off the hood, cleaned the windshield, mirrors, and back window, and checked to make sure no one had plowed him in overnight.

The defogger warred with the cab heat as Noah drove out to the trail head. At this hour, there weren't a lot of people around, but then again, there weren't many folks in the Papineau-Labelle Wildlife Reserve at this time of year.

Most of the time, Noah enjoyed the solitude. He loved capturing the perfect moment, sharing his love of nature and wild things. Maybe that came from being a shifter, but he thought it went even deeper. The smell of balsam, the rustle of branches in the wind, and how the late afternoon sun glittered on fresh snow spoke to his soul. Even the best photographs and videography couldn't completely capture how natural beauty looked to the naked eye, but Noah had sworn to come as close as possible.

He'd had remote cameras set up for a few days. They'd help with shots showing the wildlife entering and leaving the clearing his film would document as being an important crossroads for the animals who lived here.

Who knows—I might capture Bigfoot on tape someday.

What would you do with such a thing if it showed up? his lynx asked. *It would not make a good pet.*

Take a picture. But I couldn't show it to anyone because Bigfoot isn't supposed to exist.

Then what is the point? I don't understand why your picture box makes you happy.

It's called "art."

Can we eat art? Will it keep us warm? Does it fuck?

My pictures buy you the crunchy treats you like and chew toys.

Those keep my hunting skills sharp. They're not toys.

Which is why you like the ones with the squeaky?

Those are prey noises.

Whatever. Arguing with his lynx half seemed childish, but he knew that when it counted, his other side always supported him.

Noah hummed quietly as he went about setting the video cameras, checking the remotes and batteries, and brushing away the prints from his snowshoes when he was finished. At the edge of the clearing, his pup tent—camouflaged by branches—would provide shelter from the wind and damp, while giving him line-of-sight to his cameras and the entire open space. His main video camera was mounted just outside the tent, also hidden except for the lens. A heavy-duty sleeping bag would keep him from freezing, as would the chemical and recharge-able hand warmers stuffed in his pockets.

The rest of the day passed in a blur as Noah monitored the cameras, watched animals cross his clearing, and kept an eye on the feeds on his phone. Cell coverage was spotty. In between good shots, Noah read a spy thriller, texted Drew, loaded off-line content when he got a decent signal, and appreciated the view.

His love of nature had determined his career choice after one disas-trous summer when he thought being a park ranger might be a good fit. It wasn't, and Noah knew that while he wanted to spend time outdoors, he didn't have the patience to be a guide. Chaperoning clue-less city folk through the forest didn't sound like a good time. He was good at skiing and snowboarding, but not enough to become an instructor. Then Noah discovered photography and videography and knew he'd found his calling.

Most of his work came from local PBS stations and environmental groups, organizations that had a stake in preserving the area's natural beauty. Noah knew he was fortunate to make a living in a tough busi-ness. After ten years he'd won enough awards and had sufficient recognition that referrals kept coming.

Would that change if I went to Fox Hollow? I can still always travel back to Canada if that's a sticking point. Does it matter where I film a moose in a forest?

If you were in your fur, you'd be warmer. Noah's lynx spoke up.

I'm here to take pictures of animals you'd want to eat. They'd smell us and run away.

Then you could go home, let me out, and I can sleep on our bed. His lynx might be a wild animal, but he appreciated the finer things like mattresses and chew toys.

This is how I pay for food. And our apartment.

You don't have to buy food. I can hunt.

Pass. I am not eating raw rabbit—or squirrel.

Not my fault you're a picky eater, his lynx said with a sniff. *Although I like our den.*

Apartment.

Do we sleep there? Store our food? Keep ourself safe? Then it's a den.

Whatever.

What does the dog think of our den? The lynx in his mind sounded curious—and a little jealous.

Drew's a wolf, not a dog.

He barks and lifts his leg. Dog.

Noah sighed. *You've got to get over this specie-ist shit. I'm in love with a wolf shifter. Deal with it.*

He seems nice enough, his lynx admitted. *And he smells like "mate." But how are we going to fit into a canine household? Big cats...we have our ways of doing things.*

You know, that's something I like about Fox Hollow. You can be the kind of shifter you want, and no one tells you that you're wrong.

One of his brother's friends is also a cat. I caught his scent.

That's Tyler. Bobcat shifter. Maybe we can run together.

Fox Hollow might not be too bad if we're not the only big cat.

Noah smiled, realizing that his lynx had already accepted Drew as their mate but liked to give him a hard time about it.

I think one of the women in the library is a Maine Coon.

His lynx sniffed. *House cat.*

Dude, those can be almost as big as we are.

Still a pet. His lynx growled, hating to lose the argument, and stalked off, hackles rising at Noah's good-natured laughter.

It was just as well that his lynx wandered away because Noah needed his full attention for the cameras. His secondary equipment captured plenty of deer, rabbits, and squirrels, but this shoot was all about getting footage of moose, which were known to pass through the clearing at this time of year. If he could get the shots he wanted, it would complete the episode he'd been working on, leaving him only two more to finish before he could visit Drew.

Noah lost himself in the craft of his work, trusting experience and instinct to get the best shots. This was what he loved about what he did, what drove him to create.

When Noah got caught up in the videos, he lost track of time, forgot to eat, ignored the cold. He'd learned the hard way to set his phone's alarm to break the spell and keep him grounded. Out here in this weather, losing track of time could kill even a lynx shifter.

I wonder what Drew's doing. I bet he's warm and dry. Do I cross his mind as often as I think of him? Gods, I'm addled by the guy.

Late in the afternoon, Noah emerged from the tent to check the cameras. He downloaded the footage to his laptop, chafing at how long it took but relieved that he didn't have to take the cameras back into town with him.

Tonight he would check the shots and make sure he had good footage. Tomorrow was the final day here, and Noah planned to spend the next night at the clearing. Getting shots of the nocturnal activity would be worth enduring the cold.

Noah went to his tent and gathered what needed to go back to town with him, leaving the rest of his camp in place for tomorrow night after closing up the tent. That would save him time tomorrow, which meant more opportunity to wield his best camera for key shots. *And then I can go home…for a little while.*

The hike out of the forest felt longer than it had on the way in. Despite his heavy clothing and the hot coffee, the weather had taken a toll. Noah no longer cared that his only options for dinner were the diner or what he could cook on a hot plate in his room. Any food would seem like the best he'd ever eaten after the long day he'd spent.

Noah loaded his Tahoe and blasted the heat, slowly feeling his hands and feet get warm again. The drive back to the motel lasted long enough for him to thaw. As the cell signal improved, his phone vibrated with missed messages.

He decided to drop off his equipment at the motel and get a hot shower before going for dinner. Noah unpacked and plugged everything in before he took time to use the bathroom and wash up, luxuriating under the steaming water. He toweled down, dressed in jeans, a tee, flannel shirt, and sweater, and pulled on a fresh pair of heavy wool socks.

Scanning the messages, he saw most were from Drew. A few others were business inquiries he'd handle later, possible new video projects. Two were from Rob.

Noah read down through the stream of texts from Drew, chiding himself for feeling like a giddy teenager. Some were funny memes, others snide comments about a particular customer who gave the garage a hard time. Still more were replies to the texts Noah had managed to send on the shoot, and a request for new video snippets and outtakes.

Noah: *Got some amazing footage tonight. One more night in the cold and I can go back to my apartment. Wish I was coming home to you.*

He groaned when he saw what he'd texted, hoping he didn't sound too lovesick.

Drew: *Wish I were there to warm you up. Prevent hypothermia—sleep naked with your boyfriend.*

Noah: *Miss you. Want you.*

He hesitated, knowing what he wanted to say, but fearing it was still too soon.

Noah: *Care about you,* he texted instead. *Stay warm. Gonna need that body heat when I visit.*

Drew: *I'll make sure it's plenty hot when you get here. Hurry back.*

Noah sent several smiles, eggplants, and other emojis that he hoped described what was on his mind. Thanks to his constant texting and sexting with Drew, Noah had gotten better at sending explicit messages with emojis, although he still lacked confidence. *With my luck, I think I've sent him an explicit message and I've really said something utterly ridiculous.*

The sexy gif Drew sent in return reassured Noah that even if he hadn't been emoji-fluent, he'd gotten his point across.

Noah: *Talk later?*

Drew: *Poker night tonight. How about eleven?*

Noah confirmed and felt lighter, knowing he had something to look forward to besides work. Now that he'd caught up with Drew, Noah read Rob's messages. The first sent two hours ago had been before Noah had broken camp for the night.

Rob: *I got off early. Felt like taking a drive. Heading your way. Thought we could grab dinner.*

Noah shook his head at his friend's spontaneity. Rob decided to drive a two-hour round trip for dinner and didn't even question the impulse. The next text was barely an hour old.

Rob: *I'll be in town soon. Text me your motel. Let's eat!*

Noah: *I'm at the Full Moon Motor Court, Room 19. You'll see the truck. It'll be good to see you.*

His phone rang a few seconds later, and Noah had already thumbed the call open before it sank in that he didn't recognize the ringtone.

With a sinking heart, Noah realized he knew the number seconds too late. He'd erased it from his contacts, but not his memory. "Nate. Is this a butt dial or drunk dial?"

"Noah. Good to hear your voice, man."

Drunk dial it is, probably with a side of booty call.

"Are you somewhere safe? Please don't drive—trust me on this." Noah and Nate had broken up six months ago, amicably enough as partings went. Nate didn't like spending evenings alone, and Noah had photos to shoot. Noah had cared about Nate, and they'd been together for a year. Still, what he'd felt then was nothing compared to his bond with Drew.

"Awww…you're so cute. Still care, huh?"

Noah rolled his eyes. "I never stopped wanting you to be safe. You sound pretty mellow. Grab a rideshare and don't take drinks from strangers."

"I'm at a bar, and I'm horny, and I wish you were here," Nate told him. "We were good together, Noah. Damn good—best I've ever had. Couldn't walk straight for a week. Why'd you go away?"

Yep, Nate was past mellow, well into buzzed, and moving along right toward shit-faced.

"Did you go to the bar with friends?" Noah hoped his ex had the good sense not to go clubbing by himself.

"You'd never know it because they all paired off once they got here. Except for me. My date is a douchebag."

Noah sighed, then hoped Nate hadn't heard. "Get a rideshare and go home, Nate."

"We used to have fun going out," Nate protested. "You and me. Why'd we quit?"

Because you didn't like having to plan clubbing around my work. Because you loved your nightlife more than you loved me. "It was complicated, remember?" Noah said instead. "Just figured we'd both be better off elsewhere."

"We could make it uncomplicated. Friends with benefits. No strings, but lots of hot sex. How about it?" Nate offered.

Horny with a bad case of whiskey dick, Noah thought.

"Not going to happen," Noah said, wanting to shut down that line of thought. "I'm with someone. It's serious."

"C'mon, Noah. I don't mind being on the side. I can share. I tried to fuck you out of my mind, and it didn't work. So whaddya say?"

"I say no, Nate." Noah took a stern tone. He wondered if Nate would even remember the conversation in the morning. "Lose my number. We're done."

He ended the call, cutting off Nate's wheedling tone. *God, what did I see in him?* He wondered, but he knew the answer.

When he wasn't being a drunk fool, Nate could be fun—witty, interesting to talk to, good on the dance floor, and great in bed. Nate wasn't deep, but he had a playfulness that pulled Noah out of his thoughts and kept him from working too hard.

Aside from the social drinking that got out of hand too often to be accidental, Nate had been awesome at going out and impatient about staying in. He loved to go to clubs, bars, and concerts but bored quickly at the idea of watching a movie or reading if it didn't turn into sexcapades on the couch.

Noah enjoyed a social life—sometimes. But he also cherished quiet nights in front of the fire with a good book or a new TV series or favorite movie. After a while, he missed not having a conversation about more than where to go or what to eat for dinner. What he'd originally taken for optimistic and fun-loving started to seem shallow and superficial. If Nate had layers and depth, he resolutely refused to let Noah see that side of him. And he wasn't a shifter, so Noah had to keep an important part of himself secret.

Noah's inherent need for family had been at odds with Nate's nocommitments lifestyle, something he attributed as much to his inner lynx as to being a Cancer.

A knock broke Noah out of his thoughts, and he went to open the door. The blast of cold air made Noah shiver despite his sweater as Rob stomped the snow from his boots and shook off the flakes from his heavy woolen coat before coming inside.

"You sure there isn't a body under the bed? This place isn't even a Motel 6–more like Motel 2. Do you get a gallon of bleach with your room key?"

"It's not *that* bad," Noah protested as he grabbed his coat. "It's a little dated, and it could use a renovation—"

And I'd know if there was a body under the bed, his lynx sniffed.

That was a joke—I think, Noah explained silently.

I prefer our den.

Apartment.

Humph. His lynx glowered and padded off, muttering.

"Tell me you have one of those alarm wedge things for your door," Rob said, taking in the passably shabby room. "Are you sure it's okay to leave your gear here? We could order pizza."

Noah had told Rob that the hard-worn room was pretty normal for the small towns away from major tourist areas, but Rob rarely got the chance to see for himself. Cabins were nicer but also more expensive and harder to book for just a night or two.

"It'll be fine. There's hardly anyone else staying here this time of year. And while it's not fancy, the water pressure is great. Hot, too." Noah had his priorities.

"That diner the only place to eat?"

Noah nodded. "Yep. It's probably also the pizza place. Come on— I'm starving."

They took Rob's car, which was still warm. Just in the time Noah had been back at the hotel, a half-inch of flakes had settled over his Tahoe.

"Did you really come all the way up here just for dinner? What's Chris doing tonight?" Noah asked as Rob's Subaru crunched through the snow.

"Chris is cramming for exams this week," Rob replied, heading for the diner. They got behind a snowplow, which slowed their drive. "He's only got one more semester. It's been a long haul."

Noah knew that Chris was finishing a teaching degree and working weekend shifts as a barista to help pay the bills. Rob and Chris had been together for several years, and Noah had always admired their relationship—and envied them a little before he met Drew.

"I wish him luck. Glad my school days are over," Noah replied. "How's the store?"

Rob hung back from the truck to avoid any stones that might get kicked up by the massive tires. That meant they were nearly crawling. The five-minute trip to the diner looked likely to be more like fifteen.

"Been busy. Since I got promoted to senior manager, there's more to do, and I picked up a couple of extra shifts this week—we needed to put new tires on Chris's car. On weekends, I still give snowboarding lessons. So I needed a night off."

"Well, you've come to the right place for a hot time out on the town," Noah laughed.

Rob shrugged. "Hot enough for me these days. If you'd been home, I would have shown up on your doorstep with a pizza and a six-pack. Since you weren't, I had to be creative. That's okay—the drive cleared my mind."

"Well, thanks. I wasn't looking forward to eating alone. This is lots more fun."

"How's Drew?"

"Too far away," Noah replied with a lovesick sigh. He'd already confessed to Rob how he felt about Drew and probably bored him to tears recounting the news from Fox Hollow. "I'm heading down there in a couple of weeks."

Rob gave him a sidelong glance. "Are you coming back to Ottawa?"

"Yes—at least for now."

"You really are around the bend for this guy, aren't you?"

You have no idea. "Yeah. I'm pretty gone. Scares me sometimes—but not as much as I thought it would."

"If he's the one, then do whatever's necessary to keep him," Rob advised. "Getting Chris through grad school isn't always fun, but there's nowhere I'd rather be than next to him. When the right guy comes along, you can't let him get away."

The diner lights shone ahead as the snowplow lumbered past. Rob pulled into the lot, and they hurried inside.

"Sit anywhere," an older woman behind the counter called to them. "Plenty of seats. I'll be by with menus in a few."

Noah and Rob found a booth in the back. The woman behind the counter—whose name tag read *Lenore*—came with coffee.

"What brings you out on a night like this?" she asked. "It's supposed to snow straight through to morning."

"Well then, if your kitchen is still working, we'd better place our orders and maybe take breakfast home with us," Noah said.

They both ordered burgers with fries and pie for dessert, then added a dozen donuts to go.

"It looks bad out there," Noah said. "I've got two queen beds in the room. Stay over and leave in the morning once the plows go through. I need to go over footage tonight, but you can read or watch TV—it won't bother me." He paused. "Unless the motel is too sketchy for you?"

"I was mostly jerking your chain about that," Rob replied. "My freshman dorm was worse. Got anything to drink?"

"I might have brought along a bottle of whiskey to warm the blood," Noah admitted, feeling like they were teenagers who were getting away with something.

"I'll admit that I did throw a bag in the car, just in case. The storm wasn't supposed to be quite so bad so soon, but you never know this time of year."

Noah didn't mind the company. He and Rob had been in sync since the first time they met. Despite their immediate connection, there had never been anything more than friendship between them.

"How's the guide training?" Noah asked in between bites of a surprisingly good burger.

"I do classes when Chris is on break. Takes longer to complete, but this way, we should both finish at about the same time. It's hard, but we're stubborn—and there's a lot to look forward to."

Noah wished his friend all the best and loved hearing the enthusiasm in his voice. *Can Drew and I be like that? Fully committed, even when it's rough going?*

"Drew and his brother own an auto shop, right? Sounds like steady business."

Noah nodded. "It's grown into something that's more of a one-stop automotive service. Fox Hollow isn't close to larger cities, so the town's made a commitment to being self-sufficient for the times when going elsewhere isn't feasible. I imagine there are probably some things Drew and Russ can't fix, but not many."

"My uncle was a mechanic. He was never at a loss for work."

Noah snickered. "Are you arguing that Drew will be a fine provider? Trying to marry me off?"

Rob shrugged. "Nothing wrong with that."

Noah rolled his eyes. "My God—you're worse than a maiden aunt."

"My point is, it's good when you can both take care of each other. That's what Chris and I have been planning. Things seem different when you start looking ahead for the long run."

Noah felt like he was getting a big brother talk and didn't resent it. He knew Rob meant well and was rooting for him with Drew.

"I don't think I can take Drew away from Fox Hollow. He's got a good life there—and a great community. Which means—"

"You're going to have to move there. Did you just figure that out?" Rob chuckled.

"I can be slow on the uptake, as you enjoy pointing out to me."

The fries were as good as the burgers, and the pie ranked among the best Noah had ever eaten. Lenore sent them off with a baker's dozen donuts, and Noah left a generous tip.

"It's really coming down," Rob observed when they went out to his car, which took both of them to clean off the worst of the snow. "Is this going to mess up your shoot tomorrow?"

Noah shook his head. "No. People care about the weather. Moose will do what they do, regardless. But it will make for a cold night tomorrow."

Plows and salt trucks kept the road passable, but the snow fell hard and steady, and Noah hoped that he could get into his clearing come morning. Since he could do nothing about that now, Noah settled at the table to review the day's footage while Rob made himself comfortable on one of the beds and found a superhero movie on TV. Noah grabbed plastic cups and poured them both a generous measure of whiskey before sitting in front of his computer.

Reviewing hours of footage at double or triple speed assured Noah that the cameras were working and that he had usable video. He would examine the recordings more carefully later.

Between watching the recordings from the different cameras, Noah texted funny snippets he had shot with his phone now that he had decent Wi-Fi. He'd had a squirrel come right up on one camera and lick the lens. A curious raccoon looked like he'd been doing interpretive dance, and Noah got a breathtaking closeup of an owl.

Drew: *Love the photos. Can't wait to watch on TV.*

Noah: *Probably not until next year. Maybe we can watch together.*

Drew: *I'd like that a lot. Clothing optional.*

Noah: *Naked nature film watching. New kink?*

Drew: *Only with you.*

Noah: *Good thing. I miss you.*

Drew: *Call?*

Noah: *Rob drove out to meet me for dinner and got stuck with the storm. He's staying over. So unless you want an audience—*

Drew: *I'm not really into performance porn. I guess you'll just have to wait until tomorrow to hear about how I want to suck your cock and swallow every drop or how I want to ride your dick until you're fucked senseless and I come all over you.*

Noah: *Damn, Drew. Now I've got a boner and no way to take care of it.*

Drew: *Heh, heh, heh. My nefarious plan worked. You'll think of me tonight.*

Noah: *I was going to dream about you anyhow.*

Drew: *I'll dream about you too. Sleep well, be safe, and come back soon. You matter to me.*

Noah: *I promise. You matter to me. Sleep tight.*

He stared at the phone without moving after Drew's last comment.

Rob cleared his throat. "Done sexting? Because it's after one in the morning, and we both have big days tomorrow."

"Fuck—that late already? I used to stay up until dawn all the time in college. Why does it hurt worse now?"

Rob laughed. "Because we're closer to thirty than twenty. Getting old."

Noah knew that being sleep-deprived would only make the next day more miserable. He also understood from experience that the list of tasks stretched endlessly, and he would never be completely done.

"Okay. I just need to program my remote cameras and then lights out."

"Remote cameras?" Rob got up and walked to the table, looking at the screen over Noah's shoulder.

"I can control the perimeter cameras from my computer—as long as the signal doesn't crap out. It's not a perfect system, but even if I can't reach the cameras, they still record, and I can check what they're seeing from anywhere. Hence the 'remote' part."

Rob shook his head in amazement. "You've got a huge investment in equipment."

"Tell me about it. This is why I don't have a down payment for a condo."

"What's your next assignment?" Rob added a little more whiskey to his cup.

"I've got some PBS projects, a film for a conservancy, and a documentary I plan to enter for a shot at an award," Noah replied, "And when I visit Drew, I thought I might check in with the guy who handles the Fox Institute's video and see if they need a freelancer. Can't hurt."

"That's impressive. I've seen your videos online, and I might even have watched one of your documentaries. Good stuff."

"Thanks," Noah replied, touched that his friend made the effort. "Hopefully it didn't send you straight to sleep."

"Nah. It was fun watching how you turn this," Rob gestured at the cameras and computer, "into a show that keeps your attention. You've got talent."

Noah readied his gear and bag so he could make a quick departure to the clearing where he was taping tomorrow morning. He still had the hotel room for another day and night, so he'd be able to come back for a hot shower and a few hours in a warm bed before getting on the road. Noah accepted another pour from the bottle when Rob offered and left just the laptop open so he could monitor the night vision cameras if he couldn't sleep.

"Don't eat all the donuts if you wake up ahead of me," Rob teased as he got into bed.

"It's a strain, but I'll try to hold myself back."

Noah burrowed under the covers, exhausted after a long day. It was comforting to know there was another person in the room. He'd have preferred for it to be Drew snuggled against him, but just having company was a nice change.

Noah fell asleep right away but woke from a noise in the computer feed. Even though he had turned the volume down, he hadn't switched it off entirely. When he stumbled to the table and stared at the grayscale night vision camera footage, his breath caught.

Is that a Bigfoot? He couldn't take his eyes off the monitor as an indistinct figure meandered from the heavy forest and right for Noah's camera camp.

The being walked hunched, but upright—definitely on its hind legs. Night vision cameras didn't always capture as sharp an image as the daylight pictures, but while some aspects were less distinct, there was no mistaking the important details.

Why is one of those all the way down here? The Bigfoot/Yeti/Sasquatch that people thought they knew from the *National Enquirer* was a work of fiction. Plenty of cryptids existed in the far reaches of the forests beyond the prying eyes and cameras of humans. Noah had glimpsed several of these secretive creatures in the course of his projects and edited them out of the footage every time.

This was south of the usual stomping grounds for such cryptids, uncomfortably close to more populated areas. They occasionally wandered into places where people might be, which was the source of the tall tales. Noah could only hope that the lost Bigfoot headed north before the omnipresent cameras of settled places caught irrefutable proof.

Noah jotted a note of the video timestamp so he could easily find the spot to edit later. He yawned, then turned and shuffled back to bed. Rob hadn't stirred, and he was grateful that he wouldn't be forced to concoct a lie to explain away the figure on the video.

He got comfortable beneath the blankets, and his lynx's desire for a warm nest rose to the fore. Noah fell back to sleep quickly, deeper than before.

Their horses thundered down the road, sweat-flecked and dusty. The hoof beats of their pursuers were out of earshot, but that wouldn't last if they slowed their pace.

They had ridden as hard as they dared the previous night and hid by day, taking turns on watch while the other slept and the horses rested. Noah didn't recognize either man, yet he was certain he knew their hearts and souls.

The shorter of the pair had red hair and the fair skin of Scotland. The other had the darker hair and complexion some called "black Irish." Noah knew without the need for words that the two were everything to one another and that those in pursuit wished them ill for no reason except their nature.

"Not much farther," the dark-haired man—Reynold—coaxed. "I know a place, not far from here. We'll reach it before dawn, and we can rest. Hang on until then. Please, Isaiah, hang on."

His companion gave a curt nod. Just the way he moved, how he sat his horse, told a tale of pain and injury, as did the dark stain on his coat where the bullet had pierced the leather.

Fear curdled in Reynold's belly. A glance at Isaiah's face, expression drawn with pain, skin more pale than usual, told Reynold that they were running out of time.

The cabin in the woods was barely a shack, a waystation in the forest for hunters caught in foul weather. He had come upon it by accident, and its condition suggested he was the first in a very long time to set foot there. He could only hope that it remained forgotten and undiscovered.

"Easy now," he said when they found the darkened cabin still abandoned. He got down from his horse and came around to help Isaiah from his mount. "Don't be proud; let me help."

Isaiah leaned hard on him as they made their way into the shack. "Stay here," he told his partner. "Rest. As soon as I see to the horses and get water, I'll be back to tend that wound."

Reynold secured the horses in a thicket in reach of grass and a free-flowing stream. Deep in his heart, he knew they would ride no farther. He fastened the reins so that the horses could break free with some effort. "You've carried us well. Thank you," *he said, patting their necks and offering them each a bit of dried apple from his pocket, the last he had.*

He took the saddlebags and filled a canteen from the stream, then returned to the shack. Isaiah hadn't moved from his seat on a rickety chair, although his head fell forward, chin to chest.

"Let me see your arm." *Reynold bared his heart in his gentle tone. He pushed back Isaiah's cloak and winced as he saw the deep wound, blood still seeping through the cloth of his sleeve.*

"Leave me," *Isaiah murmured.* "I'm done. You can live."

Reynold shook his head. "Not without you." *Reynold and Isaiah had grown up together, fought side by side in the War Between the States, been friends, brothers-in-arms, and lovers. He would not be parted from Isaiah in battle, and he would not leave him now, at the end. Reynold could smell the wound gone bad, and he knew Isaiah had lost too much blood. He felt the fever that raised beads of sweat on his lover's brow. Isaiah was dying. Even if they found a safe haven and a doctor, it was too late. For both of them.*

"Promise me." *Isaiah's voice was fierce despite its weakness.* "Don't let them take us. I know what they intend." *He grabbed Reynold's hand, squeezing fiercely.*

Reynold swallowed hard, eyes moist. He had expected the request and long ago made up his mind. He flicked back his duster, revealing the sidearm in a holster on his hip. "I have my Colt. I'll handle it."

He laid his cloak on the dirty cabin floor and eased Isaiah down from his chair to lie beside him. "I don't regret one minute of our time together," *he told Isaiah, pushing strands of red hair from his lover's face.* "Only that we will not grow old."

"It's enough to have this. More than I dared dream," *Isaiah whispered, clutching Reynold's hand.* "Together." *He lifted their twined fingers to his lips.*

"Together," *Reynold echoed and ignored the sound of hoof beats for a few more precious minutes.*

"No!" Noah sat bolt upright in bed, shaking and sweating, tears wet on his cheeks. His heart pounded, and his breath came short and sharp. Beneath it all was a deep, desperate grief.

"Noah?" Rob's sleepy voice came from across the room. "You okay?"

"Yeah," Noah lied, scrubbing a hand down over his face, trying to regain control. "Bad dream. Go back to sleep."

He heard Rob snuffle and turn over, and a few minutes later, the snoring resumed.

Noah stayed where he was, trying to slow his breathing and temper his heartbeat. He pressed his fist to his mouth to stifle a sob. The men in his dream had seemed so real, a memory more than the concoction of an exhausted brain.

Were they real? Why did I see them? Why did I feel like one of those men was me—only "not" me? Am I being haunted by ghosts? Or are they trying to tell me something?

Gradually he brought his breath under control and felt his heart stop pounding. Noah fought the strong but irrational impulse to text Drew regardless of the time just to make sure he was okay.

Whoever I saw, whatever that was, if it was more than just a dream it happened a long time ago. It has nothing to do with me, with us. So why do I feel like I've lost the love of my life?

4

DREW

"Last day of the shoot?" Drew asked when Noah called him early in the morning. Drew and Russ were headed for the auto shop, and he was still finishing his first cup of coffee in a travel mug.

"Yeah. I checked the footage last night, and it's really good," Noah told him. "Rob just left to go back to Ottawa. I'll spend the night at the camera site, pack it all up tomorrow, and head for the city."

Drew didn't know if Noah intentionally didn't call his apartment "home" or if that was wishful thinking, but it warmed his heart. "Are you going to be warm enough?"

"I can shift if I get too cold," Noah reminded him. "And when I come to see you, I've got to show you what turned up on the video last night. A Bigfoot."

"Seriously?"

"Or something that looked a lot like one of them," Noah replied. "Night vision footage was a little grainy. I'm going to see if there are any tracks left after the snow we've gotten."

"I want to see those pictures for sure—but I can't wait to see every-thing," Drew told him. "And I want to hear your stories. We've got a full day at the garage today, and tonight, I'm helping at the party for the snowmobile relay race that ends in Fox Hollow. But call any time.

If I can't pick up at that moment, I'll text to see if it's okay to call you back."

"Thanks for understanding about me not being able to talk if there are animals nearby," Noah said, and something in his tone made Drew suspect that might have been an issue in a prior relationship.

"I'm not going to spoil a shot for you, much as I love talking with you. Whatever I have to say can keep," Drew assured him. "Don't forget—I love your texts and photos. It's all good. I just like being connected."

"Me too. I'd better go. I'll call when—if—I can, but for sure tomorrow," Noah promised. "Be safe. I miss you."

"Miss you too." Drew ended the call with a heavy sigh.

"Dude, could you be more besotted?" Russ teased. "You've got it bad for that cat."

"Have you forgotten how you mooned around after Liam?"

"Mooned around?" Russ repeated in mock outrage. "I'll have you know I courted Liam in a very wolf-appropriate manner."

Drew snorted in laughter. "Wolves howl at the moon. You were positively smitten."

Russ smiled. "Still am. That's what happens with fated mates."

I know that's what Noah and I are. And sometimes I wonder if we've found each other in past lives. How else can I explain falling so hard, so fast? And the dreams…

"Seriously, I'm glad you two have hit it off," Russ said. "I didn't want to leave you on your own once Liam and I paired up."

"I'm a grown-up, Russ. I can handle being on my own."

"But it's better if you don't have to."

Big brother instincts hadn't faded, Drew thought. *And I hope they never do, although I'm not going to tell Russ that. He's got enough of a swelled head already.*

Drew recounted the highlights of what Noah had told him about the video shoot. "I can't wait to see more. The new documentaries are going to be awesome."

Russ chuckled. "It's good to see you so wrapped up in someone. Make sure he knows that if he hurts you, Liam and I will tear out his throat."

Drew rolled his eyes. "Forgive me if I don't quote you on that."

"The snowmobile rally doesn't come through until late, so we should both make it to the event on time tonight," Russ said, changing subjects. "I'm going to be tied up for a while with the vintage car that's coming in. It's a sweet ride, but it hasn't been properly maintained."

Drew knew that his brother had been looking forward to working on the classic Corvette ever since his preliminary estimate had been accepted. A woman had contacted the garage because she was selling off her late husband's car collection and had been advised to make sure all the cars ran. The Corvette had needed work, and while the garage didn't normally see such unusual cars, Russ had trained to work on them, and they were one of his obsessions. When she shipped the car over for an estimate in a hauler, they knew she was serious.

"Is Liam jealous of the Corvette? Because I saw the look in your eyes, and that was pure love."

"It's an inanimate object. Liam's affection is safe."

"You totally eye-fucked those photographs. Just saying."

"Who taught you to have such a potty mouth?"

"My big brother." Drew grinned. "I'm supposed to meet Mutt for lunch," Drew added. "And if there's time between when I finish at the garage and when we have to be at the rally, we're supposed to go for a run in our fur. It's been a while."

Mutt's real name was Matt, but since he was a German Shepherd shifter, everyone called him by his nickname. He managed the theater, and he and Drew had been best friends almost from the time the Lowe brothers arrived in Fox Hollow.

"Sounds good. You need that. Run off some of that pent-up sexual frustration," Russ needled.

"Ew. You had to go there, didn't you?"

"Just doing my duty," Russ replied.

"You're welcome to join us," Drew offered.

Russ shook his head. "I think the Corvette is going to take all day—and probably tomorrow. And we're likely to have some last-minute snowmobile repairs come in from the rally. You know there'll be people who limped across the finish line and need to get fixed up to get home."

"I'm not going to leave you high and dry," Drew promised. "I'll help—even if it takes all night. Noah won't be able to call after it gets dark to keep from scaring the nocturnal animals away. That's why he's spending the night in the forest. Having some work to do would keep me from worrying."

"He's a lynx, not a kitten. His cat belongs in the forest, just like your wolf. We might be domesticated, but they aren't," Russ reminded him.

"I know—but I keep having bad dreams. I'll feel better when Noah is out of the woods. I can't shake the feeling that there's danger lurking. Something that's not normal."

Russ frowned. "When did you start getting visions? Do I need to pawn you off on the psychics over at the Fox Institute?"

Drew knew that humor covered Russ's concern. "I don't know. It gives me the creeps. But with Noah, it's almost like we're two halves of a coin, even though we're just getting to know each other." Drew paused to take a sip of coffee to steady his voice.

"Maybe you *should* go talk to Rich Jeffries over at the Institute," Russ said, dead serious. "You two might be a special case. We know there are fated mates and soulmates. If anyone can figure out what you and Noah are, it's the psychics."

"Maybe…but for now, I'd like for us to explore it ourselves," Drew replied. "We're still so new."

"Oh, you're so far past the point of no return that you can't even see it in the rearview mirror," Russ teased. "But I understand."

"Maybe at some point we'll go see Jeffries…if knowing is important. But I want us to discover what we are the old-fashioned way."

"Fine with me—just means you'll be doing the laundry," Russ said. "From all that 'discovering.'"

Drew punched him in the arm. "You know what I meant."

"Oh, I *know*."

The morning passed in a blur as if it were on fast-forward from the moment they arrived at the garage. Drew worked his way through inspections and slipped belts and worn brakes, while Russ devoted his time to giving the old cherry-red Corvette a thorough going-over. In between projects, Drew and Noah exchanged texts, and Noah included some great closeups of foxes, squirrels, and birds that meandered past his cameras.

Drew: *How's the weather?*

Noah: *Freezing my nuts off.*

Drew: *Hey—I have plans for those nuts!*

Noah: *Good to know.*

Drew: *Did you find the footprints from last night?*

Noah: *No. Too much snow. Saw some odd hair caught in a bush, and my lynx is twitchy. Who knows? Maybe we'll get a big surprise tonight.*

Drew: *Be careful. Bigfoot and the moose might not like it if they think you're there to photograph them.*

Noah: *Never thought about that, but I was planning to stay out of sight. Not expecting to make new friends.*

Drew: *Be safe. I'm looking forward to warming you up.*

Noah: *Take care. I'll text when I can. I have ideas on how we can warm things up!*

Drew joked about Russ and the Corvette needing some "alone time" after it took his brother all morning to go over every inch of the car before he retreated to the office to work up the final cost.

Drew knocked on the office window on his way to lunch. "Heading over to Bear Necessities to meet Mutt. Do you want me to bring you anything?"

"Nah. I'll run out for something once I get the numbers for the Corvette crunched. Have fun with Mutt."

Drew bundled up and headed down the street to the Bear Necessities Café. As soon as he walked in, the smell of fresh coffee and baked goods washed over him, sending a jolt of bliss through every nerve.

He greeted Mutt, who had been waiting just inside the door. Mutt had black hair with brown streaks like his Shepherd, and caramel-colored eyes.

"Hi, Drew, Mutt. Getting lunch or just java?" Sherri greeted them. She and her husband Nelson—both bear shifters—ran the café.

"All of the above," Drew replied. They walked to the counter to place their orders. "Coffee, the Reuben, and whatever mystical, magical donut flavor Jack invented for today." Mutt ordered the grilled cheese and a donut as well.

"Today's special flavor is piña colada filling, with a hint of mango in the buttercream icing," Jack, the possum shifter baker, called from the kitchen doorway. "It's new, so let me know what you think."

"When's that boy of yours coming back to visit?" Sherri asked as she rang up Drew's food.

"Couple of weeks. Maybe if I feed him enough donuts, he'll decide to move to Fox Hollow," Drew teased.

"Jack's donuts are amazing, but I think you can convince Noah to relocate all on your own." Sherri winked.

Drew and Mutt found a table toward the back. "How're things?" Drew asked although he had the feeling he knew.

"Not my best day," Mutt replied. "We've got projector problems at the theater, and parts are expensive. I'm hoping that what I ordered comes in soon so we don't have to cancel any showings. And one of my concession servers gave notice, so I might be dishing out popcorn until we find a replacement." He paused. "We still going for a run after work?"

"Definitely. I might even get Russ to join us for beer and wings at the hotel bar if things work out. We've got some time to kill before the snowmobiles get here."

"I always want to shift and chase them," Mutt admitted. "It's a weakness."

Drew couldn't resist a snicker.

"Don't judge." Mutt fake-sulked.

"The snowmobile engines hurt my ears," Drew confessed. "I like them just fine when they're stopped. I just hate the whine of the motor. It doesn't bother you?"

Mutt shook his head. "No—it just reminds me that the things I like to chase are coming."

Drew took another bite of his sandwich. He understood Mutt. While wolves weren't dogs, they were similar enough.

Will this be a problem since Noah is a cat? We're both predators. We chase prey. But cats don't run after cars. Does his lynx knock things off tables just to be a dick?

"Quit worrying," Mutt said as if he guessed Drew's thoughts. "You're such a Capricorn! People make a go of mixed marriages all the time. My parents were herbivore and carnivore. They did okay."

Drew snorted his latte at the word "marriage." "Getting ahead of ourselves, aren't we? We've barely started dating. Marriage—"

"You're fated mates. Why wouldn't you get married?" Mutt looked perplexed and did a head tilt that Drew always thought was adorably more Shepherd than human.

Drew wasn't going to point out that while Mutt's parents were accepted by the other dog shifters, being a canine who didn't hunt prey earned Mutt scorn and finally made him strike out for the haven of Fox Hollow. Even family ties sometimes reached a breaking point.

"I'm trying not to jump ahead or take things for granted," Drew admitted. "I mean, I've dated but never had someone serious. I don't have a lot of experience."

He hadn't meant to give so much away, but Mutt looked up at his comment.

"And when you say 'experience' you mean—"

Drew felt his cheeks flush. "You know—"

"Really?" Mutt's eyes widened.

Drew rolled his eyes. "Not completely, but yeah—"

"Second base? Third base?" Mutt's dark eyes widened.

"We're doing a baseball analogy? Newsflash—it all counts as sex."

"Yeah, but…"

Drew sighed and looked down. "No home runs, okay? We didn't have a lot of time together at the beginning. And Noah had been a prisoner of the Huntsman. He wasn't in a good headspace. What we felt for each other was undeniable—the fated mates thing. But we agreed to take it slow. Real slow."

"I thought fated mates were combustible when it came to sex."

Drew reddened impossibly more. "Gotta deal with the trauma before we can get to the thirst, dude."

"God, I can't believe you just said that." Mutt laughed. "Okay, I get it. And that's very noble. Practical, even."

"That's part of why I'm really looking forward to Noah coming to visit."

"You want to get laid."

"Shut the fuck up! Okay, that's part of it, but I want us both to be at a point where sex can be good for the right reasons."

"Being good for the *wrong* reasons can be awesome. Don't knock it 'til you tried it," Mutt replied, waggling his eyebrows.

"Ugh. TMI. I don't want to screw this up," Drew admitted. "I really, really, *really* like Noah. Maybe love him. I want to keep him, Mutt. And I'm not a player. I don't understand the game. I just know that it feels like we belong together—like we've *always* belonged to each other."

Mutt gave him a pitying smile, much like the one Russ had favored Drew with earlier. "You're fated mates. Maybe soulmates. Now I haven't felt that myself, but from what I've read—and not just in romance novels because I totally don't read those—"

"You just read gay mystery/adventure books with a romance subplot," Drew interjected.

"Don't hate on mysteries," Mutt mock huffed. "But the whole 'fated' thing means you really have to work at *not* being together, from what I've read. And since you both want to be with each other, then that's not an issue. So quit worrying."

Drew picked at his donut. "It's the dreams. We keep dying."

Mutt choked on his water. "Wait. What?"

Drew hid behind his latte for a moment, wishing he hadn't said anything and knowing it was too late now. "I keep having these dreams. They're so real. I see two people I don't recognize who are in other time periods, but I swear I know them. I think they're...us."

"Back the fuck up. Slow down. Try that again? You have dreams about people who are you but *not* you, only at other points in history?" Mutt repeated. "Like reincarnation?"

"Maybe?" Drew wished he could just slide under the diner table. "The people in the dreams don't look like Noah and me. We obviously weren't alive then. But I know in my bones it's us. And I have no idea what to make of it."

Drew knew that he sounded insane. Even so, it felt good to unburden himself to someone because he couldn't shake the worry in his gut about Noah's safety.

"Have you done any research?"

Drew shook his head. "There's nothing online except stuff from books and movies."

"You might find better resources at the Fox Hollow library and the archive at the Institute," Mutt replied. "I've heard people say that both places have good books about paranormal things that are accurate. It's worth a shot."

"Maybe. Liam will probably tease me."

"Not the worst thing in the world. And he'd joke—but he'd help," Mutt said. "The Institute probably has more than you'll ever want to know, but you could confirm what it really means to be fated mates."

Drew nodded. "Okay, you and Russ have got me convinced. I don't have time off today, not if we're going to run. But maybe I can go tomorrow." They finished their meals and paid the check, then walked back outside into the cold air. "Gotta admit I'm looking forward to the rally party tonight. If I can't be with Noah, at least I can take my mind off my misery."

Mutt slugged him playfully on the shoulder. "That's the spirit! Never underestimate the power of denial."

"Meet me at the cabin at six," Drew replied. "We can run in the woods, shower, and connect with Russ at the hotel bar before we need to go over to the rally."

"See you then!" Mutt headed back toward the theater with a cheery wave.

Drew looked longingly at the library, then sighed and headed back to the garage. *I'll start there tomorrow. Maybe Liam won't tease me too much. I don't understand where the nightmares factor in with the fated mates stuff. Russ never said he had dreams like that, and he and Liam are fated. So what's different about Noah and me?*

As much as he enjoyed spending lunch with Mutt, Drew's unanswered questions colored his mood. He also couldn't shake his worry about Noah and checked his phone. Noah had sent a few bird photos, a closeup of a fox, and a selfie of him bundled up in his camouflaged tent.

Noah: *Wish you were here to keep me warm.*

Drew: *Wish you were *here* with hot chocolate and a comfy bed.*

Noah: *That sounds awesome. Soon.*

Drew: *Love the photos. Are you sure you're safe?*
Noah: *What's wrong?*
Drew: *Probably nothing, but I've got a feeling I can't shake.*
Noah: *Details?*
Drew: *Just a sense that you're in danger. So please, be careful.*
Noah: *Always. You too.*
Drew: *Stay warm and safe. You matter to me.*
Noah: *Promise. And you matter to me—a lot. More later.*

Drew pocketed his phone with a sigh and went back into the garage. He smelled a meatball sub and guessed Russ had ordered delivery, probably unable to step away from the 'Vette.

"Well?" Drew asked, sticking his head in the office. "How bad is the 'Vette's condition?"

Russ looked up from his monitor. His hair was askew, which meant he'd been running his hands through it. The crumpled paper and foil from a take-out sub jutted from the wastebasket, and he had a large soda cup on his desk.

"Anything's possible if someone wants it badly enough and has the spare cash," he said. "But for the age of the car, and how long it's been mothballed, it's really not in bad shape. I think I can get it running without too much trouble. I gave Mrs. Porter my estimate, and she didn't even blink—approved it right off. I've been working on it since then—just broke for lunch. So it's all good. I'm not even too worried about finding parts. Except…"

"Except?" Drew frowned, picking up on Russ's uneasiness.

"Do you think a car can be haunted?" Russ blurted out his question, then froze as if he expected Drew to laugh.

"You're serious."

Russ let out a long breath and nodded. "Maybe. Yeah. The whole time I've had my hands on the Corvette, I felt like someone was watching me. Judging me. I didn't see anyone, but it felt colder than usual in the bay, and I kept getting a prickle down my spine. And my wolf has been freaking out."

He paused. "More than once, my diagnostic equipment went on the fritz, or a tool I put down wasn't where I left it. I'm serious. I think the car is haunted."

"Do you need an exorcist?"

Russ chuckled. "Just because it's got a ghost riding shotgun, that doesn't mean it's going to go *Christine* on my ass. But I intend to stroll over to the Institute and talk to Rich Jeffries. He'll know what to do."

"If the lady's late husband was a collector, maybe he's having trouble letting go," Drew said.

"So he's okay leaving his wife but not his car? That's some kind of fucked up."

The office door, which had been standing open, slammed hard enough to rattle the glass.

Drew and Russ exchanged a freaked-out glance.

"You saw that, right?" Russ asked.

Drew nodded. "Uh-huh. Kinda hard to miss."

They heard a clatter of steel on cement out in the bay, and both brothers got to their feet.

"Oh, fuck no," Russ muttered. He threw open the office door and stalked out to the bay where the Corvette sat like a work of art on display. All the tools Russ had left on a rolling cart now lay on the floor.

Jimmy and Steve arrived on the other side of the bay seconds later. "What the hell?" Jimmy asked, taking in the scattered tools.

Russ strode toward the car, looking like one seriously pissed-off wolf. "What the fuck is your problem?" he yelled at the Corvette. "Take your issues up with your wife. I'm just doing my job."

Jimmy and Steve gave Drew a confused look. "Drew, is Russ yelling at the car?" Jimmy asked.

"He's yelling at a ghost that's stuck to the car," Drew replied.

The temperature in the bay dropped, and frost formed on the 'Vette's windshield. The headlights flashed, and then the wipers turned on and off.

"Enough with the temper tantrum," Russ yelled. "I'm supposed to get this car fixed up and running like a dream. The car's beautiful, and I get that you loved it, but dude—you're dead." He dropped his voice. "Your wife is sad about selling, but I think she needs the money."

The radio blared, and the horn went off. Then—silence.

Russ stepped closer to the Corvette and carefully put both hands palm down on the roof. "I know what it's like to lose someone you loved," he said quietly, addressing the ghost. "Things and places get all tied up with the past, but they aren't the memories. She'll still remember you when the car belongs to someone else who can cherish it like you did."

Drew found himself holding his breath, afraid the Corvette might attack. When nothing happened, he relaxed a little but still feared for Russ.

You are right. There is an angry ghost. My fur is standing on end, Drew's wolf said, watching Russ and the car warily. *Not something I can bite.*

We might not need to bite. Let's see how this goes. Drew eyed a nearby crowbar and remembered from a TV show that ghosts didn't like salt or iron.

"Did you get tangled up and forget how to go on?" Russ continued talking to the ghost. "We can help. Just please stop trashing my garage, and don't hurt my people."

The turn signals blinked once, which Drew guessed meant "yes."

Russ backed away from the car, but nothing else happened. He gestured for the others to follow him into the lobby, where they filled Kerrie in on all the excitement.

"Okay, everyone stay away from the 'Vette until we get this straightened out," Russ said. Steve and Jimmy nodded and walked around on the outside to get to the bays with their cars.

"I'm going to go see Rich Jeffries, and I'll call the owner. Maybe she'd feel differently about selling if she knew about the ghost."

"Or maybe the ghost is why she's selling." Drew met Russ's gaze. "Just because *he's* still attached doesn't mean she can't be ready to move on or at least let go."

Russ looked stricken for a moment, and Drew knew his brother was thinking of how hard it had been to go on with his life after a car accident claimed his first husband. Time—and Liam—finally pulled Russ out of his grief, but it had been several hard years.

"Yeah, it'll be enough of a challenge getting the 'Vette running without it being haunted." Russ reached for his coat and then looked back at Kerrie. "If anyone calls, tell them I stepped out, but I'll get back to them."

Drew finished an inspection, replaced a set of brakes, and did a couple of oil changes before Russ returned late in the afternoon. With him was Rich Jeffries from the Fox Institute, an elderly woman, and a man Drew had seen before but couldn't place.

"What's up?" Drew asked quietly, sidling up to Russ.

"Jamie Miller is a ghost whisperer. He can help if the ghost isn't able to communicate easily. Mrs. Cooper owns the Corvette. Rich wanted to see what's going on," Russ replied. "Since Mr. Cooper's ghost has a temper, can you please send everyone else home early and then come back and help? I'm not exactly sure how this is going to go."

"Can do. Be right back."

Jimmy, Steve, and Kerrie didn't argue about the extra paid time off, especially since they'd seen the Corvette's ghost throw a fit earlier. Drew locked the door after them and flipped the sign to closed, then went back to support Russ—even if that meant being a bodyguard.

"Oh my," Mrs. Cooper said, staring at the Corvette with a smile. "Farrah looks better already."

Rich's eyebrows rose. "Farrah?"

Mrs. Cooper laughed. "Named after Farrah Fawcett-Majors, who was quite the hottie back in the day. My Eddie had her on a calendar, and when he bought the 'Vette, I suggested that he go ahead and name her Farrah after his TV crush."

Drew figured Mrs. Cooper was around eighty, and despite her age, she flashed an impish grin at the sexy sports car. "We had some very good times with Farrah," she added with a wink.

"We went for Sunday drives in nice weather until Eddie's eyesight wasn't safe. I took over driving until cataracts got the best of me. By then, Eddie's health started to fail."

She shook her head. "Even so, Eddie would go out and putter in the garage until he wasn't able to get out of bed anymore. He had other very nice cars, but Farrah was always his favorite. Sometimes he'd just go sit behind the wheel. The day before he died, he asked his nurse to push his wheelchair out to the garage. I think he wanted to say goodbye."

"I'm sorry for your loss," Russ replied.

"I held on to the cars for five years—sold all the others first. But the house and property are too much for me, even with help. Our daughter wants me to move down to Albany—the weather isn't much better, but at least I'll be closer to her," she added with a sad laugh.

"Which is why I brought Farrah to you," Mrs. Cooper said, turning to Russ. "You worked on cars for some friends of ours, and they spoke well of you. I knew you'd treat her like a lady."

"Did you suspect that Mr. Cooper's ghost stayed with the car?" Jamie asked.

"I can't say I'm surprised. I thought I felt his presence—sometimes in the house, but more so when I went out to the garage. Some of our happiest memories include Farrah. But I can't drive her, and I think she deserves someone who can enjoy her the way we did."

"Mr. Cooper got agitated this morning. We don't want anyone to get hurt," Russ said.

She smiled. "Eddie was a lover, not a fighter. I think he's just frustrated about being dead."

"We should help him pass over," Jamie said. "He deserves peace."

"Let me have a word with him." Mrs. Cooper lifted her head and squared her shoulders, and Drew could have sworn she looked decades younger as she walked over to the 'Vette.

"Eddie? I think we need to talk."

The temperature dropped, and the car's windows frosted over again. "Now stop that. You're scaring people," she chided gently, laying a hand on the cherry-red roof.

"I miss you, Eddie. And I miss the fun we had taking Farrah out on the road. But you're gone, and it won't be long before we're together again. Maybe there are cars in heaven," she added with a wistful smile. "But for now, you need to let go. For me."

Drew caught his breath as a misty apparition formed standing next to the driver's door of the Corvette. The details were hazy, but he could make out the image of a man that seemed to flicker between young and old.

"It's okay to let her move on, Eddie, just like I have to do. She'll go to a good home. I'm going to live near Lindsey until it's time for me to come to you. But for now, this is how things have to be." Mrs. Cooper's gentle, firm voice held a lifetime of affection.

The ghost nodded, then leaned forward toward the windshield. When he stood, he put a hand over his heart, looked at his wife, then at the Corvette, and gradually faded away.

A finger-tracing of a heart remained, drawn in the slowly-melting frost.

Russ stepped closer to steady Mrs. Cooper when she wobbled and Drew grabbed a chair for her. She sat, but waved away their concerns. "I'm fine. Just tired. That took a lot out of me."

"Turns out you didn't need me at all," Jamie said with a smile. He brought Mrs. Cooper a bottle of water, which she accepted with a nod of thanks.

"I didn't think he meant to be a problem. Sometimes Eddie could just be stubborn until I got him to see reason."

Russ turned to Mrs. Cooper. "Thank you."

She shook her head. "No, I owe you thanks. For taking care of Farrah and helping Eddie and me move forward."

While Mrs. Cooper chatted with Russ and Jamie, Drew motioned for Rich Jeffries to step to the side.

The psychic looked closely at him and narrowed his eyes. "You aren't sleeping well."

Drew managed a wan smile. "Do I look that bad?"

"I think you've got something on your mind."

"Is there someone at the Institute who knows about dreams and... fated mates?" Drew screwed up his courage to ask. "I don't know much about the Institute—I'm sorry, just didn't have reason to find out before now."

"We're here to educate and help solve problems," Jeffries replied. "And yes, our staff has studied both." He pulled a business card from his pocket and handed it to Drew. "Give me a call when you want to talk. Once I know more about what you're looking for, I can match you with the right person."

Drew felt a little lighter already. "It might be a couple of days, but I definitely want to understand what's happening."

Jeffries and Jamie drove Mrs. Cooper home. Drew walked over to where Russ stood next to the Corvette—Farrah—just staring at the car with an expression Drew couldn't decipher.

"Penny for your thoughts," he said.

Russ didn't look away. "Just thinking about the things we get attached to. Was it the car or the memories? Or his lost youth? Time goes by so fast, and then what you thought would last forever is just…gone."

Drew moved to stand beside his brother and bumped shoulders. It had been a long time since he'd seen Russ pensive—rarely, now that Liam had come into his life.

"Thinking about Anthony?" Drew knew that while his brother had learned to love again after the loss of his first husband, he would never forget him.

"Sometimes. It's not like I'm being unfaithful by moving on. I know he's gone. I love Liam with all my heart. Liam understands. It's just— Eddie's story brought up memories."

"Come running with Mutt and me. It's been a while since you were in your fur. Bring Liam if you want. Then we're all going to get hot wings at the hotel bar before we go to the rally party."

"I don't know—"

"Not taking no for an answer. Do you want me to mope about not being able to talk to Noah? I'm not distracting *you*. You're distracting *me*." Drew used his best innocent look, one he knew Russ could rarely resist.

Russ let out a long breath. "Okay. You're right. There's a line between honoring the past and letting it screw up the future. Anthony wouldn't want that. And I'm so lucky that I have you and Liam."

"Damn straight," Drew said with a laugh. "Come on. Let's blow this popsicle stand."

Mutt was waiting inside when they got to the cabin, talking with Liam in the kitchen. Russ greeted Liam with a kiss.

"Sorry we're late," Drew said. "We had a haunted car."

"Haunted?"

Drew recounted the excitement with the vintage 'Vette, and Mutt's eyebrows rose.

"Are you going to exorcise the car? Can I watch?" Mutt looked hopeful, while Liam just laughed.

"Already done, and it was a ghost, not a demon. So an exorcism wasn't needed," Drew replied with a chuckle. "The 'Vette is a sweet car. I guess I can understand why the husband liked it so much, but I don't think I'd want to stick around after death, even for a cool ride."

"Let's run," Russ said. "I need a change of scenery."

Drew sneaked a glance at his phone, but the last text from Noah had been a couple of hours ago, with more photos of wildlife that had wandered by his hidden tent. *He said he'd probably be out of touch at times. It's nothing to worry about. Noah's been doing this for years. I need to run, go to the rally, and keep busy.*

As soon as Drew shifted, he felt calmer. While his wolf was always with him and often made his presence known, shifting let Drew step away from the human side of his mind in a way that was difficult to put into words.

Wolf-Drew focused on the present, didn't stress about everything that might go wrong, and took joy in the freedom of existing. He ran through the twilight forest at full speed, reveling in his animal side's grace and strength. At the top of the hill, Drew howled.

It will be better when we run with our mate. Even a cat can run.

Despite his wolf's snark, Drew knew his other self was as crazy about Noah as his human half.

Russ launched himself at Drew, knocking him over and play-tussling in the snow. Liam and Mutt chased each other through the trees. By the time they headed back to the cabin, they were winded, wet with snow, and purged of the day's worries.

They changed form, dressed, and headed back into town refreshed. Russ had lost some of the day's tension, which made Drew happy. Even though he hadn't heard more from Noah, taking time in his fur had lightened Drew's mood. Knowing that he was welcome to talk to Jeffries also took some of the weight off his mind. He still wasn't sure he intended to go, but having the invitation gave him a backup plan.

"These are the best wings in the Adirondacks," Mutt said, swooning over his food when they were seated in the bar. The Fox Hollow Hotel had a formal dining room, an inside bar, and an outdoor patio bar. For a town its size, there were several good restaurants, but the wings at the hotel bar were definitely the best.

"Half the town is out tonight," Liam observed. The bar was packed, and even the dining room had a wait. Later, the rally party would be on the deck, and the celebration would go late into the night.

The conversation stayed light as they ate, and Drew guessed that no one wanted to bring down the high after their run. Shifting had a healing effect, both physically and mentally, and Drew always gave himself a stern reprimand when he forgot and went too long without changing to his other self.

You need me. I'm your better half. His wolf sounded smug.

Of course I need you. But "better" is debatable, Drew snarked back.

After they ate, Drew and the others went out to the deck, where the rally party was setting up. A DJ arranged his equipment inside a heavy plastic tent that would shield him from the wind while letting him spin tunes for the street party. The disco ball that hung from a pole outside cast a spinning prism of light over the snow. Drew and the others pitched in wherever anyone needed an extra hand.

Half an hour before the snowmobiles arrived, the main street had become a big party despite the temperature. Barricades closed it to through traffic, and amid the lights and music, the snow-covered scene looked magical.

Friends greeted them, pulling Drew and Russ into conversations that spun out into small gatherings. A cluster of people who liked to dance started the party early, grooving to the DJ's tunes on a patch of shoveled parking lot that doubled for a dance floor. Others mingled, carrying their take-out boxes and cups of hot chocolate, rushing to eat their steaming-hot food before it cooled.

Drew, Russ, and the others offered their help to the organizers but were waved away. "Go have fun," one of the men said. "We've got this."

As the evening went on, Drew felt his mood slip. He had started the night pumped up on endorphins from the run, but the cold and dark chipped away at his natural optimism. His phone's silence let Drew's worries run amok. Despite telling himself that it was all because of the photo shoot and everything would be right in the morning, Drew couldn't shake the feeling that something was about to disturb the peace.

The rally party would go on until the bar's last call, but Drew, Russ, and Liam headed home before midnight. Russ and Liam walked in from the car with their arms wrapped around each other's waists, and Drew felt a stab of loneliness, missing Noah more than usual.

He had put his phone on vibrate to keep him from checking obsessively, but the stillness was almost as bad as the silence. *He'll call when he can,* Drew reminded himself, but that didn't make the waiting easier.

That's what mating bites are for, his wolf offered. *It's a deeper connection, so we're always linked.*

We'll get there. Not going to rush things, Drew pushed back.

Why wait? I know we're fated mates, and so does the cat.

Lynx.

Whatever. We approve. So mate and get bitten already.

So much for romance.

His wolf snorted. *Flowers don't taste good, chocolate makes me sick. Do me a favor and sit on my dick.*

Wolf poetry? Gotta say I'm underwhelmed.

Bite me.

That's what we were discussing.

His wolf growled and huffed, shook himself off, and stalked away.

With his animal side off sulking, Drew felt doubly alone. They all had to get up for work tomorrow, so it was too late to start a movie, but Drew felt jumpy and restless. He said good night to Russ and Liam, then got ready for bed. Still twitchy, Drew padded out to the kitchen to pour himself a drink since he'd taken it easy at the rally. He carried his whiskey back to his room, got comfortable in bed, and scrolled through YouTube, checking for new content.

When he finally gave up, Drew opened up his playlist of Noah's videos and plugged in his computer so he could listen all night. He drifted off with Noah's voice soothing him to sleep, but even that couldn't keep the dreams at bay.

The smell of hay and sawdust would always be mingled in his mind with the taste of his lover's sweat and the feel of his skin. That's where they had first admitted their love and sated their need out in the loft.

They were older now and preferred a bed for lovemaking, although John still liked to grab Patrick for a quick kiss when they were doing their chores.

The horses wouldn't tell their secret, and they had dismissed the remaining farmhands years ago.

The little farm in the wilds of Western Pennsylvania was remote enough that no one was likely to show up unannounced. John and Patrick had done their duty in the war against King George, lucky enough to come home alive and uninjured. Back then, John's father and mother still ran the farm. After Pa died, John took over. He and Patrick made the farm as self-sufficient as possible, with crops and corn whiskey to trade for what they couldn't raise.

At first, Patrick had a room in the bunkhouse. Then John's mother had a stroke and could no longer leave her bed, wits scrambled, and there was no one to know or care that Patrick moved into the spare room in the house. They maintained that fiction, though they had shared a bed every night since then.

"Want you. Need you," John panted as Patrick's hands roamed up and down his body, strong, calloused, and just right.

"And I'm gonna take good care of both of us," Patrick assured him, pushing a lock of blond hair from John's eyes and tilting his chin up for a long, lingering kiss. Patrick's dark hair fell shoulder-length, loosed from its queue.

They fell onto the cotton-stuffed mattress, and the rope supports creaked with their combined weight. Patrick pulled his shirt over his head while John pushed his breeches down and started to unlace his lover's pants. Patrick leaned forward to kiss John on the mouth, then traced the column of his throat. He rucked up John's linen shirt to lick at his nipples until they hardened, then settled himself to lick and stroke his stiff cock until John begged for release—

Drew woke with a start, hard and aching, damp with sweat. The dream went beyond fantasy with the clarity of memory, and it only took a few strokes for Drew to chase his climax. He lay still for a moment as his orgasm faded, and his mind began to function again.

Mutt mentioned reincarnation. Could it be? Have Noah and I been drawn together in other times and places, as other selves? I thought that only happened in movies.

He slowed his breathing to calm down and wiped himself off with his shirt. *They were together for a long time. Happy.* Still, Drew couldn't shake a lingering sadness, as if there was more to the story, a tragedy just out of sight.

Speaking of safe...

Drew sat up and reached for his phone as Noah's voice, deep and steady, still played from the videos on his laptop. No new messages awaited him, and Drew realized that he hadn't heard from Noah since before supper.

Now that the glow of the dream and his climax had faded worry set in, sharp and urgent.

A glance at the time told him it was after three. He figured Noah had his phone on silent if he could even get a signal. Drew only hesitated for a moment before anxiety overruled restraint and he started typing.

Drew: *Are you okay? I can't shake a bad feeling—seems like a warning. Please be extra careful.*

He stared at his phone, knowing that a reply was unlikely and holding his breath anyway.

Noah's on a shoot. Might not even have enough bars to get my message. He promised to call at a decent hour of the morning—which isn't long to wait. What am I so afraid of? He's a lynx, a predator. There aren't too many things in the woods that will mess with him except for a bear—and he's smart enough to avoid those.

Drew felt his wolf pacing, so he knew his other half also sensed danger. More than that, he felt a surge of concern that he was sure came from Noah.

Is it possible to have that kind of connection before we've fully mated? Maybe. Do I need to understand in order to love him? Maybe it's enough that we're "special." Would I love him any differently without the bond? No.

Drew knew it shouldn't matter, and he hoped that deep down it didn't. *Everything is so new. Maybe with time, we'll know ourselves and each other better. New love is exciting, but I'm looking forward to settled and familiar.*

Once the adrenaline faded, Drew felt impossibly tired. He knew it wasn't long until his alarm would go off, but exhaustion won out, and he slept more deeply than he expected. He did not dream and woke lonely.

5

NOAH

NOAH SPENT A COLD AFTERNOON IN HIS HIDDEN TENT, MINDING HIS cameras. He'd checked them all first thing and then brushed away his footprints, retreating behind his makeshift wall of saplings and branches to ensure that the settings were just right on his video camera and on his favorite digital SLR.

He texted Drew in the morning and shared photos and short videos he had made just to amuse his boyfriend. *I'm not very interesting. I'm a camera nerd and a video geek. I know way too much about wildlife. I'm kinda boring—but the animals are cute. Maybe they'll help me charm my way into Drew's heart.*

Deep down, Noah knew he and Drew shared a connection different from anything he'd felt before. Still, old rejections bit deep. His last relationship had ended with a fizzle instead of an explosion, leaving him disillusioned. Then he'd been nabbed by the Huntsman and would have died if it weren't for Liam and his friends. Still, all those misfortunes led him to Drew, which meant Noah wouldn't change them for anything.

With spotty reception, Noah didn't expect his texts to go through, but he liked feeling closer to Drew, even if the messages were delayed.

Noah: *Wish you were here. We could stay warmer. Share body heat.*

He included a picture he shot earlier of a squirrel hanging upside down on the trunk of a tree.

Noah: *I hope the moose knows I'm waiting for him. This is all a bust if he doesn't show. Maybe I should have sent an invitation?*

He added a funny cartoon he had saved on his phone and pressed send.

Noah: *I wish I could hike out once the moose comes, but it'll be too dark. I'd probably break my neck. My lynx would never forgive me. I'm not as coordinated as he is.*

This time, he sent a selfie he had managed to take of his animal, when he had proven that paws and toe beans didn't work as well as fingers with a camera.

He scrolled up, re-reading his exchange with Drew earlier in the day and before that, reassuring himself from their chatter and endearments that he hadn't made up the whole thing. Sometimes, when they had gone too long between visits, his imagination ran away with itself, and he had to remind himself that everything they had shared was real.

That should get better with time—and closeness. I'm so screwed. All I want to do is wrap myself around Drew and lose myself in his scent. I want to be full mates—even though that's a little scary. Am I wrong to want to share the bite? When we talked about it, Drew wanted it too. They say we'd be even more connected—maybe hear each other's thoughts and feelings. That's intimidating, but I want it so much I can taste it.

I've got it bad. And that's really good.

Noah sighed and put his phone back into the small backpack he'd brought with him. He liked the bag because he could carry it as his lynx as well. It didn't hold a lot, but he could lift limited weight when he shifted, and the bag was big enough for essentials.

He squirmed, feeling oddly restless. He'd filmed more than he needed, and while he hoped for some good moose footage tonight, he could nearly finish the project without it and set up a blind elsewhere if the animal proved elusive.

A sudden wave of uneasiness washed over him, worrisome and disquieting. *Get out of here,* his lynx urged, striding to the forefront. *Danger.*

That concern overlaid an uncomfortable feeling that had been building since late afternoon. It didn't feel like his own thoughts, and Noah wondered—impossibly—if somehow Drew managed to reach him through their fledgling bond when cell phones couldn't.

They say Cancers are intuitive, maybe even psychic. Like my hunches about where I'll find the animals and get the best shots. Of course, Cancers are also supposed to be pessimistic and suspicious, so it's a toss-up...

He'd spent more than a week setting up this shoot and days freezing his ass off to get the perfect shots. Tonight was icing on the cake, and he'd hoped to get some photos that might win him an award.

Now, with his lynx and his mate shouting warnings, Noah found the decision to be easier than he expected. *Time to go.*

The tent folded down small and so did his bedroll, packing away in minutes. As the seconds ticked by, Noah's sense of impending danger ratcheted up until he practically vibrated with the stress.

Reluctantly, he pulled up his perimeter cams. They were glorified action cameras on tripods, but he had rigged them for night vision and motion sensitivity, and they delivered acceptable footage to round out his B-roll.

Noah left his video camera for last, just in case a perfect shot happened along in the final few minutes. Since darkness had already fallen, getting back to his Tahoe was going to be a royal bitch. Noah shouldered into his pack and put his tent and bedroll back in the protected area where the tent had been. He swept the snow smooth with a branch to cover his snowshoe tracks, then hunkered down once more, hoping for a lucky break.

I'm not ignoring the warning, Noah told himself. *Just ten more minutes...*

A strange howl echoed through the night, and then something large and ungainly tromped through the underbrush. Noah's ears pricked up at the sounds, and he realized that more than one large creature was on the move.

The Sasquatch burst into the clearing, running at full speed. Behind him, two other human-looking figures followed in pursuit.

The half-moon illuminated the clearing, giving Noah and his

camera a good view as the creature flailed its arms and screeched, howling and muttering at its pursuers. Then a shot rang out, and the Sasquatch dropped to the ground and lay still.

Noah saw it all lit by moonlight through the lens of his video camera. His eyes widened in horror, and he stared at the downed cryptid in shock. His camera kept taping.

Two men emerged from the trees, carrying high-powered rifles. One was in his middle years, and the other looked to be in his late thirties. The older man had jowls and small, piggy eyes. He grinned wide, elated at his kill. The other man, whom Noah guessed to be a guide, was handsome in a rough way, a guy who looked like he'd started his share of trouble.

"You did it! You said you'd find me a Bigfoot, and you did it!" The older man exulted. "Hey, gotta get a picture of this!" He handed over his camera, and his companion snapped a shot with the hunter holding the body of the dead creature like a prize buck.

The guide handed back the camera, clearly looking pleased with his client's satisfaction. The hunter kept taking pictures and chattering about "bagging the big one," heedless of being covered in the Sasquatch's blood.

Noah felt sick.

"We should get going," the guide urged. "It's going to take a bit to get it back to the truck, and we want to be out of here before dawn."

"You really think there's going to be anyone within ten miles of here at this hour?" the hunter asked, still looking high from his kill.

"I think that neither of us want to explain or deal with the expense of averting consequences if there is," the guide replied, and it was clear from his voice that he had done this before.

Then he turned and looked directly at where Noah hid behind the bushes. They didn't make eye contact, but Noah felt that gaze and tensed, expecting to be shot—either as a witness or a trophy.

"If anyone happened to see something they shouldn't, we'd have to make sure that story never got told," the guide added, and Noah knew it was directed at him.

"No one's around—quit worrying," the client prodded, still taking photos of the dead creature. "But I'm freezing my balls, so let's be done with this."

Noah was grateful for the darkness and for the caution that made him smooth over his tracks. So glad that he'd already packed up and could get the hell out of here as soon as the hunter and guide were out of hearing range.

His human side wanted to be sick; his lynx wanted to attack. Noah remained motionless, barely breathing, but the guide didn't approach his hiding place. The two men unwrapped a litter with two stainless steel poles and a canvas sling from the guide's backpack, rolled the Sasquatch onto it, and hefted their prize with a grunt.

"Gonna get him stuffed when I get home," the hunter exulted. "I've got a guy who does nice work, and he's real discreet. Knows when to keep his mouth shut. Bigfoot is going to be the king of my trophy room."

When the two men finally moved out of hearing range, Noah realized he was shaking. *I've got to get the fuck out of here in case the guide comes back. He knew I was here.*

He willed himself not to look at the dark patch of bloody snow where the cryptid fell. Moving as silently as he could manage without shifting, Noah eased out of his hiding place and looked around warily, glad he had gotten to know the area during the past several days.

He didn't dare follow the guide and hunter, who had taken a path that led to a secondary trailhead parking lot, one where their vehicle would be less likely to be noticed. Noah had parked at the main lot— he had nothing to hide, and he'd gotten a permit from the park ranger for his photography stakeout.

Shit. They could find my car and trace the plate. If the guide suspected and didn't want to raise a fuss or kill me in front of his client, he could ask the park ranger for details. I've got to get away.

He remembered his way back to the path, aided by his inner cat. Much as he wished for his lynx's sure-footedness and enhanced vision, he didn't want to leave behind his gear if he could help it. The cameras and his phone fit in the bag he could carry once he shifted, but not his tent and sleeping bag or some of the equipment he'd brought to make his long observation more comfortable.

Noah moved quickly and silently, on high alert. When he finally reached the parking lot, he lingered inside the tree line, scanning for danger. The security lights were relatively dim on purpose to minimize their impact on wildlife. The inch of snow on the gravel showed fresh footprints that led to and away from the Tahoe, the only vehicle in the lot. *Fuck. He—or someone—found my car.*

Now that he had a signal, he flicked sound on for his phone and saw a string of missed texts from Drew, as his own prior texts went through. He added a new comment, even though he knew it was an ungodly hour of the night.

Noah: *There's been a problem. I need to leave fast. I'm heading to you. Watch for me—and be safe.*

The drive back to his motel took minutes. Noah checked his rearview mirror constantly, wondering whether the guide would see his client out of the forest, then return to the location of the kill if he suspected they'd had a witness.

I know he sensed me. I don't think I'm imagining it. If he's a guide for illegal trophy hunts, then he's got to be a decent tracker. I hid my presence to keep from spooking the animals, but I wasn't trying to foil a master woodsman. Maybe he didn't want to freak his client, but he could have noticed other signs that someone else had been in the clearing.

I can't stay here overnight. And if the guide finds out anything about me, he'll be able to trace me in Ottawa.

Would he kill me? Hunting anything out of season in the preserve is illegal, but there's no season on Sasquatch. That's got to count as an endangered species. He and his client could get a big fine—even jail time. He might be willing to risk murder to avoid that.

I'm not going to hang around and find out.

Noah backed into the parking space outside his motel room, hiding his license plate from passersby and thankful the Tahoe was a common color. The motel had several other guests, and he hoped the hunter wasn't one of them. Then again, a guy rich enough to hire an illegal guide for a cryptid hunt probably rented a cabin or a house.

He rushed inside and quickly filled his duffel with everything that he hadn't taken with him to the shoot. Noah lifted up the floor in the back of the SUV and opened a secret storage bin. When he'd bought the second-hand Tahoe, he discovered that the previous owner had installed subwoofers in this space. The first owner took the speakers with him, so Noah used the area to secure his expensive electronics.

Noah took the memory cards out of his cameras and put them in a waterproof bag. The larger cameras and lenses as well as the night cams went into the storage bin. He threw his duffel, tent, and sleeping bag into the back of the cargo area and pulled out his emergency kit.

He had a modified dog backpack that fit his lynx, altered so he could work the fasteners with his teeth. Noah put his phone, the memory cards, keys, emergency kit, and wallet in the backpack.

To that he added a compressed bag that held light-weight clothing designed for hikers—a quilted jacket, shirt, leggings, wool socks, hat, gloves, and boots that squashed flat and weighed almost nothing. The emergency kit had a space blanket, survival tool, solar charger, compass, small medical kit, straw filter, lighter, and protein bars he could eat in either his human or lynx form. He locked the compartment, put the floor back in place, and threw the bag into the front seat, where he could grab it in a hurry if things went bad.

Noah had paid for the room through the next morning. He left the key and a tip for the housekeeper on the table, made a quick check to assure himself that he hadn't overlooked anything, and then got in the SUV.

He pulled out of the motel and drove carefully down the two-lane rural highway until he came to a major road. His shoulders finally relaxed when he was on the freeway headed back to Ottawa.

Dawn glowed on the horizon as Noah saw the outskirts of the city. He wanted to call Rob and Drew, but it was still too early. He took a roundabout route to his apartment, still nervous that he might have been followed.

Maybe I'm being paranoid. Now that I've left the preserve, the guide might not try to find me.

A predator will not give up the hunt, his lynx cautioned. *Run—then take your vengeance.*

Noah rolled his shoulders. *I'm not going to tear out the guide's throat —although I want to report him to the police.*

He is not trustworthy. He might hunt ones like us.

Noah had to agree with his lynx. The thought had occurred to him. He worried that heading to Fox Hollow might bring danger to the town by leading the guide there.

On the other hand, they handled a Huntsman—they can handle a guide. The sheriff is fierce. We will be safe there.

Noah didn't try to argue with his lynx, but he worried about leading trouble to Drew's doorstep.

He went around the block twice to make sure no one was watching his apartment building. *I hadn't planned on leaving quite this soon—or running for my life. Will it ever be safe to come back? There isn't time to pack all my stuff.*

Noah had been fond of his small apartment and worried that this might be the last he would see of the space that had been his base and refuge for several years. *Quit that. Rob can check on the place from time to time. I'll pay the rent and utilities until we know what's going on. It might not even be an issue. Ottawa is a long way from the preserve. I might be totally overreacting.*

His lynx growled, making it clear that he did not believe that.

This just means I get to see Drew sooner. I'll tell the Fox Hollow sheriff about what I saw, and they can take it from there. Will that be enough? Will it be safe for me to come back to Ottawa if the guide figures out my plate and where I live?

He remembered the man he had glimpsed in the woods, the one he guessed was the guide. The dead-eyed stranger hadn't been squeamish at all about slaughtering a cryptid for ego's sake. While he wasn't the one who pulled the trigger, he had led the hunter to an easy kill, and the unfair advantage didn't keep him from making a buck off the death of an endangered creature.

Killer's eyes. He'd seen calculation and malice in the man's expression and a coldness that Noah expected from a hitman. The guide's image morphed into that of the Huntsman who had kidnapped Noah, Liam, and others. Suddenly, Noah found it difficult to breathe.

I got away. Even if he finds out my information and comes looking, I won't be here.

Noah tried to convince himself that no one ever went into Witness Protection over poaching. His lynx remained unconvinced.

He parked in a different spot than the one reserved for his apartment and backed in so that his plate faced a retaining wall. By now, nearly six o'clock in the morning, a few lights were on in windows, indicating early risers. He didn't see anyone loitering, so he bolted up the steps and checked to make sure the door to his apartment hadn't been tampered with before he opened it.

Noah stood still, taking in the feel of the apartment. His nose twitched, but after a few minutes he realized that no one else had been here since he left three days ago.

What should I take, and what should I leave?

Noah gathered camera equipment and device chargers that he hadn't already packed, then wrapped clothing around them in his second duffel. He packed favorites and essentials as he careened around the apartment, shoving items into his bag. The big things would have to stay—his TV and microwave, furniture, kitchen stuff, and artwork. Noah intended to come back when it was safe—after he'd spent some time with Drew, and with luck, the guide had forgotten him.

A quick pass through the kitchen let him throw drinks, snacks, and a pack of lunchmeat from the fridge into a small cooler bag, and he hoped Rob wouldn't hate him for the request to take or toss everything else.

He was back in the Tahoe and on the road in fifteen minutes, refusing to glance in the rearview mirror as his old life vanished in the distance.

Noah's phone rang at seven with Drew's ringtone. "Noah—what happened? Are you safe? Where are you?"

"Driving south," Noah replied, still frequently checking his mirrors. "I saw something happen in the woods that I wasn't supposed to see. Cryptid trophy hunting. I'm afraid the hunting guide might have figured out I was there. I don't want to put you in danger, so if you don't want me to come, just say so. But I can't stay in Ottawa."

"Come here," Drew said without hesitation. "You'll be protected, and then we'll figure things out. We know people who can help. Just get here safely."

Noah hadn't expected Drew to turn him away, but hearing such a clear, unreserved welcome eased some of the stress that tightened his shoulders and neck. "I'm not making any stops, so I should be there in a couple of hours. I promise I'll tell you everything."

"Just be careful. You mean a lot to me," Drew said.

"You mean a lot to me too. See you in a few."

Before long, a sign reminded Noah that he neared the United States border. He always kept his passport with him, a habit that had proven helpful time and again.

He feared a hold-up when he went through Customs. Fortunately, he got to the checkpoint at the beginning of the workday when all the people who crossed over daily for their jobs were queued up. That meant the guards didn't want to hold up the line and moved cars through quickly. Noah breathed a sigh of relief as he drove across the border.

Then everything went to hell in a handbasket.

Fifteen minutes, his phone rang again. "Rob?"

"Noah—what happened to the car? Are you okay?"

"What do you mean? I'm driving it." Rob's silence unnerved Noah. "Rob? Still there?"

"Why the hell are you driving your *stolen* car?"

"Stolen?" Noah's eyes widened.

"I'm your emergency contact, remember? I got a call about fifteen minutes ago from the police. They couldn't reach you, and someone reported your Tahoe as stolen. And apparently, you trashed your hotel room, threatened the desk clerk, and skipped out on paying? They've issued a BOLO, and there's a warrant out for your arrest."

"Fuck. That's bad." Noah ran a hand through his hair and felt his heart rate spike. His lynx hissed, twitching its short tail.

"What's going on?" Rob demanded. "Noah, what aren't you telling me?"

Noah let out a long breath. "I don't want to drag you into this more than you already are."

"You're my best friend. I want to help."

Rob didn't know about shifters or supernatural creatures. Over the years, Noah had snuck in little tests like salt, silver, and holy water. None of them affected Rob in the least, and he never mentioned anything that made Noah think his friend knew about magic.

"I saw a big game poacher and his guide in the clearing. They didn't seem to notice me, but I couldn't shake the feeling that the guide knew I was there," Noah confessed. "I grabbed everything out of my hotel. I had paid for an extra day, and I swear I didn't trash anything or punch anyone. Then I got the stuff I couldn't live without from my apartment, and now I'm skipping town for a while."

"Going to Drew?"

"Better if you don't know for sure," Noah said.

"Okay—I officially don't know," Rob replied. "Will you be safe?"

"I think so—but I'm worried about you."

"I don't know anything, remember?" Rob joked. "Seriously—are you sure the guy saw you?"

"Yeah—and he got a look at my license plate, so I'm sure he's behind reporting me," Noah answered. "I've learned to trust my instincts."

"You're still not telling me something."

"Just...trust me. I want to protect you. You're the only best friend I've got," Noah said. "When things calm down, if I'm not back for a while, please drop by the apartment. I didn't have time to clean out the fridge or take out the garbage. But don't go there right away—just in case the guide shows up looking for me."

"Why would someone report your truck stolen when it isn't? Or make up stories to get you arrested?" Rob turned back to the first issue, and Noah sighed in relief.

"I think the guide wants to stop me from getting away."

"Wouldn't that just increase the likelihood of you telling the police what you saw? That would be bad for him, right?"

"If the police believed me, maybe. But now I'm a suspect with the trashed hotel room. By the time things got straightened out at home, the guide might find my cameras and take the evidence," Noah told him.

"Okay, I can see that," Rob said in unwilling agreement.

"We'll sort it out when I'm safe," Noah promised. "But now, I've gotta drive."

"Be very careful. Must have been some serious poaching. It sounds like the guy you pissed off doesn't fool around."

"You too. I don't want the crazy to rub off."

"Too late," Rob said with a chuckle. "Drive safe."

The call ended, leaving Noah alone with his thoughts. *If the guide reported my truck, then cops are going to be looking for me. Would the notice have gone to the US police as well? Probably, since the border is right here.*

I need to watch for the police. I have enough gas so I shouldn't need to stop. But I've still got two more hours—or a little more—to Fox Hollow. Fuck. I should find a way to ditch the Tahoe.

We have done nothing wrong, his lynx protested, sounding offended. *Maybe if we fought instead of running—*

We could be dead if the guide shoots us, Noah pointed out. *We need to stay away from him. The police could put us in a cage. Run now, fight later.*

We should mark our territory and defend it.

You can pee on trees when we get to Fox Hollow.

His lynx stalked off, but Noah's smirk faded quickly. As he drove, his thoughts circled around outwitting the guide. *How can I hide the Tahoe and still have it—and my equipment—be safe?*

Another sign triggered a memory of the last time he had caught a flight from Massena airport because it was cheaper than Ottawa.

Massena offers free long-term parking. I could put some mud on the license plate to make it difficult to read and then leave it in the lot there. If I back in against a wall, no one might notice. After all, it's a black Tahoe. There are tons of those around. And since I'm not flying out, why would anyone even search the airport garage for me?

When it's over, I can come back for the car or send someone for it. I might be able to catch a bus from there to somewhere near Fox Hollow and hike the rest of the way.

It's not a great plan, but it's a plan.

He stuck to secondary highways, avoiding the freeways with their speed traps. Driving into the Adirondack Mountains usually gave Noah a sense of peace. The high peaks and long drop-offs at the side of the road made him feel like he drove along the edge of the world. Snow fell without stopping, making the asphalt slick despite frequent plowing.

A sign announced only five miles to the Massena airport. *Almost there.*

Then he heard the siren.

"Shit!" Noah pounded his hands on the steering wheel. He saw the state police car coming up in his rearview mirror.

Noah sped up; the state police kept pace, lights flashing.

Maybe I should pull over, explain what happened, he thought, then shook his head. *That's never going to work.*

He tried to imagine what that discussion would sound like, how the officer would react, and what it would feel like to be detained in an American jail.

The Tahoe maneuvered well, but the slick road had other plans. Noah felt the truck begin to slide and steered into it like he'd been taught.

Noah shouted as he struggled to regain control, but the SUV's skid took it across the far lane. He tried to wrest the vehicle back into place, but the ice carried him too far, too fast. The Tahoe hit the guard rail and plunged down the steep embankment, mowing over bushes and saplings.

He didn't tumble and managed to steer enough to avoid large trees, despairing for the state the Tahoe would be in by the time he reached the bottom. The front tires hit a depression and brought the breakneck descent to a halt with so much force that the airbags deployed.

Noah sat for a moment, feeling like his world had hit pause as his head spun. Fortunately, shifters were tougher than regular humans. He didn't know if the cop that chased him would try to reach his car before the emergency vehicles arrived, but Noah felt certain he needed to be gone by then.

He released his seat belt, unzipped his parka, unbuttoned his shirt, thumbed open the waistband of his pants, and loosened the lacings on his boots. The door opened, not jammed or blocked.

Noah struggled for the focus necessary to shift. He pictured his cat, remembered the feel of fur and claws, and willed the change to happen. Bone, muscle, and sinew rearranged themselves, making him grit his teeth against the pain as he resisted the urge to rush. Force-shifting was possible, but making the change between one breath and the next brought on serious, maybe even life-threatening side effects, and Noah couldn't afford to be incapacitated when he was being hunted.

He stood beside the Tahoe, fully changed into his lynx, rapidly scanning for sound and scents that might warn of imminent threat.

Then he grabbed the backpack in his teeth and darted from the damaged Tahoe, heading deep into the woods.

6

DREW

Drew ended his call with Noah and tried to push down his worry. He felt a strong flash of fear that he knew wasn't his own, and he wondered if it came through their mate link, even though they hadn't completed their bond.

Noah's in trouble, and there's nothing I can do about it. I need a distraction.

He knew he'd never get back to sleep, so he went to the kitchen and made a pot of coffee. Looking for ways to stay busy, Drew went ahead and put frozen sweet rolls in the oven as well as a pan of bacon.

Drew tried to keep his mind blank, but that didn't fool his body. Tension thrummed through him, and his wolf pawed at the ground and howled for its mate.

He checked the clock obsessively, watching the minutes pass. At eight, he tried to call Noah to see how the drive was going but didn't get an answer. *That's okay. He needs his mind on his driving if there's snow. I can wait.*

Russ stopped in the doorway to the kitchen and gave him a worried look. Drew heard the shower running and figured Liam was getting ready for work. "Why are you up so early?"

"Noah's in danger, and he's on his way here—except he's not

answering his phone, and my wolf is climbing the walls," Drew replied miserably, clutching his coffee mug in both hands.

Russ frowned and went to pour a cup for himself, then pulled out a chair at the table and motioned for Drew to join him. "Sit. Tell me what's going on."

Drew recounted his call with Noah and his gut sense that something was very wrong.

"Maybe he's just dealing with bad weather, and he couldn't be distracted," Russ suggested, and Drew knew his brother was trying to lighten the mood. "You need to be here when he arrives, so don't worry about coming into the shop—"

"But I've got a half-day of appointments," Drew protested.

"And you've got a family emergency," Russ countered. "We'll handle it. Once Noah gets here, if he wants to talk to the sheriff about what he saw, I'll be glad to go with you two for support."

"Thanks," Drew replied, hating how shaky his voice sounded. "I just want him here, safe and sound."

Russ finished his coffee, clapped Drew on the shoulder, and ate a sweet roll and several pieces of bacon. Then he laced up his boots and reached for his coat. "Call me when he gets here. If you need anything, don't worry about interrupting. Just call."

"I promise," Drew said.

"That's what big brother wolves are for," Russ teased before he headed out.

Drew found he didn't have any appetite for food and stuck to coffee, standing at the window and watching the driveway.

Our mate is in danger. He needs us. We need to go to him. Drew's wolf paced as if caged.

We don't know where he is. We have to wait until he gets here. Then we can protect him.

Something's wrong. Can't you feel it? his wolf protested.

Yes. But there's nothing I can do right now. Drew felt miserable.

His resolve to wait lasted until nine, but the call went directly to voicemail. Drew's stomach tightened until he thought he might throw up. Coffee and nerves made him jittery. Drew's imagination unhelpfully suggested reasons why Noah hadn't called, each worse than the previous one.

By ten o'clock with no word, Drew knew something awful had happened. Noah was over an hour late, and according to every traffic report along his route that Drew could find, there were no storm warnings, road closures, detours, or traffic slowdowns. Conditions were snow-covered and icy, but at this time of year, that was the norm this far north.

To distract himself, Drew logged into the library website and searched for books on fated mates. He had intended to visit on the weekend before everything changed with Noah's call.

A surprisingly long list of books showed up, and Drew was impressed that they weren't all romance novels. He didn't know how much the library collection might reflect Fox Hollow's unique population, considering that during tourist season the town did get visitors who weren't part of the supernatural community.

Maybe my library card marks me as a resident. I'll be impressed if the catalog can tell who's in the know and who isn't.

Drew whittled the non-fiction list down to a dozen of the most promising titles, which he reserved for pickup. He wondered when he'd get to read the books with Noah arriving early, then figured maybe they could read—and figure out their unusual bond—together.

Come soon, Drew thought, closing his eyes and praying to the fates to bring his lover home to him.

His phone rang just before eleven from an unfamiliar number. His pulse raced as he answered.

"Is this Drew Lowe?" He didn't recognize the voice.

"Yes. Who is this?"

"Rob Girard, Noah's friend. There's been an accident."

Drew felt lightheaded and sat at the table, trying not to hyperventilate while his wolf howled in his mind. "What happened? How's Noah?"

"I can only answer one of those questions," Rob said. "A police car was pursuing Noah's Tahoe when he lost control and went over an embankment."

Drew's breath caught. "Is he safe? Did he go to the hospital?" He refused to ask whether Noah was still alive. *He has to be okay.*

The rest of what Rob said finally sank in. "Police? Pursuit? What the fuck—?"

Rob sighed. "Noah wasn't in the truck when the rescue crews reached it. The officer said he was able to look down at the Tahoe moments after the wreck, and he never saw him leave. The weirdest thing is, Noah's coat, boots, snowshoes, and clothing were all in the SUV, plus his bags in the back. Why would he run off naked in the snow? How did the cop not notice a naked guy in the woods in winter?"

Noah never told him. It shouldn't have surprised him that Noah didn't tell Rob about being a shifter, despite their close friendship. Maintaining that secret was drilled into people with supernatural abilities from a young age, a matter of life or death. If Rob had never needed to know before and nothing occurred to accidentally "out" Noah, Drew suspected that his boyfriend probably thought he was protecting Rob.

"I don't know. That's strange. Was there blood? Maybe he was disoriented." Drew's thoughts spun as he tried to process the information.

"No blood. The airbag deployed. He must have had his seatbelt on," Rob replied.

"Did anyone see a wild animal near the Tahoe?" Drew hoped his voice sounded steadier than he felt.

"You think he was attacked?" Rob sounded even more worried. "The cop said they saw tracks, some type of big cat, but no one got a look at it, and there weren't other marks in the snow like someone was dragged off. That doesn't explain why all his clothing was left behind."

"Are they searching? Do you know where the wreck happened?"

"Yes. It was near Massena. The cops told me they'd fan out and search until dark. But there aren't any footprints leading away from the Tahoe. Where did he go? He wasn't thrown clear. Did he fly?"

He walked away—as a lynx. Did the cop force him off the road? Noah was afraid he was being stalked. He's alive—but where?

Drew felt bad that he couldn't share the scant comfort of Noah being able to leave the scene on his own since Rob was clearly worried.

"There are a lot of woods in that area," Drew said, glad Noah could evade capture but realizing it would be tough to hike out. "That's going to make it challenging to search."

"Drew, I'm worried. Noah said he witnessed a poaching incident, and he thought the poacher saw him. Then someone reported that his Tahoe was stolen and said he'd trashed his motel room and skipped town without paying. Do you think the person who did that was the poacher?"

Fuck. "Yes—I do. Noah called me to tell me the same thing—and that he was on his way. I haven't heard from him since." Drew gave the most "normal" description he could manage. "Maybe the poacher reported his car and made a false report hoping Noah would get arrested and then he'd be findable."

"You know that suggests that the poacher has cop friends or can access their systems." Rob sounded skeptical. "That's pretty fancy for a poacher."

Drew hesitated, unsure what to disclose. "Some of these people aren't working on their own. Like the guy who attacked Noah. What did he tell you about what happened three months ago?"

This time, Rob paused. "He didn't want to say much. What he did tell me sounded like something out of a movie. Noah said he'd been mugged and then escaped, got lost in the woods, and got hurt before rescuers found him.

"That covers it." Drew sighed, sad that Rob couldn't know the full story. "It took him all the time he spent here afterward to function again—and the counselors agreed that learning to live with PTSD is a long, ongoing process."

He took a deep breath and then went on, doing his best to skirt the truth without lying. "The mugger was part of a network. And if the poacher is getting paid by rich clients, odds are he isn't working alone."

"Shit. I never thought of that," Rob admitted. "As for the PTSD, I'm glad Noah has you to help him through it. He probably figured I wouldn't understand—and I wouldn't in the same way you do because you lived it."

"You help him plenty by being a good friend. I'm glad he has you, so he's not alone all the way up there."

"Canada isn't on another planet, you know," Rob said, a wan attempt at humor.

"Seems like it sometimes," Drew admitted. "Noah's scared that someone's coming after him, traumatized from what happened before, and now he's out in the woods, lost and alone." Drew wrapped his arms around his middle, trying to keep himself from throwing up. "I want to go to him, and I don't even know where to start looking."

"His phone."

"What? He's not answering."

"If he took his phone with him, maybe it can be tracked," Rob suggested.

"Let me talk to our sheriff," Drew said. "We know for sure *he's* not paid off by the poacher. Maybe he can access Noah's phone account."

"Okay. I'll follow up with the police here and see what they'll tell me. I'm going to keep an eye on Noah's apartment and make sure no one breaks in," Rob said. "If I hear from him, I'll call you right away. Please let me know if you learn anything or if he manages to call you."

Drew promised and ended the call. He sat staring at the phone, trying to make sense of what had happened.

I'd know if he died. I'm sure of it. Our mate bond isn't complete, but it's strong enough for that. Drew took comfort from that thought. His stomach still roiled at the idea of Noah alone and scared in the forest.

On Noah's last visit, they had talked about completing a mating bite. *We didn't think there was a hurry. That we had plenty of time, even though we both wanted it. He offered—I asked to wait. I wish I'd agreed. It might help me find him or give him comfort. If something happens to him—no. I can't think like that.*

Please be okay. Please, please.

He startled at a knock on the door and ran to answer it, hoping Noah had somehow reached Fox Hollow.

Liam stood on the porch with a stack of books in his arms and a

bag hanging off his wrist. "Russ said you were home. I brought books
—and donuts. Sorry—didn't have a hand free to use my key."

Drew stepped aside to let Liam in. "There's coffee—and I can make
more," he offered.

Liam put the bag on the table. "The donuts are mango mai-tai," he
said with a grin. Somehow he always managed to channel his inner
fox, dramatic and fabulous. When Liam dressed up, he used a bit of
kohl to line his eyes, increasing the resemblance to his animal.

"Sounds fantastic," Drew said, appreciating the gesture but unable
to shake his worry.

"Linda was working front desk, and she told me about the books
you were looking for, so I brought them. You didn't make a note about
the request being a secret, so I hope that didn't violate any
confidences."

Drew shook his head. "No, that's fine. I think you and Russ already
figured out that Noah and I are mates—" His fear bubbled up, and
Drew found himself blinking back tears.

"Drew? What's wrong? You can tell me." Liam reached across the
table and took Drew's hand in both of his.

Drew told him everything, from Noah's panicked message to their
brief phone conversation, to Rob's ominous news.

Liam listened intently without interrupting. When Drew finished,
Liam jumped to his feet. He brought Drew a donut and refilled his
coffee, then poured a cup for himself. He swooned more than sat and
shoved an entire donut into his mouth at once.

"Sorry. I stress eat. It's a weakness," Liam said over a mouthful of
pastry. "Delicate constitution."

Drew snorted. "I know for a fact that you went apeshit on the
Huntsman to save Russ and the sheriff. Delicate my ass."

"It was more like rabid fox, and that was one of my best moments,"
Liam replied with a flash of pride.

"Russ said you were badass."

Liam smirked. "Of course I was." He sobered quickly. "So you need
to be the big bad wolf to protect your kitty cat."

"Lynxes aren't house cats," Drew protested, defending Noah's
honor.

"Of course not. They're predators—remember that. He's not help-less. He's in danger, but Noah is smart and resourceful, and he loves you. He has every reason to fight. He'll come back to you." Liam locked eyes with Drew. "I believe it in my soul."

In the time Liam and Russ had been together, Liam had become a second big brother to Drew. Now, Drew appreciated the strength of their connection—their pack.

"I'm scared," he confessed. "This whole thing is new to me." Drew made a vague gesture to indicate everything. "We're mates—but I don't think it's quite like you and Russ. You and Noah share the trauma of the Huntsman, which I can't ever completely understand."

"You don't have to understand to be there for us," Liam replied. "Just love him. That's what Russ does for me. We'll heal."

Drew swallowed hard. "Do you believe in reincarnation?"

Liam looked startled. "In what way?"

"I know that fated mates are real. But are some mates destined to find each other, life after life?"

Liam caught his breath. "Is that what you think is happening here?"

Drew nodded.

"Tell me everything."

Drew knew he was rambling, but it filled the silence and kept him busy. He tried to stick to the topic, but stress made his brain jump from point to point. Liam listened patiently while Drew recounted his night-mares of being someone else in different times and what Noah had told him of his dreams.

"It's clear that you're fated mates. But what you're describing is a true pairing. It's rare, but I've heard of it being real—although not nearly as common as in romance novels," Liam said.

"I always liked those stories," Drew confided.

"Me too. But you know what they say—every legend has a basis in fact."

"You think it's possible that Noah and I have been drawn to each other over lifetimes?" The scope of the idea left Drew breathless.

"It's not unknown," Liam replied. "You need to go talk to the psychics at Fox Institute."

"Maybe once we know that Noah is safe, he and I can go together," Drew replied. "Can I ask you something?"

"Sure," Liam replied. "Well, almost anything." His smirk had TMI written all over it.

"Ew. Don't want to know some things." Drew's exaggerated protest made Liam smile.

"Do you and Russ get bad dreams like this? Is it only Noah and me? You had the Huntsman trauma too."

Liam let out a long breath. "We both have nightmares. I'm surprised you haven't heard us cry out—the images can seem quite real."

Drew blushed. "I just ignore noises from your room. I assume you're in the throes of passion."

"Seriously?" Liam protested.

Drew shrugged. "I try not to think about it, honestly."

Liam sobered. "The PTSD counselor I spoke to said that's pretty normal. In many cases, they get less frequent with time and therapy. Hopefully that will work the same for you and Noah."

"We found out that the Huntsman was part of something bigger. What if the 'big game' poacher is too?" Drew worried. The bounty hunter who had initially gone after Liam and also nabbed Noah was part of a larger network of people who kidnapped and sold shifters, cryptids, and people with special abilities. Just thinking about the trafficking scheme made Drew sick.

"If it is, we'll deal with it," Liam assured him. "We have friends— we're not alone. But sometimes bad people act on their own. Now that we know what the guide's been doing, we can find him and stop him. But let's focus on finding Noah first."

Liam urged Drew to call Sheriff Armel and see if his office could trace Noah's phone. While Drew talked to Armel, Liam bustled around the kitchen, completely at home. Liam had moved in after the Huntsman incident and released the small library-owned house that came with his job. Drew figured that eventually, Liam and Russ would either build on or get a place of their own once they married, as he was sure they would.

Sheriff Armel listened carefully as Drew explained the situation.

"I'd heard some chatter about those sort of guides, but they've steered clear of our area," Armel said once Drew finished his story. "I can report the situation to the Tribunal since it involves shifters. There's no way to explain to regular law enforcement that someone just bagged a Bigfoot, although I imagine the CIA knows he's real."

"Can you track Noah's cell phone? He got away from the wreck, but there's a lot of forest between where he crashed and Fox Hollow. If he's hurt and holed up because he's afraid of being tracked or arrested, we might have to go looking for him." Drew crossed his fingers and closed his eyes, hoping hard.

"I can try. Give me his number and tell me which network he's on, and I'll make the request. They usually move fast when it's a life-threatening situation," Armel replied. "Stay home, be close to the phone, and keep checking email and social media in case Noah gets a signal. I'll keep you posted."

Drew thanked him and ended the call, then sat with his head in his hands, feeling as if the world had spun out of control.

He didn't realize what Liam was doing until he heard the oven beep.

"I made a quick casserole for your lunch so you'll eat," Liam said. "Canned chicken, broad noodles, cream of something soup, and a can of peas, plus the secret ingredients—Parmesan cheese and Worcestershire sauce. If Noah shows up in the next few hours, you'll have enough to feed him. One of my 'six canned ingredient' recipes from my bachelor days, but it's hot and filling."

"Sounds good. Thanks. I'm sorry to be a mess."

Liam shook his head. "Russ told me what he was like when I disappeared. I think you're holding up well. Don't overthink, and don't give up hope." He reached to rustle a hand through Drew's hair like an honorary big brother. "I've got to get back to the library, but I wanted to make sure you had food fixed. If you hear from Noah or the sheriff, or you need anything—call me."

Drew watched Liam leave, and his stomach rumbled at the smell of the casserole in the oven. He knew that he wouldn't have taken the time to make something for himself. *I don't know how much I can eat or whether it'll stay down, but it was nice of Liam to make me food.*

He checked his phone for missed messages, then his email and all his social media. *Nothing. Maybe Noah doesn't have a signal, or he doesn't dare shift.* His imagination provided worse options. *Maybe he's injured, or he's been captured.*

Annoyed at himself for focusing on gloom and doom, Drew opened one of the books Liam had brought and buried himself in its pages until the timer dinged. He fixed himself a small plate, unsure how it would set in his tense stomach, and felt pleasantly surprised when the food hit the spot.

When his phone rang he jumped at the sound, grabbing it and feeling a rush of disappointment when he realized it wasn't Noah.

"Sheriff—did you find him?" Drew held his breath.

"I'm sorry, Drew. His phone isn't showing up. You said he was in a wreck? Maybe it got damaged."

Drew felt his heart drop. "Thanks for trying. Please let me know if anything turns up."

"If you get a name on that 'guide,' let me know, and we'll check into him. I'll put out some feelers and see if I can find out what's behind the false charges," Armel offered before ending the call.

Dejected, Drew blinked back tears. He closed his eyes and focused on the connection he often sensed with his mate. He felt a vague presence, enough to reassure him that Noah lived, but nothing strong enough to point to his boyfriend's location.

As soon as you find him, mount him and bite him, Drew's wolf advised. *No more misplacing our mate.*

I didn't "misplace" him.

You don't know where he is. Misplaced.

You're insufferable, Drew shot back.

No, I'm right. We should go to the woods and howl to him.

That will get us shot or picked up by animal control.

Humans make these things too complicated. Howl, eat, fuck, sleep. Simple.

Drew shook his head. *Look, I don't want to fight with you. So be helpful or lay off.*

He expected his wolf to stalk off, insulted. Instead, he saw his other self tilt his head, thinking, and then sit. *We're both worried about our mate. I will stay present, so you aren't alone.*

Thanks. Although he and his wolf quibbled, Drew was fond of the beautiful creature and felt sleek and powerful when he changed into his fur. Although his other half never actually went away, it could recede from his consciousness for periods of time, giving him space. Now, Drew appreciated feeling the wolf's close, supportive presence.

He put the leftovers in the refrigerator, poured more coffee, and forced himself to settle in with the books Liam brought, deciding that he could make progress on one mystery while he waited to hear on another.

Find your way home to me, Noah. I'm waiting for you.

7

NOAH

HE RAN, LEAVING THE TAHOE AND THE COPS BEHIND. NOAH BARRELED through the forest, backpack clamped in his teeth, trying to outdistance his pursuers.

Noah finally paused, heaving for breath, tongue lolling, and dropped flat in the snow. When he could move again, he nudged the pack with his nose and rolled around until he had gotten his front paws through the harness, then he pulled the straps tight with his teeth. That settled the light bag on his back so he could carry it easily. A special clasp that he could reach with his mouth would let him drop the pack when it was time to shift.

As his lynx, Noah's sight, smell, and hearing were keen. The cold didn't bother him, and his broad paws handled both snow and uneven terrain easily.

A shifter could cover twice the distance in a day as a regular lynx, but would it be fast and far enough? His range was still less than that of a wolf—or a human.

I was about eighty-five miles from Fox Hollow when I went over the side. That's an eight-day hike as a lynx. If I push hard and don't hit bad weather, I can probably do it in a little more than three if I switch back and forth to human. I don't dare go to town and ask for help or use my credit card on a bus ticket. I'll end up arrested—and extradited.

He stayed in his lynx all morning, then caught and ate a rabbit for lunch. His human self retreated far into his mind to avoid thinking about the crunching bones and raw flesh.

Delicious, his lynx proclaimed. *It's been too long since I hunted.*

Glad you're enjoying running for our lives, his human side snapped, out of sorts.

At this moment, we have a full belly and are in no danger. The sun is bright, the woods are full of prey, and we can stretch our legs. It is all good.

Noah bit back a retort, realizing that his cat was right. He hadn't heard any pursuers, and the thick forest would hide him from helicopters—which wouldn't be looking for a lynx anyhow, though one wearing a backpack might catch some notice. For the moment, things were as good as they could be.

He took stock of the situation. *I'm not bleeding, no broken bones, just rattled. I've got my backpack, so when I shift, I'll have clothes. The Tahoe is a mess, but if they called Rob about it being stolen, then maybe they'll call to say it was found, and he can retrieve it. With luck, my gear isn't ruined. I'll worry about repairs if I survive.*

Rob and Drew are probably worried sick. I need to shift and call them—if I even have a signal.

Noah found a protected place out of the wind, a relatively dry, sheltered outcropping. He focused his energy and shifted back to a naked and shivering human.

He pawed open his backpack, removed the bag of compressed hiking clothes, and dressed in a hurry, hoping the goosebumps would eventually fade. His thick-furred lynx snickered at the mostly-hairless human's reaction.

The quilted coat provided adequate protection from the cold, especially with Noah walking at a brisk clip, and the boots, along with thick woolen socks, kept his feet dry and reasonably protected. The rest of the serviceable clothing was unremarkable, but functional.

Once hypothermia was no longer a major risk, he reached for his phone, only to find the screen shattered and the body cracked. The damaged phone didn't even turn on.

Shit—the pack hit the console hard when the Tahoe crashed. Drew will kill me once he finds out I'm not dead.

That also meant figuring out the direction to go with just his compass and dead reckoning. His lynx senses, muted by not being at the fore, still provided helpful input.

I like to sleep during the day, his lynx informed Noah, sounding miffed.

Since I can cover ground faster, but my night vision sucks by comparison, we're going to do most of the traveling when I can see. You can come out at night to keep me warm.

Do I get a vote? The lynx sounded grumpy.

You can pick where we sleep. Don't get your hackles up on the daytime bit. We don't really have a choice.

Noah tried to pace himself, and his shifter endurance served him well even in his human form. Beneath the trees, the snow wasn't deep, which saved him from tramping through drifts. A tracker who knew where to look could certainly follow his trail, but since he stayed away from cabins or pathways, he hoped that picking up his footprints in the vast forest would be like a needle in a haystack.

Still, the fear of pursuit made Noah push on. He filled his bottle with clean snow and let it melt before using his special straw to purify.

I can eat and drink from the land, his lynx reminded him smugly.

My legs are longer.

With a growl, his lynx withdrew, leaving Noah alone with his thoughts.

He tried to keep his focus on the path ahead and checked for threats, reminding himself that a bear or a startled moose could be just as lethal as a man with a gun.

Under other circumstances, the hike could be pleasant. Far from highways and not on a major flyover path, the sounds of nature came to the fore. If he hadn't been running for his life, the change of scenery might have been restful.

He paused long enough to drink, refill his bottle, and eat one of his protein bars.

Once we stop for the night, you can hunt, he told his lynx.

Oh, goody. I'm your furry meal delivery service.

Sarcasm doesn't suit you.

Bite me, Short Tooth. Looking pleased with himself, the lynx retreated.

Sun didn't filter down much through the trees, but Noah glimpsed clear sky, which made the threat of snow unlikely. He took comfort from the chatter of birds and the nattering of squirrels knowing that meant other humans hadn't invaded the area ahead of him.

The sun, his compass, and his lynx's instincts guided him, navigating a route that kept well away from roads or settlements. He walked at a steady pace, glad that going into the forest for his photo shoots had prepared him for long hikes.

By the time it grew too dark for him to safely continue, Noah figured they had covered close to twenty miles. *Three more days of this, and I'll be at Fox Hollow—what's left of me.*

He stripped, carefully packed his clothing and boots and replaced them in the backpack, leaving a corner of the space blanket easy to find in case he needed extra warmth during the night. Noah shifted and slipped into the harness. His lynx shook himself, fluffing the thick fur. He sniffed the air and purred, content.

Glad you're enjoying yourself while we're outlaws.

Unclench. I'm just scenting for predators—and dinner.

Better find us a place to spend the night so we don't freeze.

Eat first, then I'll look for a den.

An unlucky raccoon became dinner. Much as Noah disliked eating raw meat, he was ravenous after a full day of walking. In lynx form he could drink his fill from a stream. Sated, his cat made short work of finding a recess beneath a rocky outcropping that provided shelter from the wind and protection from larger predators.

Only humans hunt lynxes, his cat reassured him. *Bears and bobcats won't bother us if we don't take their food or young. The cold is our only enemy tonight, and in our fur we're protected. The bad man won't hunt in the dark.*

Noah hoped his other half was correct. He wriggled out of his backpack, opened the zipper with his teeth, and tugged on the flat square-folded space blanket, being careful not to let anything else fall out. Then he closed the pack, looped it over his back, and pulled the blanket under and around him to fend off the damp and the chill of the hard ground. Thick fur would keep him warm enough, but his human side preferred a bit more comfort.

How is Drew holding up? I can't even call to let him know I'm alive. Please don't let him do something stupid, like try to search the forest for me. I hope he stays home, safe, and trusts me to find my way to him.

He thought about sleeping in Drew's bed, curling around each other the way they had before he returned to Ottawa. How good it felt to be with his mate and how healing it had been to lie skin to skin even though they hadn't completed their mating.

Why did I leave so soon? Why didn't we complete our mate bond? Nothing is more important than my mate.

You had to go away to understand, his lynx replied as if it were obvious.

Maybe so. I knew it was real between us by how much the separation hurt.

You're pretty smart for not being a cat.

And you're pretty badass for being a pretty kitty, Noah teased before falling into an exhausted sleep.

8

DREW

"I wondered when you would come to see us." Rich Jeffries looked up from the papers on his desk and rose to welcome Drew to his office at the Fox Institute. The Institute's director was friends with Russ and Liam, so Drew felt comfortable talking with the older man. Jeffries wasn't a shifter, but he *was* a psychic with a deep commitment to Fox Hollow and its residents.

"Noah and I are mates, but I think there's more to it," Drew said, struggling to put his thoughts into words. "I keep dreaming about us in different centuries. We're us...but we're not us. I think Noah has had similar dreams."

"Curious," Jeffries looked intrigued instead of telling Drew that it was all in his imagination.

"I know it sounds crazy. Like something out of a TV show. But is it possible? Could Noah and I be more than mates—be reincarnated to find each other time and again?" Drew held his breath. Saying it out loud seemed preposterous. But something deep inside felt the truth of his words.

"Tell me what you've seen." Jeffries leaned forward, intent on Drew's story. "The more I understand, the better I can match you with one of our people who has the right skills to get to the bottom of this."

Drew told him about the dreams in as much detail as he could remember and shared what Noah had told him about his nightmares.

"Did you have dreams like this before you met Noah?" Jeffries asked.

Drew nodded. "I've had those dreams on and off my whole life, but since I didn't recognize the people and didn't see much of a story—I thought I'd seen something in a movie or read a book that stuck with me. Then I'd forget until they happened again."

"But since you met Noah, something changed?"

Drew ran a hand over his face, a nervous gesture when he felt unsure. "When we touched for the first time, I felt a connection I can't even describe. It was like getting hit with lightning, only in all my veins and nerves. He looked startled too. Later, he said he felt the same. After that, the dreams became more detailed and lasted longer, got clearer. It was like a channel opened. They feel like memories. Real." Drew knew he sounded crazy.

Jeffries sat back in his chair. "They *are* real, Drew. It's just that most people aren't accustomed to remembering past lives. Many folks believe that we've all had other identities. It's a lot to wrap your mind around."

Drew shook his head. "It seems like a movie plot. I swear I'm not making it up. And I get the feeling that at least some of the past pairings didn't get their 'happily ever after.' I think they died young."

Jeffries reached out to touch his hand. "I believe you. And so will folks here at the Institute."

"I don't know how to untangle it all. I remember some dreams with swords and horsemen, like back in the Middle Ages, as well as more recent times. I think if I could recall everything, we might go back farther. Maybe we were cavemen together," he said with a nervous laugh.

"Souls are eternal," Jeffries said.

Drew caught his breath. "That's kinda romantic. In a scary sort of way."

He looked down. "None of this matters if we can't find Noah. No one's heard from him since the wreck. Can your people help? Then, we'll have all the time in the world to figure this out. But right now, with him missing? I'm afraid time is running out."

"I'll talk to Isabel, one of our senior witches. Her coven is powerful. They may see possibilities we haven't considered yet," Jeffries told him. "The sheriff already alerted us and asked the coven and our far-seeing psychics to try to find him. We don't have a lock on his location yet, but I'm sure we will soon." He paused. "Back to the reincarnation topic, have you ever read about past life regression?"

"Isn't that something on daytime talk shows? Like someone finds out she used to be Cleopatra?" Drew hid his nervousness with humor.

"There are plenty of frauds and charlatans in every business," Jeffries replied. "Their existence doesn't negate the truth."

"That sort of thing is real?" Drew was starting to feel as if he'd fallen through the looking glass.

Liam and Russ had nagged him into coming to get him out of the cabin. He left a note on the front door in case Noah showed up. Liam drove him, doing his best to keep Drew distracted so he didn't climb the walls worrying.

Sheriff Armel had put out a call to law enforcement units in the towns near the area where Noah disappeared. Unfortunately, because of the false report of Noah's car being stolen, and what Drew was sure was a dishonest report of him skipping out on a trashed motel room, Noah had a warrant for his arrest. That meant asking other police departments for information, but not pulling them in on a manhunt—or a lynx hunt.

"Yes, past life regression is real—when done by someone with training and ability," Jeffries said with a rueful chuckle. "What worries me is that at least some of the memories you've seen have a tragic ending. That's not the usual."

"It isn't?" Drew tried not to focus on the impression that the people in his dreams came to a too-early end, hoping it wasn't as ominous as it felt.

Jeffries shook his head. "I'm not the one to ask. My role here is to know a little about a lot of things outside my area. But from what I've read, you've got a special situation, and I think it's going to matter at some point. I know you're worried about Noah's current problem, but once we find him—and I believe we will—I think we need to get to the bottom of the bad luck. It may be possible to change your future."

Drew looked up, hopeful. "You don't think we're fated to die young?"

"No. That's not part of the normal reincarnation cycle. Someone has tampered with your timeline."

"It might be possible to change it?" Drew looked up, hopeful.

Jeffries smiled. "I don't think it's inevitable. I'd bet that dark magic is involved. Figure that out, and the curse ends."

"Curse?" Drew asked sharply.

"That's what we usually call magic that hurts people."

Drew buried his face in his hands. "I'm so confused. Noah is missing and charged with crimes he didn't commit. We might be cursed—by someone long ago—to have bad luck and die young. Why can't we just be in love and be happy?"

"Let's get some experts involved," Jeffries replied. "Do you want to go down to the dining room and get a snack, and I'll check with Isabel?"

Drew checked his phone and saw no messages from Noah. "Okay. I'll go get some food, and when you have something, call me. I'm off today, so if anyone can meet with me, I'd like to dive right in. It'll keep my mind off worrying about Noah."

Jeffries smiled at him. "You're very brave."

"No. I'm scared shitless for my mate. But I'll do whatever's necessary to bring him home and free us from the curse."

"Do you have anything with you that belongs to Noah that I could lend to the remote viewers? It might help the psychics focus," Jeffries said. "Different people have different clairvoyant abilities. I get visions. Some folks have telepathy or can channel ghosts, and others are able to see things in real-time that are happening a distance away—the remote viewers. Some people call them 'far-seers.' We have a couple of those on staff, and they're doing their best to find him."

Drew peeled off Noah's flannel shirt, which he wore over a T-shirt. "This is his. Just...I'd like it back, please."

"Absolutely. They won't hurt it." Jeffries gave Drew a voucher for the Institute's cafeteria and promised to call him as soon as he could rally the people to consult on his situation. Drew was so nervous that he didn't know if he could keep food down, but the dessert selections looked appetizing, and he found he was hungrier than he expected.

By the time he finished a piece of blackberry pie, his phone rang.

"If you're done eating, come back to my office. There are some folks here I'd like you to meet."

When Drew arrived at Jeffries's office, he found two women he didn't recognize eyeing him with speculation.

"Drew, come in. I'd like you to meet Isabel, our senior witch." Jeffries nodded toward the older woman, "and Becca, whose specialty is reincarnation." He indicated a woman with a blonde bob who looked like she should be at the PTA. "I'm a psychic and an empath, and if—when—they've explained things you want to trance, I'll help you."

Drew nodded, hoping he hid his nervousness. "Whatever it takes to make this right with Noah. Did the remote viewers find anything?"

Jeffries shook his head. "Nothing actionable yet, but they said the shirt did help them focus. He's alive, and he's in the forest. But they couldn't pick up any landmarks to tell us where. Maybe if they can check again when the stars come out, they can get a better idea."

He's alive.

Drew was grateful for any bit of information. "So how does this work?"

"Here's what will happen," Jeffries filled in. "Isabel warded the room so no dark energies can enter—and no one outside can pick up on thoughts or feelings. She's also our protection in case poking at memories triggers any long-ago magic. Becca will guide you, and I'll feed energy to her and take my own psychic 'readings' to gain a different perspective."

"Sounds good. What next?" Drew knew he didn't have time to get comfortable with the idea of trancing. Noah needed him.

"Let's start with you telling Isabel and Becca what you told me—and if you remembered anything else, please add it," Jeffries said.

Drew told his story again, describing his dreams in as much detail as he could recall. To his surprise, they listened without questioning his sanity. He fidgeted, aware that his wolf had retreated, and felt alone.

Noah's missing, my wolf is having a snit, and when I tell my story out loud it sounds insane. I should be at the cabin waiting for a call or out in the woods looking for him.

Isabel put a hand on his arm. "We don't think you're crazy."

He didn't know whether she had read his mind or could guess from his expression. Then again, she *was* a witch.

"Fated mates are uncommon," Becca said. "A true pairing isn't unheard of, but rarer. It means that your souls are tangled together and keep finding each other when separated. There are theories," she added with a shrug. "Some say that a true pair have a single soul split between them. Others think that it's a quirk of creation energy that caused souls to imprint on each other so deeply. The 'why' doesn't really matter."

"Is it a good thing or a bad thing?" Drew's voice barely rose above a whisper.

Becca smiled. "It's a wonderful gift to have an unbreakable bond with someone who loves you. To find each other across time and space, like your 'true north.'"

Drew met Becca's gaze. "Do we have a choice? Fated mates can still choose. It would be terrible to be forced into something like that forever."

"Do you want to escape the bond? I thought you and Noah were a couple," Jeffries asked, concerned.

"We are. I love him. It's just I wanted to make sure this wasn't a trick of some kind."

Jeffries smiled. "I know this is new and rather difficult, but the feelings are real, and they haven't been forced on you. They're a natural part of your existence."

"What about the curse?"

"One thing at a time." Jeffries looked to Becca. "Can you confirm the true pairing?"

Becca reached for Drew's hand and twined their fingers together. She closed her eyes and wrapped her other hand around both of theirs. After several minutes, she opened her eyes.

"I can sense your connection and that the energy could be ancient. No, I can't tell where Noah is right now, only that the bond extends beyond a single lifetime. But it is real and strong," Becca told him.

"Now about the curse." Isabel broke in after she studied Drew closely and read his energy. "We've got a problem. The spell is relatively new—and badly done. All fucked up, to tell you the truth."

Drew's surprise at Isabel's comment must have shown in his face because the others chuckled. Isabel just smiled.

"What I mean is the witch—and I can tell it was a man—who cast the curse had some power but probably hadn't been trained. So he did the spell wrong. It worked...but since it's cobbled together in ways it shouldn't be, the magic is unstable. That also means that breaking the spell isn't going to happen in the usual ways," Isabel explained. "It's like someone who doesn't know anything about electricity doing the wiring in a house. It might function at the beginning, but over time it breaks down, and it'll be dangerous."

"So the guy who's after Noah is a witch?" Drew caught his breath.

Isabel shook her head. "At one time, but not necessarily in this life. And he wasn't a very good witch—perhaps more malice than talent, and self-taught. Curses have always been a type of magic someone without a natural gift can access—which has caused a lot of problems."

"Can we do the regression thing? I'm waiting to hear from Noah and the sheriff, and I'm itching to do *something* that might get answers." Drew's frustration came through in his voice. "Maybe if we can see my past, we'll get some clues about who the bad guy is in this life."

Jeffries smiled. "We can do that right now if you want. And I've arranged for you to have lunch with Jamie Miller and Austin Williams, who might also be able to help. Jamie's a historian on staff here at the Institute, and Austin—his partner—is a private investigator who's been part of cracking open the trafficking cartel."

Drew's eyes widened. "Do you think the 'guide' who is after Noah is part of that?" *This just keeps getting worse and worse.*

"Not necessarily, although I think there are probably points of intersection," Jeffries replied. "My intent was for you to tell Austin everything Rob relayed about the guide. Maybe Austin can find more details. The more we know, the faster we can track down the guide—and hopefully, Noah."

Drew rubbed his hands together nervously. "So...how do we do this?"

They left Jeffries's office and went to another room with a comfortable recliner, soft lighting, three side chairs, a small writing desk, and a recording set-up. The walls were a peaceful shade of blue, and a fuzzy blanket lay across the armchair. Everyone silenced their phones, but Jeffries promised to keep an eye on Drew's in case Noah, Sheriff Armel, or Rob called.

"Make yourself comfortable in the recliner," Becca told Drew. "I'd recommend loosening any tight clothing, taking off your shoes, and getting snug under the blanket. Once you're ready, I'm going to take you through a hypnotic sequence in a guided meditation to open memories you can tap into with your conscious mind."

That didn't sound so bad. Drew sank into the recliner, leaned back, and lifted the footrest, then pulled the blanket over him. His wolf came closer in his mind, curious.

Why not sleep at our den?

This is different. They're going to help me remember things. Drew wondered how to explain the situation to a wolf.

This will help find our mate?

I hope so.

It looks like sleeping, his wolf said. *Are you sure this isn't a nap?*

Stick around and find out. Maybe you can keep me awake. Do you remember our past wolves?

We are all one wolf. The fur changes, but the wolf within stays the same.

Drew decided he needed to remember that, in case it was important. *Did the long-ago witch know he cast a spell on shifters? Maybe that's where it went wrong.*

"Ready?" Becca took a seat near Drew, facing him. Jeffries sat against the wall, observing but out of the way. Isabel sat beside him, leaning forward with an intense gaze as if sending some of her power into the process.

"I'm going to paint a word picture for you," Becca told him in a soothing voice Drew knew was going to make it hard to stay awake.

"Focus on my words, let them create a scene in your mind. Try to engage all your senses to make that scene real. Don't let other thoughts distract you. We'll take a walk together, and when we get to the bottom of the steps, you'll look around and tell me what you see in as much detail as you can. Here we go."

"You're walking in a beautiful garden," Becca began, "the sun is warm, a light breeze touches your skin, and the flowers smell amazing. Birds are everywhere, singing. Wind chimes sound like bells, and there's a fountain and a koi pond. You know you are safe here, and you feel happy...relaxed."

Drew pictured the garden and let go of his worries, following Becca's voice. His wolf canted its head, confused but not alarmed, and trailed Drew on the garden path.

Becca's soothing voice described flowers and trees, pointed out lizards and butterflies, and lulled Drew into feeling happy and relaxed. They paused to watch the koi. Drew's wolf lay down on the path, resting his chin on crossed front paws while his tail wagged lazily.

If you don't watch out, you're going to be rolling over for belly rubs, Drew joked. His wolf just stuck out a pink tongue.

"The garden has many levels, all of them lovely and safe. It's been a while since you've visited these other levels, but you miss them, and today you want to see them again. You're excited about going to the lower garden, so you carefully descend the steps." Becca's voice guided him, and Drew relished the feeling of warmth and safety. Even his wolf seemed comfortable.

"When you reach the bottom, you are in a new part of the garden. You feel completely safe and relaxed. Nothing can hurt you. Tell me what you see," Becca said.

Drew blinked, needing a moment to make sense of his new surroundings. The garden remained, but subtle differences told Drew he was not just somewhere different, but some*when*.

New statues peeked from within the greenery, with a very Art Deco look. Drew looked down at himself and saw that his clothing had changed. Instead of a T-shirt and jeans, he wore a starched shirt with an old-fashioned collar, dress pants with suspenders, and spats.

"What do you see?" Becca prompted. Drew told her, describing everything in detail.

"Who are you?"

Drew hesitated, but the answer came to him almost immediately, second nature. "My name is Trevor Keeg. I'm an architect."

"Tell me about the ring you wear," Becca prompted.

Drew looked down at the garnet ring on his right hand and saw its sapphire twin in his mind. "It was a gift from a friend," he replied, uncomfortable at the inquiry, although he pictured the man who wore the other ring right away. *Partner. Lover. Mate.*

"Tell me about your friend. You can trust me," Becca told him, and his reflexive panic eased. "Nothing bad will happen to you."

Drew believed her, although silence and secrets equaled safety. "Dorian Fitzgerald. He's my partner in the architecture firm we own." He blushed because their relationship was far more than professional.

"You're mates?" Becca asked.

Drew knew that she hadn't meant friend or classmate. "Yes. We are. For years. Forever." He lifted his chin defiantly, afraid but feeling strength in speaking the truth.

"It's time to come back to the upper garden," Becca said. "Return to me, Drew."

Drew felt reluctant to leave the garden. The sculptures resonated with him, and he wanted to go home to be with Dorian. But a powerful compulsion brought him back to the staircase, and as he climbed step by step, his connection to the lower level faded.

When he reached the top and stood in the sunlight once more, Drew remembered who he was.

"It's time to leave the garden for now," Becca told him. "You will be able to return, and you won't be afraid of what you'll learn. You will remember what you see here, but the other levels will be long-ago memories, real but unable to harm you. I'm going to count backward from three, and on one, you'll wake refreshed, remembering every-thing, completely yourself."

"Three."

The garden shimmered in Drew's vision, and the sun went behind a cloud.

"Two."

The brilliant colors of the flowers faded, and the edges of the garden grew hazy.

"One."

Drew opened his eyes and found himself in the quiet room at the Fox Institute, emotionally wrung out.

"Was it real?"

Becca pressed a bottle of water into his hand. "As real as memory can be. You found one of your past lives. How did it feel?"

Drew paused to drink the water, trying to sort through the swirl of emotions. Now that he was back in his own time, his fear for Noah's safety returned like a gut punch.

"Trevor loved Dorian like I love Noah. They were husbands in every way that mattered, except they could never be open about it in their time. And I sensed a sadness clinging to them." He looked from Becca to Jeffries and Isabel. "They didn't get to grow old together."

The images came to him as he spoke. "There was a car accident. They died young." Once he said the words, the rightness of it sank in. Grief clenched his heart, fresh, strong, and personal.

Becca reached out to lay a hand on his arm. "That happened a long time ago. It isn't you and Noah now, and we're going to fix this so it won't be you two later."

Drew nodded, too overwhelmed with emotion to answer.

"You made a good start today," Isabel said as she got up and stretched. "That's one life. Come back tomorrow, and if you do well, we can reach back farther."

"Can't we do more today? Noah's in trouble, and what I remember might hold the key to fixing all of this," Drew argued. "We don't even know who put the curse on us, or why. Please?"

The others exchanged a look. "How about you go to lunch with Jamie and Austin and see how you feel afterward?" Jeffries replied. "We're willing to go farther, but not if it drains you too much."

"Noah is already running for his life. How can I play it safe? When we find him and save him from the guide, we'll still have the curse hanging over us. Who knows how quickly it might strike in this life, and then we lose our chance for another century?"

Isabel made a shooing motion. "Go. Eat. Thoughts are clearer on a full stomach."

Drew huffed, but he left the building and walked the short distance to the Full Moon Diner. He had met Jamie a few times before but hadn't talked much with Austin. Knowing the man was a private investigator felt a little intimidating to Drew.

"Over here!" Jamie called and motioned for Drew to join him and Austin in a booth toward the back.

"You've met Austin?" Jamie asked as Drew took his seat across from them.

Drew smiled and nodded, distracted. He didn't want to be rude, but what he'd seen at the Institute weighed on his mind, and his worry for Noah never strayed from his thoughts.

"Yes, we've met—but we didn't have a lot of opportunity to talk."

"Good to see you again," Austin replied. "Hard to believe that it's possible not to run into someone in a town the size of Fox Hollow, but I guess it goes with being busy."

"Let's order before I starve," Jamie said, handing Drew a menu. "I love the fried chicken here, and it's on special today."

They gave their orders to the server, who brought water for all of them and coffee for Drew.

Once the waiter retreated, Austin leaned forward. "Rich Jeffries said your boyfriend's being stalked. He thought it might be connected to a case I'm working on. We don't know each other well, but will you trust me with the details of what's going on? I swear that if I'm able to help, I will."

Drew filled them in while they waited for their food. He sipped his coffee, trying to quell his nervousness. *Time is passing, Noah is missing, and I feel like I haven't accomplished anything to make him safe.*

"I think this guide is taking clients into the forest to hunt cryptids," Drew finished. "Who knows if he works with a Huntsman too?"

Austin sat back and crossed his arms while Jamie looked worriedly between the two. "Do you think that's possible?" Jamie asked his partner.

Austin shrugged. "Anything's possible. Is it likely? Can't rule that out. You know how small the paranormal world is. Sooner or later, people run across each other—especially if they're in a similar business."

"Does it matter?" Jamie asked. "Can't you figure that out after you save Noah?"

"It might make a difference if the guide draws more people into Noah's situation. That could make it more dangerous for Noah—and for us trying to get him to safety," Austin replied.

"Can you investigate the guide? Try to figure out who he is? Rob— Noah's friend—is going to call me back with any details he can find." Drew didn't try to hide his desperation.

Austin gave him a comforting smile and slid his card across the table. "I'll do my best. Call me as soon as you hear something."

Drew thanked him, and they ordered dessert. While they ate, they talked about the weather, what was playing at the theater, and what everyone was saying about the ice fishing this year. For a few minutes, everything felt normal.

Then fear and guilt came rushing back like a riptide, threatening to drag Drew under. *I'm sitting here with friends having a nice meal and dessert, and Noah's trying to stay ahead of a killer. How could I forget that, even for a moment?*

"Hey," Jamie said, jostling Drew's plate to get his attention. "It's okay to have some good moments in a bad time. That's what keeps you going. Keeps your strength up for the fight."

"Don't feel guilty," Austin agreed. "You've got friends—and we'll help you get to the bottom of this."

Jamie and Austin walked back to the Institute with Drew. When he went into the lobby, they stayed behind talking. As Drew went up the stairs, he glimpsed them kissing through the large windows.

I want that kind of relationship. I miss Noah—and if I can find him, I hope he decides not to go back to Canada after this. I have to save him. Then we can make a plan afterward—together.

His phone rang before he reached Jeffries's office, and a glance told him it was Rob.

"Rob—please tell me you've got news about Noah." Drew's heart was in his throat.

"I do, but not the good kind," Rob replied. "I'm back in Ottawa, in our neighborhood. I just live across the street from Noah. A friend at the coffee shop said there was a man he'd never seen before looking for Noah, saying he wanted to hire him to take pictures, but he didn't really seem to understand the kind of photography Noah does. My friend said that he didn't tell the guy anything, but it creeped him out."

"Doesn't sound good."

"I did some online searches and found 'Exclusive Outdoor Expeditions.' It's new, definitely pitches itself upscale, and dangles a carrot of 'unique' and 'uncommon' hunts. The guide's name is Oliver Grantham." Drew's phone pinged as Rob sent a text with the web address.

"Shit. Is Grantham the guy who was asking about Noah at the coffee shop?"

"He gave my friend his name and number in case he saw Noah. It was Grantham. His tip is what led me to the website."

"Shit," Drew replied. "Anything else?"

"Yeah. Noah had asked me to stop in at his apartment to take out the trash. When I got there, someone had broken in and tossed the place. They didn't break anything valuable that I could tell, but made a big mess. I don't know if anything was stolen."

Drew caught his breath. "Grantham? What do you think he was looking for?"

"My bet? Cameras. He could have asked the Park Ranger who had a permit to do commercial photography, and tracked Noah from that. Grantham's probably scared that his poaching got caught on camera."

Drew doubted Rob knew what, exactly, Grantham had poached—and why that made the stakes even higher.

"I cleaned up the apartment the best I could," Rob went on. "Didn't want Noah to come home to see the place wrecked. I don't think it was a regular burglary, because they didn't take any of his big electronics—the TV, stereo, and speakers were all there. I figure he had all of his camera stuff with him. Lucky for Noah."

"Yeah, that's real lucky," Drew replied, thinking that Grantham was probably scared and angry enough to make a dangerous enemy—more so if he was part of an illicit network. "Thanks for letting me know. We're trying to find Noah from this end—if you hear anything—"

"I'll call, and you do the same," Rob confirmed. "Hang in there. We'll find him."

Drew set the phone down and rubbed his eyes. He texted Grantham's name to Sheriff Armel, Austin, and Jeffries.

His phone rang and Drew grabbed for it, hoping to see Noah's name, and instead realized it was Mutt. "Hey," he answered, "what's up?"

"I was going to ask you," Mutt said. "Russ asked me to check in on you. What's going on?"

Drew gave him the recap.

"Wow," Mutt replied. "I'm sorry to hear that—but think positively until there's reason not to. Noah's a smart guy. Don't count him out. Do you want to come hang with me at the theater if you aren't going to the garage? You can watch us set up for the next show, and I'll give you free popcorn."

Drew smiled, grateful for his friend's offer. "I might take you up on that another day. But I'm at the Fox Institute right now—we're trying to figure out the reincarnation angle, and the psychics are looking for Noah."

"Okay—I'll let you off the hook this time," Mutt said. "But I'll check in on and off to make sure you're okay. If you need anything or get word about Noah, call me."

Drew promised and ended the call. Drew felt lucky to have friends like Mutt—and now Rob—in his life.

He still felt sick with worry, jittery from bracing for the worst, and exhausted from the emotions that he'd experienced during the hypnosis journey into the past. *Now's the time to rely on those Capricorn traits—relentless, dedicated, won't give up. I'm going to need that to handle this mess.*

Jeffries's office door was closed, so Drew went down to the café and got a cup of coffee. Needing to clear his head, Drew did an internet search on Trevor Keeg and Dorian Fitzgerald. The citations he found gave him a sense of borrowed pride. In their time—the 1920s before the Crash—Keeg and Fitzgerald had won awards for their beautiful

Art Deco buildings throughout the upper Northeast. Some were still standing, while others had been lost through the decades but remained immortalized in pictures. Drew bookmarked the sites to read them more closely later.

One fact that did not escape his notice—Keeg and Fitzgerald were in their mid-thirties when they died in a head-on collision on a rainy night in 1928.

The curse. We'll find a way to break it. But first, I've got to find Noah.

He gulped the last of his coffee, got a refill to go, and headed back to Jeffries's office, ready to explore more of the past.

We're going to bring you home, Noah. Keep fighting on your end, and we'll keep looking on ours.

9

NOAH

NOAH SPENT THE NIGHT IN HIS FUR, WITH HIS LYNX CURLED UP NOSE TO tail and sheltered in the space blanket, out of the wind beneath a shallow overhang. It had been a long time since he'd stayed all night in his cat form and never before out of necessity.

We're fast and clever. We will find our way to our mate, his lynx reassured him, staying close in his consciousness.

You're not being snarky. That's how I know I must be screwed, Noah replied.

Ha, ha. Perhaps since I'm better suited to the wild, this doesn't bother me. It's an adventure. A holiday.

Noah's human side snorted. *We slid off the road, there's a dangerous hunting guide trying to get us in trouble with the law, and we're far away from Fox Hollow without a car. Screwed.*

The squirrel is fatter in the morning, I always say. His lynx's tone sounded like he was dispensing great wisdom.

Is that supposed to mean something? Noah knew he was being unreasonable. *I'm scared. That guide—he's not just going to let me go. Not if he thinks I've got photos of him and his client shooting the Bigfoot. He's going to hunt us. I don't have any way to contact Drew or ask for help because everyone thinks I'm a criminal. We might not make it out of the woods alive.*

Now who's dramatic? His lynx teased, but without heat in his voice. *Stick with me. I'll get you to somewhere safe.*

Don't have much choice, since we're in the same body. But...thanks.

Noah appreciated his lynx's effort to console him, and for the sake of his cat, he kept his gloomy thoughts at bay as best he could. *I'm a Cancer—my sign is tenacious, a defender, protective. I'm going to need my cat and those traits to get through this alive.*

Dreaming felt different in his lynx. Images came in flashes instead of a movie. Noah saw a sedan from the 1920s, long and sleek. Two men inside joked and laughed with a fondness that in the privacy of the vehicle went far beyond friendship.

The image changed suddenly, and he saw the same car driving through heavy rain. Lightning flashed, reflecting on the slick road. Tires screeched, and the Ford sedan skidded into the blinding lights of an oncoming truck. Metal screamed as it tore and twisted, glass shattered, and there was so much blood...

The jolt of the impact woke Noah, and even in his lynx form, he shook and panted.

Why does it hurt? I feel like I died with them—or that I was them. But it was just a dream. Just a dream.

What did you see? His lynx stirred, hackles rising, immediately on defense. *I don't smell a bear. I don't hear a human. Where is the danger?*

I dreamed about dying. Except the person in the dream wasn't me—but it was.

You make no sense, his lynx protested. *You, and not you? So human. I am lynx. I am always lynx.*

Go to sleep, Noah muttered. *Make me dream about rabbits.*

Rabbits?

I'm hungry. And it's better than dreaming about death.

Humans are very strange.

No more dreams came that night. Noah tried not to remember the way the car lurched, the feel of broken glass slicing skin, sharp metal, warm blood. His blood—and his lover's. Noah didn't know how he knew, but he felt the certainty in his marrow.

There's no time to think about dreams. We have to get out of the woods, get to Drew. If we live through the trip to Fox Hollow, I'll have time to figure it out.

He woke in the morning stiff and chilled despite his fur and the blanket. His whiskers twitched, and the dampness clung to him. Noah's stomach growled, and he felt parched. Smells and sounds were far more vivid, like a sensory assault.

Time to move our furry ass. Breakfast won't catch itself, his lynx prodded.

Noah stretched, arching his back and flicking his tail. He twitched his ears and whiskers and sniffed the air. When the scent of a rabbit caught his attention, Noah bounded off, giving himself over fully to his lynx to track and hunt their breakfast.

Pick a fat one this time. I'm hungry.

His lynx growled, enjoying the chase. He brought down an ample hare and gulped it before the flesh cooled. Noah withdrew to the far recesses of their shared mind to avoid the taste and smell of fresh blood and the sound of crunching bones.

Noah waited until the meal started to digest before changing form. The rising sun painted the snow-covered forest in shades of gold. Noah shifted quickly, dressing as he shivered. He put the space blanket back in his bag and pulled the backpack over his shoulder, then he filled his water bottle and headed off at a brisk pace.

He knew he needed to stay alert for danger, but his thoughts spun, nonetheless. *I'm late—Rob had Drew's number, and he would have called about the arrest warrant and the wreck, so Drew at least knows that much. I hope. But what can Drew do? I'm nearly seventy miles of forest away—too much for them to search. And they don't dare involve the police and the search and rescue squads, or I'll end up in jail.*

We'll save ourselves, his lynx assured him staunchly. *We are tough, wild, and smart.*

Noah smiled at the support. *We're still a long way from safety. On top of all those things, I hope we're lucky too.*

He had a rough map of the area in his mind from his visits to Drew. Noah avoided the town of Brasher and knew that the next danger lay between two parallel highways. That area was comparatively more exposed thanks to smaller roads running through it.

If I can get past the second road, I'll hit a long stretch of forest park land. When I get that far, it would be tough for the guide to find me. I don't think even satellites can see through the trees.

The trouble started after he crossed the first road.

Still in human form, Noah slowed after darting across the asphalt. He focused on his lynx senses, although it was harder to concentrate with the smell of exhaust and motor oil, the distraction of old road kill, and fast-food wrappers.

If the guide wants to hunt me, this is his best bet. Easy access, but few people, Noah thought, practically vibrating from the tension.

My whiskers are twitching. Be careful, his lynx warned.

Noah ran into the forest on the other side, doing his best to stay between the roads. Despite the distance from settled areas, Noah couldn't shake a sense of foreboding.

We got away from the guide? He wouldn't know to track a lynx. He'd be looking for a man, right? How could he have followed us?

Maybe because his job is hunting wildlife, his lynx replied. *Guide—remember? And he has a car, so he could get ahead of us. We will have to out-fox him—even though we're a lynx.*

How am I safer—human or lynx? Noah debated.

For now, human—because you can move faster, go farther. I'll do the smelling and hearing—you do the moving.

Noah set out at as fast a pace as he could sustain. Normally the balsam forest would give him a sense of peace, but all he felt was fear and tension. He had to pick his route carefully since he wasn't sticking with a trail. That meant weaving between the trees and finding a path between the large boulders left behind eons ago when glaciers dug the lakes and earthquakes formed the mountains.

His lynx remained alert, scenting the air and listening to the sounds of the forest. Noah knew that while he couldn't see the small roads through this area, they weren't truly far apart. Easy enough for the guide to park and head into the woods if he guessed Noah's route—or if he found out Noah had a lover in Fox Hollow.

Could he have learned about Drew? Will he come after Drew to get to me? I don't think that would go well for him after what happened to the Hunts-

man. Still, he feared for Drew's safety. *What if I lead the guide right to a town full of shifters, just because I'm trying to save my own life?*

You think too much, and at the wrong time, his lynx said, swatting at Noah with his big paw. *We're being followed. I smell a person. He's behind us but not too far away. Keep moving, but sneak.*

Sneak but be speedy? How the fuck am I supposed to —

The sound of a rifle broke the stillness, echoing from the rocks. Noah dodged, choosing a zig-zag course. He saw no promising hiding places, nothing that wouldn't quickly be revealed.

Another shot rang out, barely missing him and hitting a boulder, sending shards of stone into the air.

Is he a lousy shot or just toying with me? Somehow, Noah doubted that the guide would miss on purpose.

Noah ran, trusting his lynx for sure-footedness even in his two-legged form. He hopped over roots, skidded on wet leaves, and hoped he didn't turn an ankle on the many rocks. Forest parkour was a dangerous sport. But while his lynx wouldn't have needed to worry about dexterity, Noah's endurance could carry him farther, faster. *Am I charging away from danger — or toward it?*

When exhaustion took him, Noah searched for a place to hide. He eyed the large trees around them, near a rocky drop-off. *I've got an idea.*

He stripped off his clothes and boots, shoving them into his pack. Then he shifted as fast as he dared and pulled the pack over his shoulders. Climbing the pine tree in lynx form was easy, and he headed for the high branches that might conceal him from anyone beneath.

What if he looks up? Noah doubted the wisdom of his plan.

Humans never look up.

I couldn't run anymore. I needed to rest and catch my breath. But if I stop down there, he'll find me.

Noah reckoned that they had covered about fifteen miles yesterday, and he had hoped to get twenty today—but if he had to dodge someone hunting him, reaching Fox Hollow might take much longer.

Not much I can do about that. If I get caught, I won't get there at all.

He waited with the stillness of a predator, listening. Footsteps sounded on the forest mat of old pine needles and dead grasses. Noah dug his claws into the branch and waited.

A man he didn't recognize passed beneath the tree, carrying a rifle. *Not the guide I saw that night.* Still, the man had shot at him—twice. *Who is he?*

We could pounce on him from above and rip out his throat like a rabbit, his lynx suggested.

I'd rather not. He's still human.

He is rival. Predator. He would make us prey. Killing him is the way of things.

I don't want to rip out his throat. I would remember. Yuck, Noah protested.

He will not hesitate to kill us with his gun. Staying alive would be worth some bad dreams.

Once the hunter had passed beyond hearing range, Noah climbed down carefully and headed to the right, hoping to avoid the hunter by taking a parallel path. Despite his wide paws, the lynx moved silently and sure-footedly, though not as quickly as his human side.

He put as much room between himself and the hunter as he could, but the lynx never lost the scent of him. *This is what it's like to be hunted. It's not the guide. Did he sell me to a client for a hunting "experience"? And if that man shot at me in human form, he must know I'm a shifter, and he doesn't care.*

Fear thrummed through Noah. *Will he capture and not kill to put me in a private zoo? Or will he shoot me and do taxidermy on my remains? Would that trap my soul? If I don't make it to Fox Hollow, will Drew ever know what happened to me?*

If he could cross Route 118, he'd be in a more thickly wooded area, a sparsely inhabited preserve without as many roads. He'd still be a long way from Fox Hollow, but it might be harder for his pursuers to keep up or find his trail.

Noah stopped to rest. His lynx drank his fill from an ice-cold stream and made a meal of a feckless rabbit before surrendering his form to Noah's human side. He popped a mint into his mouth to remove the copper penny taste of blood and dressed quickly.

If he shoots me when I'm naked, I'll haunt his ass for eternity, Noah thought bleakly, although there was nothing funny about the situation.

It's dangerous for you to be in your skin, not fur. You're bigger. Easier to see. Can't climb trees, his lynx protested.

I have longer legs, more endurance—and you've hit your limit, Noah reminded his other half.

I will keep watch, the lynx promised in a solemn tone.

Things were quiet for a while. Noah wondered if he had lost the hunter. *Maybe it had nothing to do with the guide. Could have been a guy out hunting regular game, and he mistook me for an animal.*

Comforting a thought as that was, Noah couldn't let himself believe it.

He'd made progress, putting several hours of hiking at a brisk pace behind him before his lynx signaled danger.

A bullet seared through Noah's left arm, digging a furrow against his bicep—a near miss. He stifled a shout and clapped his hand to the wound to stanch the blood. He ran, slipping and sliding on the patches of snow and the wet leaves and needles. Two more shots missed him but not by much.

Twigs tore at him as he ran, and scrub bushes caught at his pants. He doubled back, trying to lose his pursuer, and waded up a shallow stream to obscure his tracks.

Hide, his lynx advised. *Get out of sight.*

Where?

He felt his lynx come to the fore. *In there.*

Up ahead, the path veered thanks to a heap of boulders left behind from the last Ice Age. Noah couldn't really call the cleft between two of the large rocks a cave, but he saw that he could wriggle into the space and get out of sight.

Once he slipped through the opening, a larger space gave him room to sit and open his pack. Noah's head spun, and he felt nauseous. *What's wrong with me? I'm not usually squeamish.*

Silver bullet, his lynx provided. *Poison. The hunter knows his prey.*

Shit. He's really hunting me. And he definitely knows I'm a shifter. Noah recoiled from the thought, even as he knew it to be true. Silver bullets weren't practical for anything except supernatural creatures, especially given the price of the metal.

At least I know he probably can't afford ammunition for a machine gun,

Noah thought with gallows humor. He dug out the mini med kit in his backpack, wincing every time he moved his injured arm.

Noah mopped up the blood with his shirt, cleaned the wound with an alcohol wipe, and spread antibacterial ointment. He leaned back against the rock and closed his eyes.

If his stalker found him now, he was a sitting duck.

Eat something, drink, and do what you can for pain, his lynx nudged. In Noah's mind, his cat nosed him toward the backpack.

He swallowed a couple of ibuprofen, unwilling to take anything stronger because it would keep him from running—or fighting. Noah gulped down water and ate one of his protein bars, appreciating the non-bloody taste of chocolate and peanut butter.

Once he caught his breath and the pain dulled, Noah stripped off his clothing and packed it in his bag, then shifted and shouldered his backpack. This time, the transition felt sluggish and required more concentration than usual.

It's the silver, his lynx reminded him. *Slows you down. Takes a while to go away.*

The silver caused a low fever and all-over ache he hoped would pass soon. Still, shifting accelerated healing and closed the graze on his arm—the lynx's front leg. He tested his weight on the injured limb, and once he realized it wouldn't collapse beneath him, Noah bounded from rock to rock until he could climb out of the pile at the top.

No one shot at him immediately, which he counted as a win. From here, he saw in all directions, although branches obscured part of the view. His lynx sniffed the air and reckoned direction by the sun, then led him on the steep decline back to the forest floor.

He took off at a lope, unwilling to put too much stress on his healing leg or to deplete his cat's range too quickly. To have any hope of getting close to twenty miles behind him today, Noah knew he'd have to shift back to human as soon as it seemed safe. He doubted he would get that much distance, which meant even longer before he would be back with Drew in Fox Hollow.

Drew has to be worried by now. Please don't let him try to find me. He'll end up in danger too. I need to know he's safe.

Noah remembered the map. If he could cross the second highway, he could lose his pursuers in a large stretch of undeveloped forest. Those woods were unbroken by roads, making it much harder for the guide to find him.

But first, he had to live long enough to get there.

Danger! His lynx warned, picking up the scent of a man—different from before. He didn't have time to ponder as a shot barely missed his haunches.

Fuck. There's more than one hunter.

Noah plowed into a thicket of bushes, staying close to the ground, ignoring the burrs that tugged at his fur and the thorns that scratched through his thick pelt. More shots sounded, and he realized that the hunter was firing blindly into the brush.

He dropped to his belly and kept his head low, remaining completely still so as not to reveal his position by making the scrub move. *Silver's not cheap. If he can't see me and he's not sure where I am, it's expensive to keep firing.*

Noah heard a man cursing and realized he had eluded the hunter —for now.

The thick brush would dissuade the hunter from wading into the tangle of bushes to search. Noah's heart pounded so hard he could barely believe the man couldn't hear it. *Guess that proves he's just human. But why is he chasing me? He doesn't have the same scent as the guide.*

The guide leads hunts for money? his lynx asked.

Noah nodded, trying to slow his breathing and calm his heart rate. *Yes.*

Then perhaps he has made a sport of catching us.

Cold horror filled Noah at his lynx's theory. The guide's customers didn't have second thoughts about shooting a cryptid that did them no harm and considered a rare beast to be a trophy to be shown off.

Would it bother them to hunt a shifter? But even as he wondered, Noah knew the answer. If someone had no conscience over killing a Bigfoot, they wouldn't hesitate to kill a shifter, even in its human form.

He remained still until boot steps receded. The day was only half over, but Noah feared coming out of his hiding place in either lynx or human form.

How do I know there are only two hunters? Maybe the guide announced a bounty and declared "open season" on me. Will they still hunt at night? Maybe if I rest now, I can make up time tonight. I'll have to stay in my lynx, but at least I can put a few more miles behind me.

While the gunshot graze had closed, it still hurt, and the silver in his bloodstream made Noah feel like he was coming down with the flu. He wondered whether the effects would be better or worse in human form. Unfortunately, he didn't dare find out until he had lost the men hunting him.

While he waited for twilight, Noah slept. His lynx roused when unwary birds ventured too close and moved quickly to smack them down. That and an unlucky mouse became a snack to stop his stomach from growling but hardly passed for a meal.

When Noah woke once more, darkness had fallen. He listened carefully, but heard nothing except the sounds of the forest's "night shift" growing active. An owl hooted overhead, and small animals stirred in the underbrush.

He belly-crawled out of the thicket, ears twitching and whiskers quivering to catch any scent that indicated danger. After a few moments' vigilance, he stood and stretched. Noah followed the sound of running water and found a stream, where he drank his fill. His lynx provided a rabbit for dinner, and despite his hunger, Noah struggled to choke down the warm meat.

Noah still felt the silver poisoning, making him sluggish, queasy, and sore. He forced himself to move once he finished eating. He started at a trot, hoping to put the hunters far behind him by morning, moving at the quickest pace he could sustain.

The road. Snow glistened in the moonlight, making the highway a ribbon of white. Noah knew that out in the open he had no way to hide his footprints. Once in the forest he could pick a path where patchy snow, rocks, and fallen logs would let him conceal his passing.

The two-lane state route didn't get much traffic at this hour, and the absence of overhead lights let Noah bolt across safely. He didn't stop running until he was safely inside the tree line on the other side, heading into a large area preserved from development.

Once beneath the tree cover, Noah sighed with relief. The cold didn't bother him while he kept moving since the lynx's thick coat protected him from both the temperature and the damp.

I can't smell anyone near us, his lynx spoke up. *For now, we're safe.*

I won't get as far like this. Even as a shifter-lynx, my range is only about ten miles, half of what I can do as a man. I need to be in human form to travel faster.

You can't get far as a dead *man,* his lynx pointed out.

Funny, really funny. Noah's mental voice lacked heat. He was glad for his lynx-side's company. Under other circumstances, he might have found the dark, still forest to be a place of meditation and solace. Now, he twitched at every sound, constantly scanning for threats. *It would have been nice to do a photo shoot here.*

Do one later, when the bad men are gone, the lynx replied.

I'm doing my best, but we might not make it out of this. The night felt ominous, and the silver made Noah's muscles ache and his head hurt. Solitude closed in, and his thoughts grew shadowed remembering troubled dreams and the tragic couples whose fates felt far too personal.

Drew and I've barely gotten started together. If we're fated mates, what will happen to him if I don't survive? Will my death cause his as well? Those dreams, are we cursed to misfortune?

Could those people in the nightmares—us and not us—be past lives? Are we always unlucky? Always taken from each other once we fall in love? The events of the past two days weighed heavy on Noah, and his hope had worn thin.

Who plucked your whiskers and stepped on your tail? His lynx broke into the gloomy train of thought. *If you've given up already, then at least find a comfortable place to sleep. Although if the hunters find us, they'll skin us and stuff us full of straw. Our soul might be trapped. But by all means, surrender and doom us both.*

You've made your point, Noah mentally muttered.

Just thought you should remember that your decisions affect more than you and Drew. My fabulous existence would also come to an end.

Noah knew he was being morose. His body hurt, the wound stung, and he couldn't shake a mix of fear and fatalism. *I didn't say I was going to give up. The odds just seem to be against us at the moment.*

That's the problem with humans. You try to live in all the moments, all at once. Be like lynx. Live in this moment. Right now is not so bad.

We're being hunted, Noah protested.

Not at this moment. We had good rabbit and cold water to drink. Our belly is full, and this forest is nice. It is good in this moment.

The thought made Noah stop in his tracks. *The lynx is right.*

I'm always right.

Don't get a swelled head.

Noah's trot slowed to a walk, and by the time he stopped just before dawn, he was staggering. Before the sun came up, his lynx spotted a hidden cleft in a rocky hillside, and Noah managed to drag branches to cover the mouth of the shallow cave before collapsing inside.

The silver is getting worse, his lynx said. *And the bullet didn't stay inside. How are we this sick?*

I thought you knew all about silver.

I've never been shot before.

Don't you know secret lynx things? Noah fired back.

I know the mystery of rabbits in the brush and how to find good water. I can swat a bird in the air and trap a lizard by its tail. Those are secret lynx things.

Will the silver go away? Will it kill me? Is there an antidote? Noah demanded.

Those secrets I don't know. But I hope for the best. In this moment, all is not lost.

Noah found his lynx's reassurance strangely comforting, despite the odds against them. He tugged the space blanket from his pack, chewed through a protein bar package to eat it, and settled with his chin on his paws, trying to ignore his sore feet, the way his joints and muscles ached, the burn of the silver in his blood. He hoped that tonight's dreams would come easy.

They did not. This time, the images were like flashes of a slideshow. *Two men from the Civil War era, hiding from a posse, lives ended by bullets fired by love before the mob could reach them. A century earlier, a farmer and his farmhand, claimed by a barn fire one could not escape and one would not abandon. And before that, a prince and a young nobleman, cursed because their love upended kingdoms and successions.*

He startled awake with a growl. *So many times, Drew and I found each other—and lost one another. Are we always fated to be apart, or can we break the spell and live to be old together?*

Go back to sleep, his lynx insisted. *You need to heal, and this much feline beauty doesn't happen without a good night's rest.*

What if it's true? What if we're fated mates—and fated for tragedy?

Does that change tonight? No. Sleep. In the morning, eat and drink. Sniff the air. Avoid the hunters. Fate will take care of itself.

10

DREW

"Do it again." Drew gripped the armrests of the recliner. "There's more—I'm sure of it."

Drew's head pounded, and his vision blurred from concentration. They had been doing one guided regression after another since returning from lunch, and Drew knew they were all ragged from the effort.

We were farmers after the Revolutionary War. Former soldiers out West after the Civil War. Professionals in the big city in the 1920s. And apparently, a baker and butcher back in the 1500s. But if we are born new each century, there are still lives I haven't glimpsed. When did the curse begin? Isabel was able to guess the time period by the clothing I described, but we missed a century—the 1600s. Did the curse happen then? Or before what I've seen?

"Why can I only see glimpses? Is there a way to see more of their lives?"

Becca shrugged. "Not to my knowledge. We can't remember everything that's happened to us in our current lives. They say that the brain stores all our memories, but some go into a sort of long-term storage that are harder to access on demand. With past lives, it might be the soul archiving the memories—and that's even harder to retrieve."

"I just wish I knew a little more about them—us. Some of the bits I saw made me think we were happy, but in others, I felt foreboding, especially the Civil War life. Not like we didn't get along; more like there were outside dangers. I hope we don't find each other time after time just to get pulled apart," Drew said, worried.

"A curse might shift the natural path, but a true pairing is chosen by the universe," Isabel spoke up. "I prefer to believe it's an extension of soulmates, two halves that make a soul. There's a shadow that isn't supposed to be there."

"Shadow? The one who placed the curse?" Perhaps that malice was part of the foreboding he sensed.

Isabel nodded. "Yes. He accidentally made himself your tormentor in each life—but in doing so, he has denied himself eternal rest."

Drew thought back over the dreams. "The farmers worried about a nosy neighbor. They were afraid of being exposed as lovers. The former soldiers were being hunted by a posse—did their love make them outlaws?"

Becca looked at him with compassion. "Such things have happened."

"The ones from the 1920s, they had to hide their relationship," Drew speculated. "Someone with a grudge or a bad cop could have turned them in…" He paused, thinking. "I didn't sense danger for the butcher and baker. Maybe that was before the curse? Or perhaps at that point, their love wasn't forbidden?"

"That's certainly possible," Jeffries spoke up. "There have been times and places where relationships were accepted—more often throughout history than many people realize."

"If the curse happened in the 1600s, why is that the century hidden to me so far?" Drew felt like he'd been beating his head against a wall, trying to force his memories to give up their secrets.

"Our minds protect us from pain by making us forget," Becca suggested. "Trauma survivors sometimes don't remember anything about the incident. The memories can come back later—but occasionally, they don't."

Drew met her eyes, and from her sympathetic gaze he suspected that he looked a bit crazed. "I have to remember so we can stop the bad luck. I want to live a long and happy life with Noah. And if there is a life after this, I want us to be safe from the curse and happy then too."

"It would help to have the memory of when you were cursed, but it's not essential to the breaking of the spell," Isabel said. "My coven is researching the old texts. Just narrowing it down to probably the 1600s helps. The one who cast the curse wasn't trained, so he wouldn't have found the spell in a grimoire. It would have been hedge witch magic, the petty love potions and hexes done by those with a bit of ability and no real instruction."

"How does that help?" Drew felt adrift, unable to help the man he loved.

"The lore is vast. Those details help us narrow our search," Isabel reached out and patted his shoulder. "We're witches, not mind readers."

Drew looked hopefully at Jeffries. "You're a psychic. Can you—?"

Jeffries smiled sadly and shook his head. "My gift doesn't work like that. We have some folks on staff who are telepaths. But to read your mind, you would have to possess the information in waking knowledge. If the memories of your past lives have been tucked away in 'cold storage,' so to speak, they wouldn't be visible. If you don't know something in this life, no one else can retrieve it."

Drew sank into his chair and buried his head in his hands. "I don't know how to save Noah. There's so much to find out, and we're running out of time." He bit back a sob. "I get flashes of strong feelings —Noah's emotions. He's scared, and he's hurt. He needs me to help him, and I'm so far away."

He glanced up and met Jeffries's gaze. "If we are a true pairing— and I believe we are—if one dies, does the other go as well?"

"The lore is...unclear," Becca replied. "It might happen at the same time or soon afterward. The life energy is linked. One might die of a broken heart or fade away from grief. But without the other half of the pair, one will not survive long alone."

"Don't tell Russ." Drew's voice was barely a whisper. "He worries enough. And if it's fate, he can't stop it if we can't...if we don't..." He couldn't bring himself to say the words.

"We'll help you find Noah in time," Jeffries assured him.

The concern in Becca's eyes made Drew look away. "You're tired. We're all tired—"

Drew raised his head, stubbornly refusing to acknowledge his exhaustion. "Noah is out there, pursued, maybe injured, and a long way from home. We have no way to find him. But I can do *this* and maybe figure out how to end the curse."

"Drew—pushing yourself too far isn't going to help Noah in the long run." Jeffries's placating tone set Drew's teeth on edge, even though he knew the man had good intentions.

"I can't go looking for him because the territory's too big. I'm not a hacker or a private investigator, so I can't try to figure out who's after him or how to get him back. Don't you understand? This is all I can do—and I have to do something," Drew argued, hearing the desperation in his own voice.

"At least this is *useful*. When we rescue Noah, if I can find where the bad luck started, then we can fix it." Drew knew he was being unreasonable. Jeffries, Isabel, and Becca had worked patiently with him from lunch to past sundown.

"We're all for continuing," Isabel said, rising from her chair and stretching so that her spine gave an audible *crack*. "But beating a tired horse won't get you anywhere. How about you have a good dinner, go home, and see where your dreams take you, and we'll start again right after breakfast tomorrow."

Drew opened his mouth to protest, but Jeffries laid a hand on his arm. "I'm going to pull rank here," he said gently. "For everyone's benefit—even Noah's. We're not going to find him tonight—but we might be able to take action tomorrow once we hear from Austin and Noah's friend. That won't do any good if you've pushed yourself to collapse."

Drew realized that the others were right and that his single-mindedness put them all at risk. "Okay. But we start first thing tomorrow."

"Absolutely," Becca agreed. "Now, let's get dinner. I'm starving."

They all headed to the Full Moon Diner and found Russ, Liam, and Mutt holding a long table in the back for them. "Figured this was the best bet for getting a meal tonight," Russ said with a grin as Drew sat beside him. "Rich called and said he was going to get you to take a break and eat."

"Plus, neither of us wanted to cook, and we figured you'd be worn out." Liam leaned around Russ from the other side.

"And I thought it would be more fun to have dinner with you than to keep bugging you on the phone," Mutt added.

The normal dinner rush had cleared, so the diner's servers brought their food quickly. By unspoken agreement, none of them talked about Drew's marathon session at the Institute, or Noah's disappearance, although the latter cast a pall over the get-together.

Drew found himself picking at his food and pushing pieces around on his plate without actually eating.

"Hey," Russ said quietly, gently bumping Drew's elbow. "If you don't eat, you won't have the strength to help Noah. Eat at least a few bites, okay?"

"I'm not really hungry," Drew said. "I shouldn't have ordered anything." The diner's usually excellent food tasted like sawdust to him.

Fortunately, no one seemed to expect Drew to join in the conversation, and he suspected that Russ and Jeffries had engineered the dinner to distract him. It didn't lift the burden on his heart, but the gesture filled him with warmth at the love of his brother and their friends.

Everyone had dessert—even Drew, who couldn't turn down the Full Moon Diner's homemade pie.

"C'mon," Russ said, slinging an arm over Drew's shoulders. "Let's go home. I picked up a bottle of a new blended whiskey. Seems like a good time to break it out."

Drew remained quiet in the truck on the drive back while Russ and Liam traded anecdotes about their workdays. Once they were finally settled in the living room, and Russ had poured drinks, Drew knew he needed to give them as much of a recap as he could manage. *They're worried about Noah too. And about me. They need to be in the loop.*

Liam and Russ listened closely as Drew recounted his day. Liam's eyes grew wide when he got to the part about glimpsing past lives.

"That stuff is real? I thought it was just talk show shit." Liam looked a little star-struck at the idea.

Drew shrugged. "Apparently so. Even with Becca's help, I only got glimpses—sometimes less than what happens in my nightmares. But I recognized the couples as being ones I'd dreamed about—and I'm certain now that they were Noah and me in another life. Except the four most recent ones didn't come to a good end."

Russ frowned. "Before that, they had happier lives? What happened?"

"Isabel thinks there was a curse placed about four hundred years ago, but I haven't gotten that vision yet. That's why I didn't want to stop trying—if we knew what happened, we'd have a better idea how to fix it."

Liam drew his legs up under him, and the gesture was so very foxlike that Drew could almost imagine a swish of his elegant tail. "Maybe you had to see the things you saw today and have time to digest them before you can tap into the rest. You did a lot. Don't beat yourself up."

Drew's phone rang before he could reply. "It's Austin," he told them and put the call on speaker. "Did you find anything?"

"I've got some info—and I'm working on getting the rest," Austin told them. "Rob and I have been busy. He's been my boots on the ground in Ottawa and fed me information to flesh out the queries I've made. We've got some solid leads."

"I'm here with Russ and Liam, and you're on speaker," Drew told him. "We could all use some good news."

"I'm not sure I have that—yet. But I'm making progress. First, the not-good stuff. Grantham has a long record for poaching and breaking game laws. It looks like he decided to chase a higher-paying type of customer with his cryptid hunts," Austin said.

"The Sycamore Rod and Gun Club is a swanky outfit with some shady history and shadier—but rich—members," he continued. "That seems to be where Grantham is getting his well-heeled clients. Thanks to my friends who have magically-enhanced hacking skills, we've found out more about Grantham. Just yesterday, he posted a note in a members-only forum about a special hunt with a cash bounty."

Drew felt himself pale. "Shit." Russ reached over to grip his shoulder in support.

"—and he's received three large payments to his bank account from members of the club," Austin went on. "Now for the good news—"

"How can anything be good? They're hunting Noah!" Drew thought he might throw up.

"We know the names of the hunters," Austin told them, with a tone in his voice that said he was about to go in for the kill. "I've got some very good people working on hacking their phone accounts. Once we do, we can track their whereabouts by *their* phones—even though we can't track Noah's."

"Find the hunters, and we'll know where they think Noah's hiding," Russ completed the thought, and Drew looked up sharply, feeling a mix of hope and terror.

"Then we can ask the psychics to hone in on that area and narrow the search even more," Liam said excitedly.

"Exactly. So you can bring *our* version of the hunt to them." Austin was a psychic, not a shifter. He was most valuable chasing information and leaving the fighting to those with teeth and claws.

"When do you think your team might get into their phones?" Russ asked, and Drew gave him a grateful nod since his throat seemed to have closed up.

"Soon, I hope, now that we know what we're looking for. I'll call once I know more. You might want to get your rescue party arranged," Austin said. "And figure out how to explain to Sheriff Armel where you got your information in a way that doesn't put me and my friends in jail."

"Definitely," Russ agreed. "Thank you." He ended the call and looked at Drew. "Talk to me. You look freaked out."

Drew took a shaky breath. "There are three men—plus the guide—hunting Noah. For money. And he's alone in the woods…"

"He's got his lynx," Liam said reassuringly. "And it's night—humans won't hunt in the dark. So he's safe until dawn."

"If they'd already found him, that forum would have had an announcement of the winner," Russ pointed out. "So he's still out there. That's a good sign."

"Once we know where the hunters are, we've got to go after Noah," Drew begged, looking from Russ to Liam.

"How about you and I call the sheriff right now?" Russ suggested. "We'll put frozen pizzas and snacks in the oven, everyone can meet up here, and we can plan a rescue."

"And while you do that, I'll let Brandon, Justin, Mutt, and Tyler know. We'll need backup," Liam volunteered.

Drew knocked back his whiskey and tried not to notice how badly his hand shook. He listened while Russ and Liam alerted their friends and made plans to gather at the cabin.

Fox Hollow was a small town. Before the oven had fully heated, a knock came at the door. Russ opened it to find Sheriff Armel filling the doorway. It wasn't a stretch to picture him as a bear shifter with brown hair and dark eyes. His human form had broad shoulders and a stocky, powerful body.

"Do I smell pizza? Good thing—I'm hungry. An army runs on its stomach." He brushed past Russ. Behind him were his cousin, Sherri from Bear Necessities Café, and her husband, Nelson. They were both bear shifters and large people, so the kitchen felt suddenly full.

"Is that a meaty pizza?" Nelson asked. "I'm starving."

Russ glanced at Drew. "I'll get more snacks out of the freezer," Drew said. Liam bustled around the living room, setting out folding chairs.

Another knock at the door announced Brandon's arrival. He had to duck to get through the doorway, and while he was taller than the bear shifters, his muscular form and wide shoulders took up nearly as much space. *Then again, a moose isn't small as an animal or a person.*

Drew helped Liam find seats for everyone, then went back to the kitchen to set out plates and cups and give Russ a hand with the sudden onslaught of snacks.

Brandon and the sheriff moved into the living room. Sherri laid a box on the kitchen table. "Jack's been baking—these are some of tonight's donuts. I figured we can't plan a rescue without plenty of sugar," she said with a broad grin.

Justin had a late chartered seaplane flight, so he couldn't make the meeting, but he promised to be available whenever they needed him. Jeffries showed up along with someone Drew didn't know.

"This is Hudson—one of our remote viewers. We're here to help however we can," Jeffries said. Austin begged off attending in person to spend more time chasing leads online—and to avoid awkward questions on his methods from the sheriff.

Mutt straggled in with a case of beer. "Gotta keep the spirits up," he said as he put the beer down on the counter.

Tyler was the last to arrive. The bobcat shifter had the same compact, muscular build as Noah, animated with a restless feline energy. "Hey, everyone. Hope we're not late." He shuffled into the kitchen, and Drew saw Tyler's family behind him—all of them bobcat shifters as well.

"What's cooking? Is it ready yet? Can we eat while we plan?" Tyler asked. His mother smacked Tyler's head.

"Behave. You'd think we never feed you," she admonished.

"But dinner was a long time ago," Tyler replied.

"An hour," his father said, rolling his eyes.

"Forever," Tyler bemoaned.

Everyone chatted until the pizza and snacks were done, then filled plates and moved into the living room.

"Now what's this about an unofficial rescue?" Sheriff Armel asked. He wasn't in uniform, but he still had an air of authority.

Drew told the story for everyone who crammed into the cabin's living room, starting at the beginning for those who hadn't heard any of the tale before. His only omission was how he received the information that Austin and his team had supplied.

"Noah's in the forest, running from men who want to kill him for a bounty. We couldn't go after him because we didn't know where he was. But now that our friends have gotten more information, we should be able to track the hunters' GPS—maybe as soon as daybreak," Drew finished his story.

Sheriff Armel gave him a look. "I'm going to pretend I didn't hear that."

Drew managed a wan smile.

"That doesn't mean I can't guess," the sheriff said, wagging his finger. "So don't push your luck." His half-smile softened the gruff rumble of his words.

"We need a plan," Russ said, and Drew appreciated his big brother taking the lead. "We're waiting on the cell phone data. Once we have it, we'll be able to narrow down Noah's location—and maybe with the help of the far-seers, pinpoint his whereabouts. We just have to get to him before the bounty hunters."

"Well, then—if we need a plan let's get to it." Tyler's mother Brenda spoke up. She was a no-nonsense sort who ran the family motel with friendly efficiency.

Drew felt a little better. Brenda was a force of nature. He had seen her organize local fundraising dinners and rally volunteers to help deal with an emergency.

"Even when we get the coordinates, there's probably going to be a lot of territory to cover to find Noah," Brenda said. "Some of us move faster than others. I suggest that the bobcats go in first. We're a family—we're used to working together. We'll slow the hunters down and fuck them up, draw off their fire. Then once we have their knickers in a twist, we'll bring in the heavy hitters—the bears, wolves, dog, and moose."

"Just remember, I'll be out of my jurisdiction," Armel noted. "I can't arrest anyone. And I don't think we want to trigger an official manhunt—not until we get that false warrant and car theft charge cleared up. I reported it as fraudulent, but it takes time for a report to work through the system."

"Whether anyone needs to make an arrest is going to depend on how the bounty hunters react, now isn't it?" Brenda replied with a predatory smile.

"If we needed him to, Justin would do a fly-over," Tyler offered.

"I'm not sure how much he could see through the tree cover with all the pines, but if there's a lake nearby, the seaplane might come in handy for airlifting Noah if he's injured."

Before long the food was gone, and they had a plan in place. Everyone helped carry plates and glasses to the kitchen, and Russ walked them to the door.

"I'll call everyone as soon as we have news about Noah's location," He promised. "Keep your phone on and with you—once we know where to look, we'll be moving out quickly. And—thank you."

The house felt quiet and empty after everyone except Liam and

Drew were gone. Russ locked up and grabbed beers on his way back to the living room.

"I'd say that's a big win. The sheriff is good for an unofficial, off-the-books rescue. Sherri and Nelson want to join us, which gives us three large brown bears," Russ said as he joined Liam and Drew, taking a seat next to his mate on the couch. "The bonus of being one of Bear Necessities' best customers."

"Brandon and Tyler—and his whole family—didn't even hesitate," Liam reported with a grin. "Neither did Mutt. So we have a German Shepherd shifter, a bobcat clowder, and a moody moose on our side. Along with psychics, detectives, two grumpy wolves, and a fierce, fabulous fox," he added with a toss of his head.

Russ looked to Drew with a confident smile, and Drew fought back tears. "Once we get a location, we'll roll out. Those hunters will learn not to mess with Fox Hollow."

Drew nodded, overwhelmed.

"Go get some sleep," Russ ordered. "We might move as soon as first light."

Drew managed a shaky smile. "I'll be ready. We're going to bring him back."

He left Russ and Liam in the living room and went to bed, although he didn't know whether he would be able to sleep—from worry over Noah or anticipation of a rescue mission.

I saw our lives—some of them at least. I didn't see how they ended, but I know that after the curse, it wasn't good. But before the curse...we lived to be old men—I saw that history at least once. We were happy together, even when our lives were short.

I want a happy—and long—life with him now and in the lives to come. I think we've earned it.

Drew drifted off quickly once he lay down and got comfortable.

As he dozed, he tried to remember the meditation Becca had used to lead him down the garden steps in his mind into memories of his past. He had heard them so often today he could recreate the gist of it even if he didn't get the exact wording.

He opened a door and stepped into a palace. Gold leaf glittered everywhere, from the walls to the frames around oil paintings, to the candlesticks and chandeliers. The ornate room felt familiar. Comfortable. Home.

A glance down at his clothing revealed a tunic of brocade over silk leggings and a silken shirt. A signet ring on his right hand bore a royal crest, while a plain gold band adorned his left. His long hair was caught back in a queue. A wide, flat jeweled neck-piece rested on his collarbones, a mark of his rank as crown prince.

Beside him stood a dark-haired young man, equally well dressed with a matching ring—the prince's consort. The prince held out his hand, and his consort gripped it nervously.

They stood before two older men. A crown clearly marked the king, who looked regal—and displeased. Beside him stood another man in the robes of a palace advisor.

Even in the dream, darkness surrounded the advisor. Drew recoiled from him, loathing rather than fearing. The stranger reminded him of a spider, clever and deadly. His graying, close-cropped beard softened a gaunt face with deep-set, light blue eyes that looked nearly colorless in the sun.

The men argued. Drew couldn't hear their words, but he knew the heated exchange went badly. The king grew red in the face. The prince held tighter to his consort's hand and shouted back. Clearly, two stubborn men would not compromise.

Infuriated, the king turned to his advisor and shouted an order. An unpleasant smile spread across the other man's face, and a blue glow limned his body. The advisor pointed at the two younger men and spoke words Drew could not hear. They stumbled backward as if stricken, expressions of terror on their faces.

Drew woke, shaking and sweating. The bedclothes pooled in his lap, chilling him all the more as the cool air hit his soaked T-shirt.

Russ tapped on the door and opened it looking worried. "Are you okay? Liam and I are just heading to bed, and I thought I heard you cry out."

Drew looked up at Russ, feeling like he had when they were kids, and he woke crying and screaming from a bad dream. "I had a nightmare," he confessed in a soft voice. "Sorry to bother you."

Russ came into the room and sat on the end of the bed. "Want to talk about it?"

"I tried to remember the way the psychic led me into seeing past lives, and I think I saw when we got cursed. I can look it up tomorrow, but from the clothing, I'd guess 1600s. We displeased the king—my father—and his mage cursed us." Drew was shaken to his core.

He turned to meet Russ's gaze, still feeling adrift. "Four hundred years of lives cut short, four different lifetimes, damaged for an old man's anger."

"Did you hear what the mage said? Maybe if you can tell Isabel the curse, she can reverse it," Russ replied.

"I didn't hear the words in my dream, but now that I know where to go with the regression, maybe I'll get a clearer memory." Drew fidgeted, twisting his hands in his lap. "I'm scared, Russ. I'm afraid I'll lose Noah before we've even really gotten started—and there won't be anyone else for me. We're fated and a true pairing. If he dies…I don't think I'll survive it."

Russ reached out to grab his wrists, eyes wide as Drew's words sank in. "Then we're just going to need to keep both of you from dying, aren't we?"

11

NOAH

THE DREAM CAME JUST BEFORE DAWN. NOAH FOUND HIMSELF IN THE PALACE *again, holding the prince in his arms, comforting the man he loved more than life. Noah couldn't hear what was said but figured from both men's frightened expressions that this was the decisive moment.*

From the tender touches the prince and his consort exchanged, the way they sought and gave consolation, it was clear they were deeply in love.

They squared their shoulders and faced their adversary with pride and defiance, hands joined, unwilling to be parted.

No one could mistake the triumphant malice in the advisor's scornful expression. Even at a distance, in silence, Noah sensed darkness and evil in the man. Noah didn't have to hear the king's words to gather that the punishment for defying the monarch's will meant death or banishment.

A blast of blue light enveloped them, leaving the two men clinging to each other in fear and confusion.

The fierce growl of a pissed off lynx roused Noah from his nightmare. Even in his cat-form, wrapped in the blanket, he shook from fear instead of cold.

Time to go. The sun is rising, his lynx prodded.

He caught a rabbit and gulped down his breakfast, then drank from a stream. Noah shifted and dressed, determined to cover more miles even if his human form was harder to hide.

Sense anything? he asked his lynx.

No. But the wind is blowing the wrong way. Be careful.

Noah saw the trailheads and ignored them, trusting his cat-side to guide him going overland. Striking out off the path frequently turned fatal in the Adirondacks. The vast, unforgiving forest had a reputation for killing the arrogant, unprepared, or unwary. Children and adults went missing here, never to be found—not even the bones.

Bears, bobcats, and wolves would scent Noah's lynx and stay clear. At this time of year, few hikers would brave the temperature and snow to explore this part of the forest, and they'd stay on the path if they knew what was good for them.

That meant anyone Noah encountered was likely to be here for one reason—hunting him.

I'm a day and a half late to meet Drew. I might have put thirty miles behind me, but that leaves more than fifty to get to Fox Hollow—bad enough if I weren't silver sick. But I can't leave Drew wondering what happened. And I don't want my carcass eaten by vultures.

He felt the silver like a fever. It cut into his stamina and made over-worked muscles and joints hurt worse than mere exertion. Still, he plowed on until a sharp pain in his chest made Noah double over. He thought it might be a heart attack, but when he didn't die, he realized the pain came from his mind more than his body.

Drew. I'm feeling his emotions. He's in pain because of me. Don't, Drew. Let go. I never meant to hurt you.

Even as Noah thought the words, he knew his partner wouldn't rest until he got an answer about the disappearance—even if that came too late for Noah. *Soulmates. True pairing. I can't die and cause Drew's death. I won't let the hunters kill both of us.*

Enough snow had fallen that Noah couldn't help leaving a trail. He avoided as much of the snow as he could since there was no telling what lay beneath it, and breaking a leg would be a disaster. Any decent tracker could follow him—if they were within miles in this remote stretch of forest.

Noah quickened his pace, knowing he couldn't sustain that speed for long but eager to put as much distance between himself and his last encounter with the hunters as he could.

Instinct, intuition, and his lynx made Noah duck seconds before a razor-tipped arrow zinged over his shoulder. He didn't stop to look for the archer. Noah changed course, running a reckless zig-zag through the woods. He didn't doubt that the arrowhead had been silver, and he knew that more poison would bring him down. So he ran as hard as he could, praying he didn't trip or slip.

This section of the woods must have been the edge of an ancient glacier that furrowed the land, pushing boulders and gravel ahead of it. Thin dirt barely covered loose rock. Moss and lichen shrouded boulders the size of cars, which formed a gray wall, separating the trees that grew above the rocks and those that stretched beyond.

The rocks gave him cover, obliging him to dart between them, hiding him in crevices as he worked his way over the uneven terrain. The archer chased him, but the treacherous footing assured that trying to stop long enough to fire off another arrow was unlikely until they reached flat ground again.

In some places, moving forward required a mix of climbing and running, and before he'd gotten halfway across the field of boulders, Noah's fingertips bled, and his nails tore. His only consolation lay in hearing the gasps of his pursuer, realizing that the man was wheezing with the effort to keep up.

Even silver sick, Noah had an advantage in his youth and the additional stamina his shifter side lent him. The archer continued to heave for breath as he ran, making Noah wonder whether the guide had misled his clients on the ease of the hunt.

Noah reached for the next boulder ahead to steady him. He stumbled, and his hand left a bloody streak as granite scraped down his palm like sandpaper. The edge of the rocky field lay ahead, and Noah knew that once he got down to flat land, the archer would use the advantage of high ground to fire more arrows—and this time, he probably wouldn't miss.

He stopped and crouched, gathering rocks the size of his fist in hand. He counted to ten, then sprang up and hurled stones in an effort to drive the hunter back.

One rock struck the man's left shoulder, and he shouted in pain. Noah got a good look at him—a man in middle years. Another rock caught him on the ear, while a third hit in the center of his chest. Angry and bleeding, the hunter rose and reached for the bow slung on his back.

Rocks shifted beneath his feet, and the hunter windmilled, bow forgotten as he tried and failed to remain upright. He fell back, hands clawing at the air for traction and hit the stony ground with a heavy *thud* and an audible *crack*.

Noah hesitated, unsure. He crept closer, needing to know.

The man lay sprawled across a boulder, blood pooling beneath his head. Noah couldn't tell if he was still alive, but with that injury, he wouldn't be posing a threat.

One down. How many to go? At least one other—and what about the guide?

Noah had hoped that his early start would have put him ahead of the hunters, figuring they had gone back to motels or at least the shelter of their cars. Now he reckoned they had slept rough, all for the chance to murder him.

He scrambled down from the rocks, relieved to be on flat land once more, and forced himself to jog until he was again hidden beneath the pine canopy.

We can't linger. Others are close.

How many others? Noah wondered as he leaned against a tree, catching his breath. He pulled out his nearly empty water bottle and took a long swallow, ignoring the fever and achiness. After a few seconds of rest, he filled the bottle with snow and set out again as fast as his body would carry him.

The hunters might not know where I am, and they might not know about Drew, but they've probably figured I'm going south. I don't have the energy to lead them on a chase and switch directions, even without the silver in my system. I'm not sure whether I can get the whole way to Fox Hollow. Every obstacle makes it that much less likely I'll ever see Drew again.

The hunters probably have maps and satellite images. Maybe they don't need to chase me. They can plan their ambush, look for the best spot, and wait for me to blunder into it. I might never see them before they get me, not with rifles and hunting bows. They'll be too far out of reach to make it a fair fight.

Sadness threatened to suffocate him as he jogged on. *I don't want it to end between us before we've barely begun. Will I disappear, one of the missing people claimed by the forest? Hard enough on Drew for me to die, but for there to be no body and no explanation is especially cruel.*

Unfair to him if my death hurries his. I never meant to hurt him.

A terrifying thought occurred to Noah. *The hunter who killed the Bigfoot talked about having him stuffed. If I'm caught, killed, and...taxidermied...will I still be reincarnated? Would preserving my body like that, keeping me shifted, fuck with the true pairing? Could it lock me in to some hellish purgatory where I can't die, but I also can't be reborn?*

I can't think of anything worse than that.

He ran beneath the trees, balsam-scented air thick in his lungs. Noah knew he couldn't go much farther without rest, but finding somewhere safe when it seemed his pursuers were close on his heels seemed unlikely.

A rifle shot hit the tree in front of him, sending splinters flying. Noah veered right, and another shot struck the dirt on the path ahead in a spray of dust. He turned left, and a third shot sank into a felled tree trunk.

"Give up, Noah. You're caught," a man shouted. Noah recognized it as the guide, and his heart sank.

"Fuck you."

You tell him, his lynx growled.

"You've led us on a good chase, lost one of the hunters, killed another. Definitely worth the money," the guide gloated.

"Go fuck yourself." Noah didn't bother being creative.

I can drop in my tracks from exhaustion or slow until they catch me and take a bullet.

This part of the forest had hills and gullies. Off to his left, the ground dropped out of sight, and Noah wondered how far down it went. He sprinted toward it, thinking that it might provide a way to hide him from view, and realized that the ravine sloped down to a lake at the bottom.

The sharp crack of a rifle reverberated, sending birds winging and wildlife fleeing. Pain seared through his right thigh like a hot poker.

Guess it's a bullet, then. Not a kill shot. He's probably saving that honor for one of his paying clients.

He knew the slug lodged in his thigh was silver from the way it fanned the fire already in his blood. Noah staggered, one hand clapped to his bleeding leg.

A commotion sounded nearby. Noah recognized the snarl of a bear, and not too far away, a wolf howled.

I wish the son of a bitch had gotten eaten before he shot me. Then again, if there are predators out here, I'd rather not be eaten either. Wounded, I'm easy prey. Not that the guide would let anything gnaw on a client's trophy.

I don't want to die like that.

He knew he had lost blood and that he couldn't elude them this time.

I've lost, but maybe I can still cheat him out of his prize. If the god of the woods takes pity on me, maybe I'll bash my head into a rock on the way down and be spared bleeding out alone in the forest.

Noah flung himself forward to tumble down the muddy slope, limp and blood-soaked. Rocks battered him as he rolled, and bushes tore at his skin until a glancing blow from an exposed root left him seeing stars.

Dazed from his injuries, drugged with silver, and woozy from blood loss, Noah drifted, seeing snatches of past lives as his nightmares came to the fore of his thoughts.

This is a new way to die. I don't think I've gone out like this before.

He heard the wolf howl, closer this time, along with a dog's frantic growls and barks.

Drew? Hope flared, only to fade just as quickly. *Drew can't find us. Just wishful thinking.*

Noah came to rest near the bottom of the slope, caught by what remained of a fallen log.

Fight! his lynx argued, but Noah knew his cat felt oblivion reaching up to swallow them.

Good kitty, he thought, loopy from his injuries. *I'll miss you.*

Keeping his eyes open was a struggle. Noah thought he heard

voices and saw movement as something slalomed down the bank to reach him. He braced himself to feel the killing shot, sure that the guide or hunter had found him.

The wolf regarded Noah, then raised its head and howled. It padded over and nudged Noah with its nose, whining, then licked his face before taking a guardian stance beside him.

"Drew?" Noah didn't really believe his mate could have found him, but the fantasy comforted him, and soon, it wouldn't matter anymore.

The wolf's sandpaper tongue licked his cheek.

"Drew." Noah didn't question whether this was real or a hallucination. That didn't matter. All that counted was that the scent of his mate filled his nostrils, immediately easing his tension and blunting his pain.

"I've got silver in me," Noah explained to the wolf. "It's taking me fast. I'm glad you're with me, but I'm done for. I've doomed us both."

The wolf just maneuvered closer, watching him with inscrutable green eyes.

"Not much longer..." Noah strained to keep his eyes open. If the wolf was his subconscious manifestation of his mate, he would gladly accept company—even imagined—at the end.

The wolf gently pawed at Noah's uninjured arm, making sad noises. Then it raised its head and let out a mournful howl that sent a shiver through Noah's soul.

I wish you were real. I wish Drew were here with me. I don't want to die alone.

The noise of something big crashing through the underbrush made Noah strain to focus his attention. He saw a large brown bear barreling toward them.

Fuck. I'm going to be eaten after all.

The wolf gave a sharp bark, then stepped back.

If Drew's wolf isn't real, then neither is the bear. Just a dying man's delusions.

The bear lay down next to Noah. The wolf nudged Noah onto his belly, then grabbed the collar of his shirt in its teeth and hauled him over the bear's broad back.

Definitely hallucinating.

Except the rough fur felt real, as did the motion of powerful muscles as the bear carefully lumbered toward the lake. The wolf padded alongside, keeping up a chatter of encouraging yips and barks.

Noah faded in and out of consciousness, still questioning whether any of this was actually happening. *There's no way Drew could have known where I was. This is just the universe doing me a kindness to ease my passing.*

He closed his eyes and felt his lynx near him. *So tired. Everything hurts. I'm done.*

Sharp teeth closed on Noah's skin and sank deep, through his shirt and into the juncture between neck and shoulder. *Mating bite,* his lynx supplied, as groggy and spent as his human side.

Noah let his head loll to one side, baring his throat and neck. With the silver and the other injuries, he barely felt the pain of the bite.

I wanted this, when Drew and I were together again. Seal our bond. Guess my mind is serving up my last requests.

"You're a fucking idiot," Drew's voice sounded in Noah's mind. "*I love you, but you're slow on the uptake.*"

"*Are you real?*"

"*Do I need to bite you again?*"

His lynx snickered.

"*How?*"

"*Long story. Tell you after we save your ass.*"

Noah heard a commotion and lots of swearing. Then he saw Russ in human form joining the bear and wolf near the edge of the lake. The bear shrugged and let Noah slip off into Russ's grasp.

"Easy," Russ said, and Noah remembered Drew saying that his brother was an EMT. "Hang on, Noah. Help is coming. We've got you."

He wanted to ask about the guide and the hunter or warn them about the silver in his system. Most of all, Noah longed to tell Drew how much he loved him, missed him, and wanted to be with him forever.

"*I can hear your thoughts now. So I know. Rest easy,*" Drew's voice said in Noah's mind.

"Silver," Noah managed.

"You're in pretty rough shape," Russ said as he used supplies from his backpack to put pressure on the leg wound and apply a field dressing. The wolf whined, long and pitiful. In the distance, Noah heard a plane. "We need to get you to the hospital in Fox Hollow. They'll know how to handle this kind of injury."

Russ withdrew a syringe from a pack. "I'm going to give you a shot to fight the silver in your system. It will help stabilize you until we can get you proper care. I'm sorry, Noah—they say this burns like hellfire, but it should keep you from dying."

The shot *hurt*. Whatever Russ injected into Noah's veins felt like molten lead. Drew's wolf whimpered sympathetically and licked Noah's face, nosing at his cheeks and chin.

Russ looked at the wolf with mild annoyance. "And since you *bit* him, we'll have to get you a milder version of the shot at the hospital, or you'll be silver sick too." In response, the wolf whined and covered its eyes with one paw.

"Drew will explain everything once we get you taken care of," Russ said, looking back to Noah with worry in his eyes. "I'm going to give you a second shot for pain. Right now, you just need to hang on. Justin will be here any moment."

Right on cue, a seaplane roared overhead, and Noah watched through blurry vision as the plane touched down and landed on the small lake. It puttered closer, and Russ stepped away to guide it until the pontoons rested on the shore.

"Time to go," he told Noah, lifting him in a fireman's carry and wading to the side door, which opened with Justin framed inside.

"My God, Noah. You look like shit. Hurry up, Russ." He gestured for them to get a move on.

Justin reached out and dragged Noah aboard. Drew's wolf walked and then swam to keep up, jumping into the seaplane after Russ.

"Don't worry—the hospital's on standby. We've got him," Justin assured the bear, who remained on the shore. "Just get the sons of bitches who did this to him."

Noah heard the cold tone in Justin's voice, something that seemed so alien to his affable friend.

Shit. I must really be in a bad way.

The plane's door slammed shut. Noah lay on his back in between the seats. Russ continued to triage Noah's injuries while Drew stayed nearby.

Justin turned to them. "I'll do my best to make it a quick, smooth up-and-down," he said, then climbed into his seat.

Noah heard the wolf's grunt of pain, and moments later, a human hand grasped his own.

"Thank the fates we found you," Drew said, back in human form. Noah let his head flop to the side so he could watch as Drew pulled on the sweatpants and a sweatshirt Justin had left for him. He and Russ carefully lifted Noah into the seat between them and strapped him in as the plane taxied, barely getting his seatbelt buckled before they were airborne.

I should be appreciating Drew commando in sweatpants. I must really be half dead.

Drew cupped Noah's face in his hands and drew him in for a long, lingering, desperate kiss.

"I thought I lost you," Drew confessed, leaning into Noah's shoulder. "You've been through so much—I was afraid we wouldn't get here in time. We almost didn't. God, Noah—it was too close."

Whatever Russ injected let Noah float adrift from his damaged body. "Missed you," he slurred. "I was 'fraid I wouldn't see you again."

"Sorry I bit you without asking," Drew said ruefully. "But we both know we're fated mates—and a true pairing. My wolf took initiative. I hope...I mean, if you don't want—"

"I want." Noah had never wanted anything more in his life, and while right now his body failed him, he prayed with all his might that he'd get the chance to show Drew the truth of his words.

"Good," Drew said with a nervous smile, still as handsome as Noah remembered. "That's really good. You've just got to hang on until we get you to Fox Hollow. You've done so well. So brave. Just a little longer."

The fear in Drew's eyes and the hitch in his voice told Noah just how bad things were.

"Gonna try not to die," Noah promised, and Drew bit back a sob. "Want to stay. Hurts so much. So tired…"

"Hang on," Drew urged, grabbing Noah's shoulders in a fierce grip. "Fight. If you die now, we lose each other for a century. Please, Noah—I need you to fight. I love you."

Noah wanted to promise that he would. His shoulder throbbed where Drew's wolf had sunk its teeth into the tender flesh. The link was nearly complete, letting them speak in their thoughts. *Binding us tighter, so he dies if I die.*

Fuck. I can't let go—not without killing Drew. Dammit. He bit me because he knew I'd fight harder. I just want to go to sleep, but now I can't—not without risking Drew's life.

"Love you," Noah managed. He couldn't focus his eyes, he sounded like he'd chugged a bottle of whiskey, and his body throbbed with pain despite the medication.

But Drew was with him, and Drew said he had a plan. Noah surrendered himself to his partner's protection and let his eyes drift closed, permitting sleep to take him as the plane roared into the sky, secure in the touch and scent of his partner.

If this is just a dream, it's a really good one.

12

DREW

Flashing lights painted the beach on Fox Hollow Lake as Justin taxied the seaplane to the dock. An ambulance, fire truck, and police cruiser awaited. Beyond the vehicles, curious onlookers huddled despite the cold.

Two rescue crew members offloaded Noah, with Russ and Drew close behind. Drew recognized them from the firehouse, friends of Russ's.

"Keep me posted," Justin yelled to Drew as he followed the medics.

"Shit," Calvin, the taller of the two medics, said as he and Ash carefully maneuvered Noah onto a gurney. "We need to get him stabilized before we roll out. He's lost a lot of blood."

Russ and Drew hung back to stay out of their way as Carter Franks, the sheriff's deputy, shooed away the onlookers and kept the crew from being disturbed.

Drew reached out and grabbed the sleeve of Russ's coat, the way he'd taken comfort as a boy. Russ didn't move away or chide him. Instead, he took a half-step closer so that their shoulders bumped.

Drew watched, sick at heart, as the medics hooked Noah up and checked his stats, then started an IV. Russ had called ahead on the flight to let them know Noah's condition, so they were as prepared as possible. Liam battled his way past the barricade and came to stand beside them, taking Russ's hand in silent solidarity.

"Can you hear Noah? Through your bond?" Russ asked.

"Yes, but the pain meds make it harder," Drew replied, frowning as he concentrated. He wondered if the bond Russ and Liam shared was different in the ability to share thoughts. "Everything's jumbled and blurry. It's like someone took bits of a bunch of different movies and mixed them all up, put them together without a plot, and then showed them out of focus."

Our mate is hurt. We must protect, his wolf argued, agitated as the medics took him from the plane.

He's getting help we can't give him. They're saving his life, Drew told his wolf.

We are stronger when mates are together. His voice in our head is too quiet.

I'll go to him as soon as I can—we're silver sick, Drew explained.

Shift. I can bite and claw. We can fight our way to him.

Thanks, but he's safer letting them take care of him. Drew said.

I will keep watch.

Drew felt the dose of silver he'd accidentally gotten from the bite. Not nearly as much as what coursed through Noah's blood from the bullet wounds, but on top of racing through the forest to search for his lover and then the stress of worrying about Noah's condition, it was enough to make Drew a little woozy.

"Hey, are you okay?" Russ asked as Drew wobbled. Russ grabbed for him just as Drew's knees buckled, easing his drop to the ground.

"Got a fainter!" Russ yelled to the guys in the ambulance.

"Fuck you. Not fainting," Drew muttered.

"You're white as a sheet, clammy, and you aren't focusing your eyes," Russ replied, getting a shoulder under Drew's arm and half-dragging him to his truck. "Come on—we'll race them."

Drew hated nearly passing out, and he didn't want to distract the EMTs from Noah.

"Are you silver sick?" Calvin asked Drew as he tumbled into the front seat of the truck.

"I bit him," Drew replied. Calvin's eyebrows rose.

"Mating bite," Russ explained as he got behind the wheel. "Bad timing."

"Good to know." Calvin ran back to the ambulance and returned in a moment. "The sooner we get the antidote into your system, the better you'll feel." Calvin got a syringe ready. "Sounds like you got less exposure, so I'm going to start with a lower dose."

Drew tried not to flinch as Calvin administered the shot. Ash stayed beside Noah, watching the monitors that provided a readout from the sensors checking Noah's vitals. *I'm glad someone is taking care of him, even if I can't right now.*

Our mate is safe at the moment. Let them fix you, so we can go to him later. Drew's wolf stayed protectively close, and while he didn't growl at the EMTs, he never took his gaze off them.

We'll see you at the hospital," Calvin said, running back to the ambulance. The doors slammed shut, and the vehicle drove off, sirens blaring.

When they reached the hospital, Calvin and Ash surrendered the gurney with Noah at the Emergency Room bay doors as a swarm of people in white coats came to meet them.

Russ came around to the passenger side of the truck, and Drew practically fell out of his seat before Russ caught him.

"I need help!" Russ yelled, and two orderlies rushed to meet them with a gurney.

"Noah—" Drew reached out, but his mate was whisked off in a different direction as he was lifted onto the stretcher and wheeled into the hospital.

"We need to have a look at you before you run off," a nurse told him. "Let them take care of him, and we'll take care of you."

Drew was starting to feel better, so now he fidgeted in frustration as he waited for someone to assess his situation. Before a doctor came to check on him, Russ stepped around the curtain.

"How are you feeling?" Russ looked worried and stretched thin, making Drew wonder what else was going on.

"Better than before but still not back to normal. I'm scared for Noah. Did you hear anything?"

Russ shook his head. "No. They won't be able to talk to me without legal paperwork. For you, the mating bite might count, but they still may not give you details until Noah can okay it."

"Is he awake? Alive?"

"Alive? Yes. Awake—I don't know. Sheriff Armel left orders to update him on Noah's condition—he's law enforcement, so he can get around the rules. He's got his hands full processing the charges against Grantham and his trophy hunter. He's also following up to get Noah cleared on the bogus arrest warrant and car theft charges, and he's calling in a few favors to get him an emergency visa."

We need to go to our mate, his wolf demanded.

I'm working on it.

Drew let out a deep breath he didn't realize he'd been holding. "Thank you...and thank Sheriff Armel for both of us."

"I suspect there will be a lot of paperwork," Russ replied, clapping a hand on Drew's shoulder.

"I need to get off this bed so I can sit with Noah," Drew fretted. His wolf-side stayed on high alert, watching for threats.

"There's no reason to rush," a new voice said as the curtain fluttered to admit Dr. Fisher. "Noah's still in surgery—and I can tell you he's responding well to treatment. It will be a few hours before you can visit, so why not use the time to rest? That way, you'll be in better shape to support him."

"He's my mate," Drew said, lifting his chin, challenging the doctor. "I'm worried about him."

"Guess that's your bite then—and how you ended up with silver in your system?"

Drew nodded. "We'd planned on making things official when he got to Fox Hollow, and I didn't want to risk losing him and never having made the bond."

Dr. Fisher paused as if having an internal debate and then nodded. "We do recognize a mated pair for confidentiality purposes. I'm going to trust you on this because he's a long way from home with no other family."

"We're his pack," Russ spoke up. "We'll be here for him."

"Here's the situation," Dr. Fisher said. "Noah lost a lot of blood. On top of the silver and everything else, it put a real strain on his system."

"He's going to make it—right?" Drew hated the desperation in his tone, but his heart felt like it might stop depending on the physician's answer.

"The odds should be in his favor," the doctor replied, a less definite response than Drew wanted.

"*Should* be?" Drew echoed, eyes going wide. Russ moved closer and put his hand on Drew's shoulder.

"There's something blocking the healing—and we haven't figured out what, but we're working on it," Fisher said earnestly.

Drew's heart clenched. "It's the curse."

"Curse?" The doctor looked up sharply.

He listened as Drew and Russ explained what they had learned about the curse, their suspicions that Grantham's soul had also been caught in the spell, and what Drew had learned with the psychics at the Fox Institute.

"That might make things more complicated." Dr. Fisher frowned. "I don't know how to battle magic. My focus is on healing his body, and I can make a referral for PTSD once he's well again. If this curse has a physical impact, I need to find out right away. Noah has a good chance of pulling through, but right now he's vulnerable. A wild card like a curse could tip the scales in the wrong direction."

Drew tried not to panic.

How do I find this curse and bite it in the throat? his wolf asked, hackles raised.

You can't bite magic.

Can I bite the one who cast the magic?

Be my guest—if we can find them.

Russ spoke up quickly. "I'll call Dr. Jeffries and see if Isabel and Becca can brief you. Maybe by now, Isabel has a better idea of how to break the curse."

"I'll be glad to talk with them. My training included supernatural patients—like shifters. But it didn't cover outright magic." Dr. Fisher offered a wan smile. He checked Drew thoroughly. "The silver is gone from your bloodstream, and its effects should have disappeared. You've all been through a lot and pushed yourselves to the edge. Rest seems simple, but often it really is the best medicine. I can't block curses, but I can make sure Noah rests—and you should take that advice as well."

"When can I see him?" Drew needed to reassure himself that Noah was alive and had escaped. He could hear the low growl of his wolf in the back of his mind.

"As I mentioned before, it will be a few hours. He'll be taken to the ICU after surgery, and I'm keeping him there overnight. I want you to sleep late tomorrow, but I can arrange a brief visit. Tomorrow, when he's moved to a regular room—assuming everything continues to go well—I can put a note on his chart to allow you to stay with him as much as you want."

Drew thanked him and promised to help with Noah's recovery in any way possible. After he left, Drew closed his eyes and sank into his pillow.

"Talk to me," Russ said. "Liam says it helps."

Drew couldn't resist a chuckle. "Since when did you get in touch with your feelings?"

"Have you met my mate? 'Talking it out' came with the deal."

"I'm scared," Drew said after a long pause. "Noah and I are so new as a couple. The fated mates thing and the true pairing draws us together, but it's not the same as knowing each other. Now we're mate-bound and tangled up emotionally, but there's still the curse. We got lucky with Grantham and the hunter, but with Noah's injuries—can we cheat the spell again?"

Russ sat on the edge of Drew's bed. "I hope so. I'm not like the people at the Institute. I can't see the future. But you and he have been going round and round since time began. Compared to that, the curse is new. It wasn't intended to be like this. The dark magic is messing with the natural order. So there must be a way to change it."

Drew closed his eyes, trying not to cry as feelings overwhelmed him. He still felt wrung out after the silver poisoning, and the after-effects of panic and terror left him exhausted. After more than two days of not knowing whether Noah was dead or alive, now that they found him, they still weren't sure Noah would survive. Drew didn't know how much more his heart could take. His wolf stayed close in his consciousness, protective and worried.

"I want to believe that so much," he replied in a strangled voice. "And I'll move heaven and earth to make it happen. I'm just afraid—"

"Don't make the fear any bigger than it already is," Russ advised, laying a hand on Drew's arm. "We have friends helping, playing defense. Take it one step at a time."

Drew nodded, hoping he could follow his brother's advice.

Rich Jeffries showed up once Drew was settled. "Glad to see you awake. Isabel and the coven have been sending healing energy to you and Noah. Once you two are in your longer-term room, she'll be by to do wardings. Our remote viewers were also keeping an eye on both of you, so we could keep the visitors to a minimum while you got patched up."

"Thank you," Drew told him, grateful for all the help the Fox Institute folks had provided.

"You're very welcome. We're not done yet. Our people are working with Austin's team and the sheriff to find others involved with Grantham's 'expeditions.' We intend to make sure those hunting trips end—permanently."

"Please let me know if there's anything I can do," Drew replied, struggling not to fall asleep.

Jeffries chuckled. "Get better, and help Noah recover. We've got you covered."

Go to sleep. I will stand watch, his wolf told him. Drew didn't argue.

Drew slept on and off while they waited to hear about Noah. Every time Drew woke, Russ was beside him with food and drink. He had been okayed to eat anything and admonished to keep up his strength. Drew thought he was entitled to a bit of stress eating as well, and Russ knew all his comfort foods.

Since the hospital cafeteria seemed to specialize in those dishes— hamburgers, milkshakes, macaroni and cheese—Drew guessed he wasn't the only one to eat his feelings.

When he woke next, Mutt sat next to his bed, looking worried. "Hi. I stopped in to see how you were doing, and Russ needed to run to the garage, so I said I'd stay. I tried to call, but you didn't answer."

"I'm still a little out of it. Did you get hurt in the fight?"

Mutt shook his head. "No. But I did bite the hunter right on the ass.

He won't be sitting down for a long while!" he reported with a proud grin. "Lucky for him, I've had my shots."

Between snacks, Drew slept. He thought his worry for Noah would make sleep impossible, but his exhausted body had other plans. Even his wolf dozed, though always nearby and on alert. Sometimes when he woke, Liam, Mutt, or one of their other friends was there, checking in with Russ, who had apparently become everyone's central point of contact. Rob had called at least twice since the rescue to check on Noah and Drew, report the leads he'd uncovered, and provide a brief distraction.

"I need to use the bathroom." Drew had awakened from a deep sleep feeling unsettled and generally not right. Russ was seated next to his bed, and for once, their friends were all gone.

"Okay, let me steady you to get from here to there," Russ said, crooking his arm and standing close to the bedside so Drew could grab onto him.

"I can do it myself," Drew pouted.

"Once you get inside, you're on your own. I just want to help you get across the room."

Drew took hold of Russ's arm, and together they made their way over to the door. Drew tried to figure out why he felt worse now than with the silver sickness.

"Not much farther," Russ encouraged, misunderstanding Drew's hesitation.

Sharp pain in his chest doubled Drew over, and he sank to his knees. He clutched at his heart, gasping for breath.

"Drew! What's wrong? Shit—stay right there. I'll get help." Russ sprinted back to the call button by the bed.

Drew's blood rushed in his ears, and his chest felt like it was in a vise. In his mind, his wolf howled. He heard running footsteps in the hallway and a distant alarm. A moment later, the door burst open as a nurse and orderly answered Russ's call.

"He collapsed," Russ said, sounding scared and helpless. "I think he's in pain. Please—do something!"

Russ stood aside as the nurse and orderly carefully got Drew on his feet and back into bed. "Get a doctor," she told the orderly. "I think it's his heart."

She turned back to Drew. "Do you have a history of heart trouble?"

Drew was still breathing hard, so Russ answered for him. "No. There's no family history, and he hasn't had any problems. How can it be his heart?"

The orderly returned with a female doctor Drew didn't recognize. "I think it's a cardiac event," the nurse told her. "He's clutching his chest, clearly in pain, with dizziness and cold sweats."

"Let's get him on monitors," the doctor—Larkin according to her name tag—replied, stepping closer to do a thorough triage. "Must be the night for it," she muttered. "Someone else just coded."

Noah? Please don't let him die.

Drew lay back, panting from the pain, paying no attention to the bustle of the nurse and doctor beside him or the noise of the monitors.

"Russ." His voice was a choked rasp.

"I'm right here, Drew."

"Noah and me...hearts...curse?" Drew managed, finding it momentarily difficult to organize his thoughts.

"I'll call Isabel," Russ promised.

"Get the tests going," the doctor ordered. Her demeanor softened as she turned back to Drew. "It's probably stress, but we need to check it out to be safe."

Drew heard Russ talking to someone on his phone in the background and hoped that Isabel and her coven had come up with a solution.

"That alarm, the person who coded—was that Noah?" Drew asked in a raspy voice.

"I don't know," the doctor answered. "Right now, you need to worry about you."

Drew surrendered to being poked and prodded, then was briefly whisked off for more tests. When they brought him back to the room a while later, Russ was seated by the door, and he shot to his feet.

"How is he? Is he in danger?" Russ's words came out in a torrent.

The doctor didn't answer until she had Drew comfortably arranged in bed, hooked back up to all the monitors. "He's fine, for someone who may have just experienced a mild cardiac event."

"Heart attack?" Russ echoed, sounding shocked.

"We're not sure yet," Dr. Larkin replied. "The tests should tell us more."

"But he's only thirty-three," Russ protested. Drew felt like an onlooker to his own life as everyone talked about him like he wasn't there.

She shrugged. "I've heard a little bit about what went on. Sounds like he had the kind of day that could trigger an event. It's important to get the right treatment and take it seriously, but there's no need to panic."

But if Noah and I both had an "event" at the same time...it's got to be the curse.

Finally, the doctor and nurse left. Russ came back to Drew's bedside and laid a hand on his shoulder, clearly freaked out.

"Sorry," Drew murmured.

"Nothing to apologize for," Russ replied. "I called Isabel. And I think you're right—the timing on this is suspicious as fuck."

"Noah—"

"He's in the ICU," Russ answered. "Which is a good thing because even if you two shared a cardiac event, he's in the best place for care. We'll figure this out, Drew. Hang in there—for Noah. Why not close your eyes and rest while you can?"

Why can we not go to our mate? Drew's wolf fussed.

They know we're shifters. They'll let us see him as soon as its safe.

Mates belong together. Even his cat would agree.

Drew wanted to argue, but his body felt heavy and his mind sluggish. He thought of a dozen things he wanted to say, but sleep took him under before he could put any of them into words.

He woke to Russ gently shaking his shoulder and saw that they had a visitor.

"I have a report on Noah's surgery," Dr. Fisher said, pushing an empty wheelchair into the room. "It was touch and go for a while—his heart stopped at one point, but we got it going again. Oddest thing— that shouldn't have happened given his condition."

"Told you—curse," Drew muttered.

The doctor cleared his throat. "You can visit if you like, whenever you're ready," he said, apparently leaving the further discussion of magic for another time. "For now, I'd like you to keep the visit short and use the wheelchair when you're coming and going. If he does well overnight and can be moved to a regular room, we'll move him in with you so you can stay together."

Drew felt a rush of gratitude that made his eyes blur with tears. "What else can you tell me?"

Dr. Fisher sighed. "Noah is doing better, but he's not out of the woods yet. We've gotten his blood volume back up—he'd lost a lot, between the bullet and the surgery itself—and the silver is out of his system. Hydrating him isn't a problem, and for the moment, he's on a feeding tube. There was also the problem of…worms."

Russ bit back a snicker, and Drew leveled a death glare in his direction. "Worms?" Drew echoed. His wolf's bark sounded a lot like a chortle.

"I was told that he's a lynx shifter. And I suspect the worms are a side effect of living off the land. Since lynx prefer rabbits as prey and worms are common for them, it's a natural hazard. A regular animal can often coexist with them, but parasites become much more of a problem in shifters," the doctor told them. "So we had to administer a de-wormer. Not fun, but necessary."

He's not going to like that when he wakes up, his wolf snickered.

Shut up. As long as he's okay, I don't give a damn.

Russ helped Drew into the wheelchair. Drew hated how shaky he still felt, but he kept his mind on Noah instead of his fears, which helped a little.

When Russ pushed him into Noah's room in the ICU, he couldn't stifle a gasp.

"Can you hear his thoughts yet?"

Drew shook his head. "No—at least, not anything that makes sense. More like a 'thought blender.'"

"Doc Fisher gave him some heavy-duty sedatives and painkillers," Russ said. "Maybe if the memories and dreams are scrambled, Noah's getting some real rest without any nightmares."

"He's so still," Drew fretted. His wolf paced and howled, scratching at the ground.

He doesn't smell right, his wolf complained as Drew took a deep breath to accommodate his animal side, but he refused to lick Noah's face. At least, not here in the hospital.

Nothing smells right in a hospital. It's all cleaning supplies and medicine and disinfectant, Drew told his wolf. *I guess you did the right thing, with the bite.*

He will fight harder now, his wolf replied.

I should have asked first.

We are fated mates...a true pairing. What is left to discuss?

That's not how people do things.

You had talked about it. Both of you wished to complete the mating bond. Now, he can draw on your energy.

He can?

The wolf nodded. *I can feel that, even if you cannot. You help to sustain him. That is a good thing.*

"How about if I go get us coffee and give you two some time alone?" Russ asked, and Drew flashed a grateful smile for the best big brother ever.

Drew wheeled himself the last few feet to Noah's bedside. He took his mate's limp hand and twined their fingers together.

"Hang on, Noah. You're in Fox Hollow, and you're safe from the hunters. They can't hurt you here. I'm with you, and I'm going to take care of you."

Drew pressed a kiss to the back of Noah's hand. He sat back and took a good look at his lover. Noah was never completely still, and his expressions were a window to his thoughts. Seeing him drugged into unconsciousness hurt Drew's heart.

"They won't let me stay long, but tomorrow they said I can be with you all day and night. So you've got to get better. We have a lot of living to do together. I need you. You're my mate."

Drew shifted his weight forward, locked the wheels, and planted his hands on the bedrail, steadying himself enough to stand. He leaned forward and kissed Noah's lips, then sank back into the wheelchair.

"The sheriff is working things out so you can stay in town without getting in trouble," Drew told him, unsure what Noah could hear, but knowing that unconscious people often remembered things that were said near them. "And he's got Grantham and his trophy hunter in custody. The psychics and witches are working with Austin to hunt down any accomplices. We can be together and be safe. You just have to get better."

Russ and the doctor arrived at the same time. "I'm afraid I need to ask you to go back to your room," Dr. Fisher said. "But I'll arrange things as we discussed for tomorrow, assuming he moves out of the ICU."

Drew thanked the physician and let Russ wheel him back to his room. When he arrived, Sheriff Armel and a man Drew didn't recognize were waiting in the hallway.

"Hello Drew, Russ," Armel said with a nod. "This is Tribunal Inspector Chatham. We'd like to talk with you."

Drew shot a nervous glance at Russ, who nodded reassuringly. "It'll be okay," Russ told him. "The sheriff and I talked while you were with Noah."

Drew trusted Sheriff Armel, but like many in the supernatural community, he regarded Tribunals with deference and trepidation.

"We're investigating Oliver Grantham and the Sycamore Rod and Gun Club where he found his trophy hunting clients," the inspector said. "Unfortunately, Noah isn't able to give his statement right now, but I understand you and he had several phone calls before the car ran off the road—"

"Before *someone* ran him off the road," Drew interrupted. "Noah was being chased by a police car because Grantham made false reports."

The inspector held up a hand. "Stop. Go back to the beginning. Tell me everything. Don't leave anything out—a case can turn on small details."

"Can I please have my coffee? There's a lot to say, and my throat is dry," Drew gave Russ a beseeching look, and his brother handed over his cup.

Russ pulled a chair up to sit beside Drew, who was still in the wheelchair.

Drew gave Russ a grateful smile and held the insulated cup in both hands like a security blanket. He started from the time Noah accidentally recorded the Bigfoot and then described his fear when he witnessed the trophy hunter shooting the cryptid, and explained Noah's hurried escape.

"Grantham tracked him. Noah managed to get away each time, but Grantham was right behind him. Noah thought Grantham wanted his cameras to get rid of the footage about the Bigfoot and the hunt," Drew told them.

"I guess when Grantham couldn't take care of stopping Noah himself, he cooked up the false police reports to stop him from getting away." Drew paused to drink some coffee. "The last time I heard from Noah, he was on his way to Fox Hollow. Later, Rob called me and told me about the accident and Noah's apartment being ransacked. Rob kept looking into the guide, which is how we found out his name was Grantham. That's all I know."

"The sheriff explained that a rather *unorthodox* alliance of skilled friends helped you narrow down Noah's location," the inspector said, and Drew glanced at Sheriff Armel, whose stony expression softened with a hint of an encouraging smile.

"Fox Hollow is good at taking care of its own," Drew replied, staring down the inspector. "Everyone pitches in to help with what they're good at. If we hadn't gotten to Noah when we did, he would have died, the guide would have made off with the footage, and he'd still be out there booking cryptid hunts."

"We got a warrant to go through the backpack Noah had with him," Sheriff Armel said. "He didn't have any cameras—but he did have the memory cards. They're still being processed, but I'm betting we'll have enough evidence for the Tribunal to put Grantham away for a long time."

"Can they do that? Aren't he and the trophy hunter humans?" Drew never had a reason to pay attention to the Tribunal's workings before.

"It's complicated," Inspector Chatham said. "But we do have interagency reciprocity. We handle anything involving the supernatural, and the other organizations are happy to leave us to it."

"He's not going to get off easy, right?" Drew's tone grew fierce. "I don't want him coming after Noah again—or anyone else. We don't know how many other cryptids he led hunts for before he and Noah crossed paths."

Inspector Chatham shook his head. "He's not going to get off with a warning. I can assure you, this case is being taken seriously."

"Are you going to make Noah testify?" Drew thought about how vulnerable Noah looked, still and quiet on the bed.

"Eventually. When he's able to do so without suffering harm," Chatham replied. "We have enough to hold Grantham and the hunter for now. We found a second hunter lost in the woods and the body of a third who fell to his death. We'll want both you and Noah to give a statement. I'd prefer not to bring his Canadian friend into the matter since he doesn't know about the paranormal world."

"I think that's a good idea," Drew said, glad they could spare Rob from getting more involved.

"We're tracing Grantham's contacts—and the membership at the Rod and Gun Club. Like with the Huntsman problem last year, I'm afraid we're going to learn that this goes beyond one Bigfoot and the attack on Noah," the inspector said.

"Drew, I know this is a hard time for you. I'll be in touch and keep you updated," Sheriff Armel said as he and the inspector turned to go. "I'll also have a guard on Noah's room."

Drew's eyes widened. "Do you think that's necessary—here in Fox Hollow?"

Armel shrugged. "Better safe than sorry. Just until we know Grantham doesn't have any minions who could cause problems."

"Will Noah get his memory cards back? He needs that footage to finish a project." Drew realized that was a less urgent issue for the sheriff but likely to be of high importance to Noah.

"Yes, we'll make sure they're copied and returned promptly. He doesn't need to worry about that," Armel assured him.

Russ watched the sheriff and the inspector leave and turned back to Drew. "You did good talking to them. But you'd better get back in bed before the doctor catches you."

Drew had barely gotten settled when a knock came at the door.

Rich Jeffries poked his head inside. "Is this a bad time? I have news from Isabel."

The brothers waved him in. "Does she have a way to break the curse?" Drew asked.

Jeffries cleared his throat. "Hopefully, yes. She wants to bring the coven here to the hospital to work the spell, and she's asked Sheriff Armel to bring Grantham too."

Drew tensed. "Why would she want that guy anywhere near Noah?"

"Grantham in this life isn't the one who worked the curse. But Isabel believes that it's the same soul. So to untangle the magic, he needs to be present since he got himself caught up in the spell."

Drew didn't like the thought of Grantham being anywhere except in a jail cell, but he understood the need to have all the players together. "After that, he goes right back to jail?"

"I assume so," Jeffries replied. "I don't think the sheriff has gone to all the effort of a rescue mission to let the guy walk out. I imagine the Tribunal will want to be present too."

"It needs to be soon," Russ said. "Drew and Noah both had suspicious heart problems that weren't part of their conditions. Noah's heart stopped in the operating room. The curse isn't fooling around."

"Isabel told me you'd called. She and the coven have been working hard, gathering what they need and preparing," Jeffries replied. "As soon as Noah moves into a room and out of the ICU, they want to work the counter spell. She's with him now, placing protective wards to mute the curse until it can be broken. I imagine she'll come here to do the same once she finishes."

"They told us Noah would be moved tomorrow," Russ replied. "We'll let you know the second it happens."

They chatted for a few more minutes, then Jeffries left. Russ sat in a chair next to Drew's bed. "Talk to me," he said. "I know your wheels are turning."

Drew sighed. Ever since they were boys, Russ had always been good at knowing when he was upset. That bond had been part of the reason he left the pack with Russ and why they worked so well together.

"I know Noah needs to be under observation tonight, but after what happened, I'm afraid to wait," Drew confided. "And when I try to think on the bright side, then I find myself worrying about how we'll all fit in the cabin and whether Noah will be able to stay and—"

"Slow down," Russ said with a fond smile. "Noah is where he needs to be right now, and all those monitors mean if the slightest thing goes wrong, a whole team of people will come running. Add Isabel's wards to that. And, fortunately, you have me," he added as his smile widened to a teasing grin.

"If the sheriff is working on getting Noah's visa and taking care of the charges against him, there's nothing for you to worry about until or unless something falls through. So you can take it off your list," Russ added.

Drew made a face at Russ's list comment, but he knew it was true. "Fair."

"As for the cabin—we've got two bedrooms, and while it's a little snug, there's room for four people. I'm glad we added that half-bath. We're all out during the workday, so we only have to trip over each other on evenings and weekends," Russ reasoned. "Noah may do a lot of editing from home, but he isn't going to shoot wildlife from inside."

"You've got a point. But still—"

"Once we get the current emergency handled, we'll figure out alternatives," Russ went on. "Liam and I have been talking about looking for a cabin nearby—or even building on the property. We won't be far away, but we also won't be underfoot."

"I like the idea of building on the property," Drew mused. "Keeps the pack together."

"Or if you would rather build new, Liam and I can keep the cabin," Russ offered. "We have options."

"You don't think Liam will mind if we're crowded for a little while until we get things worked out? I know you two have been together longer, but we're all still fairly new with our partners." Drew had been worrying about that since the possibility of Noah moving in sooner than expected had surfaced.

"If I know Liam, he's probably already filling the freezer with meals and making sure we've got four of everything," Russ said with a laugh. "Of all the things to worry about, that's one that isn't going to be an issue."

Drew smiled, sleepy. "You and Liam are the best."

They looked up at a knock, and Isabel poked her head inside. "You're awake and decent? This won't take long." She hustled inside, carrying a large tote bag, and gave Drew a once-over.

"You're looking better, but the stain of the curse is still there. We'll fix that soon enough."

She took several items from the bag, mumbling to herself as she worked—or perhaps she was reciting a spell, Drew thought. Isabel walked widdershins around the room, uncoiling a length of white rope along the walls and taping it down across the doorway. She circled the room clockwise and taped a piece of paper on each wall which she chalked with sigils. Then she dusted her hands together, returned her materials to the bag, and said something that made the sigils flare for an instant before they darkened once more.

"The cord is soaked in salt and protective herbs and colloidal silver," she explained. "Less messy in a public place than loose salt. The sigils amplify my warding." Isabel withdrew an amulet on a leather strap from a pocket of her dress and put the necklace over Drew's head.

"Keep this on whenever you leave the room. It'll protect you in the between places."

"Thank you," Drew said.

Isabel grinned. "Oh, I'm just getting started. As the saying goes, you ain't seen nothing yet."

Not long after Isabel left, a nurse brought Drew's dinner tray and checked his vitals. Russ stood. "I'm going to meet Liam in the cafeteria for a bite to eat and call Kerrie to make sure everything went okay at the garage. Then I'll be back."

"You don't have to stay." Drew felt guilty about keeping Russ away from work and Liam. "There's a guard at the door."

Russ huffed. "Like I'd leave it up to the police to protect my little brother. Besides, it's just for tonight. Tomorrow they'll move you and Noah to the same room. It'll all work out."

By the time Russ returned, Drew had finished dinner and settled into bed for the night.

"How's Liam?" Drew asked, already groggy.

"He said to say hi. He's worried about you and Noah. And if I know my feisty fox, he wants to find a way to rip Grantham's ears off."

Drew smiled, figuring the same thing. "I'd like to see that."

Russ chuckled. "So would all of Fox Hollow."

Sleep proved elusive. Drew blamed the naps he had taken, but he knew he was exhausted enough that he should have slept soundly. Nightmares combined his fears about rescuing Noah with dark memories from past lives. In his dreams, they arrived too late to save Noah, either finding Grantham with his body or seeing nothing except blood.

He startled awake, cold with sweat, eyes wide, and sat up in bed.

"Hey—easy there," Russ soothed. He splayed his hand on Drew's back and rubbed circles between his shoulders as Drew tried to steady his breath.

"In every dream, we couldn't stay together," Drew said in a whisper. "I lost him, over and over again. Some were the past lives, others were 'what if' versions gone wrong." He rubbed his fist over his sternum, where he'd felt the pain the day before. "I'm scared."

"I can't blame you," Russ said. "Anyone would be frightened after seeing all those scenarios play out. But it doesn't make them real."

"Some of them were. We've lost each other too soon in four lives, four centuries. Now, just as we have a chance of stopping the curse, what if I lose him anyhow?"

Russ gripped his shoulder. "We're going to do everything possible to keep that from happening."

A knock at the door made them both look up. Dr. Fisher stuck his head in. "Good. You're awake. Noah is stable enough to move out of the ICU, in spite of having a rough night. I think he'll do better if you're with him, even though he's still sedated to help him sleep."

"When will he wake up?" Drew asked.

"By noon, I expect." Dr. Fisher's eyes narrowed. "Did you have trouble sleeping too?"

Drew couldn't hide a yawn, and he suspected that he looked hung-over. "Nightmares. I guess my brain wanted to game out every possibility—and most of them were bad."

"I can give you sleeping pills if you think that would help," Dr. Fisher said. "But if the cause is magical, I don't know if that would help or hurt. If they'll come anyhow, it might not be a good thing to not be able to wake up."

"Pass," Drew said. "And maybe when Isabel breaks the curse, the bad dreams will go away for both of us."

"I heard that Dr. Jeffries met with the hospital administrator to get special dispensation for whatever ritual this requires," Dr. Fisher said. "So I'm guessing it's a bit more involved than lighting candles and reciting a spell."

"Whatever it takes," Drew replied, exhausted but resolute.

"I came to let you know about the room change. We'll be moving Noah in just a few minutes. You'd better get cleaned up so you're ready. As soon as Jeffries gets the okay from the administrator, the witches will be here," Dr. Fisher said, then closed the door.

Drew managed to get to the bathroom on his own today, a feat he'd never thought would make him feel so proud. He stood under the hot water, grateful for good pressure, and let the spray ease his worries.

He dressed quickly, pleased that he didn't need assistance, and tried to ignore the worried buzz in his mind.

We'll do the spell, break the curse, and everything will be okay, he repeated to himself like a mantra. Drew resolutely refused to let the dark thoughts rise from where they lurked at the edges of his consciousness.

A knock on the bathroom door roused him. "C'mon Drew. Noah's settled in. The witches are on their way."

Drew opened the door, still toweling his hair. "I bet that's a sentence you never expected to say."

"Since we've been in Fox Hollow, a lot of things no longer surprise me," Russ replied.

Drew realized that while he was taking a shower, Russ had helped the nurses get Noah settled on a second bed. The wheelchair he despised was waiting by the bathroom door.

"I guess there's no avoiding that?" he asked with a jerk of his head toward the wheelchair.

"Not unless you want us to get jumped by the safety squad," Russ replied. "Why make it complicated? Sit. I'll push."

Drew sat with a huff, pretending to be annoyed. The others hadn't arrived yet, and Drew was grateful for a chance to greet Noah without visitors present. Russ pushed his wheelchair closer.

"I'm going to get coffee. If we're going to do spells, I need caffeine. I'll bring some back for you—don't worry."

Drew appreciated the chance to say hello to Noah with some privacy. He thought Noah's skin looked less pale today, and the shadows beneath his eyes had faded. A glance at the monitors told him that Noah's readings were stronger as well.

He took Noah's hand and kissed it, holding on with a gentle but firm grip. "I'm here. They didn't let me stay with you last night, but you're doing better, and now they moved you so we can sleep in the same room."

He reached out to brush a hand over Noah's shoulder where the bite was hidden by gauze and his hospital gown. "I'm sorry we didn't have more time to discuss the mating bite, but because of it, the hospital recognizes our bond and doesn't shut me out. We can work out the details when you wake up."

Drew rested his cheek against Noah's hand. "The witches are coming. They think they know how to break the curse. I was so scared when you disappeared. I kept thinking that if something happened to you, we wouldn't have another chance to find each other for a hundred years. Please, Noah, you've got to fight to get stronger and come back to me."

For the next several minutes, Drew filled the silence with a recap of what he and Russ had watched on TV in his room and the gossip Liam had provided.

"Apparently, you and I are the talk of Fox Hollow," Drew told him. "It was quite a stir when we got a team together to rescue you. Coming back in the seaplane was dramatic, and enough has leaked out about witches, spells, and reincarnation that I guess we're small-town celebrities, for the moment."

Drew clasped Noah's hand between both of his. "When we do the spell, I need you to be strong. Whatever it takes—so we can be together without the curse and have long, happy lives with each other. Please, hang on." He didn't try to hide that he was begging. If there was a chance that Noah could hear him, Drew needed to get through so his lover could grasp just how desperately he wanted this to work.

Noah murmured, then turned his head toward Drew and opened his eyes. "Drew?" he asked in a raspy voice. "Are you real?"

Drew let out a whoop of joy and lurched forward to kiss Noah on the lips. "I'm here, and I'm real. Welcome back." He held a cup of water with a straw for Noah to sip.

"How did you find me?" Noah sounded groggy, and Drew guessed that the sedatives and painkillers hadn't all worn off.

"Long story for later." Drew grinned from ear to ear because Noah was awake. "The coven is on its way to break the curse. It's still messing with us, and we need to be rid of it for good."

Noah tightened his grip on Drew's hand. "I didn't think I'd see you again," he murmured. "I was afraid I was going to die in the forest— and be stuffed for a trophy."

Drew shivered at the implications and figured that image would haunt his nightmares. "Yeah, but that didn't happen. You're safe. And once we get rid of the curse, we can look forward to a ripe old age together filled with Geritol and Viagra."

Noah smiled. "I bet you'll be a cute old codger."

"You'll be a handsome geezer," Drew teased back, hoping with all his heart they would get the chance to find out.

"I'd better let the doctor know you're awake." Drew pressed the call button. Dr. Fisher arrived with Russ—bearing a tray of coffee cups —right behind him.

"He woke up!" Drew announced.

"I see. That's good news." Dr. Fisher moved to Noah's bedside. Russ handed off a coffee to Drew and then went to stand out of the way by the wall.

"How are you feeling?" the doctor asked Noah.

"Like I got shot with silver and fell down a ravine," Noah replied. "But better than before."

"I should hope so." Dr. Fisher checked Noah's vitals and looked at the readout from the monitors. "You've stabilized, which is great news. I'd expect some soreness and fatigue after all you've been through. We'll deal with that after your visitors finish. Drew tells me there's more going on here than medicine alone can account for."

The door opened, and Isabel strode in, followed by two other women and Dr. Jeffries. Drew figured Isabel had to be in her seventies, but with her timeless haircut, a trendy tracksuit, and Uggs, her true age was difficult to guess.

"Figured I'd find you here," she said to Drew. "These are my coven sisters, Patrice and Megan." Drew suspected the women were all over sixty but looked at least a decade younger. Patrice wore a red flannel shirt over a T-shirt, jeans, and Timberlands. Megan cut a sharp figure in khaki leggings, a black shirt with poet sleeves, and high black boots.

"We knew there wouldn't be enough room for everyone, the others will be watching on livestream and lend their magic to us from a distance," Isabel continued as Jeffries stood with Russ out of the way.

"That works?" Drew asked, surprised. "You can do magic over the internet?"

Isabel and her friends laughed. "Of course. Why not? Magic requires knowledge, intent, and will. Talent helps. We have enough people present to make the connection—the others will add their strength from afar."

While Isabel set up her computer on the tray table, Patrice laid down a braided cord in a large circle around Noah's bed and Drew's wheelchair, but left Isabel's larger cord in place. She murmured words Drew couldn't catch as she walked, and he felt a sense of peace when she linked the ends of the braid together. Patrice went back to the small duffel she'd carried in and returned with four LED candles, which she placed at the quarter marks of the circle.

Megan carefully replaced the pieces of paper Isabel had taped on the room's walls and then chalked new sigils. "We have to improvise sometimes," she said at Drew's questioning look. "The hospital wouldn't take kindly to us lighting candles, marking up the walls with runes, or laying down a salt circle, so we use LEDs, a blessed cord that's been soaked in salt and silver, and make our symbols removable. The purpose is still served."

Isabel stepped away from the laptop, and Drew saw the faces of nine more people in the open video meeting. Then Isabel laid down a braided circle rug and put a silver chalice in the middle. Isabel knelt beside the goblet and took a variety of small sachet bags from the duffel, then she poured out each one into the cup with a murmured phrase.

She looked up and met first Drew's gaze and then Noah's. "The powders and leaves form powerful protection," she told them.

Patrice stepped to the edge of the braid, holding out a mirrored box in her hands like an offering. Isabel accepted it with a nod and set it next to the chalice.

"Mirrors reflect magic," Isabel said. "In this case, the mirrors trap the curse inside the box."

She held up a photograph, and Drew recognized Grantham from his pictures online. Isabel folded the picture and put it into the box, then took a few more items from her bag.

"A photograph of the one who cast the curse. Black salt and bay leaf for warding. A knot to bind the dark magic and selenite to protect from evil," Isabel intoned as she placed each item in the box.

She set the box on a silver plate atop the braided rug and placed a black candle on top. Then Megan took out a piece of parchment and held it up for Drew and Noah to see. "I have written the curse on this paper," she told them, and they watched, wide-eyed, as the parchment burned with a purple flame in a shallow agate cup. "Fire will cleanse it."

Megan rolled a piece of clay in the palm of her hand to warm it, then pressed it into the ashes in the cup and flattened it into a disk. She put the disk back into the cup and held her hand over it as her palm glowed with warm golden light. When she held the disk up, it had hardened. She crumbled it into dust over Isabel's larger chalice.

"We just need one more thing to end the curse," Isabel said as the door opened and Sheriff Armel led a manacled Oscar Grantham into the room.

Drew recoiled and Noah gasped. Russ moved to get between his brother and the guide, but Jeffries shook his head and grabbed him by the arm.

"He's not going anywhere," Armel said, keeping a firm grip on the man, who regarded the others with a baleful glare.

"Apologies, but since he's tangled up in the magic, we thought it best for him to be here when we break the spell," Isabel said.

"I want my lawyer," Grantham spat.

Isabel rounded on the man, and the aura she projected was far more fearsome than her usual appearance. "When what's left of your soul is severed from the curse, mind that I don't just cast it into utter darkness."

Grantham shrank back, sliding partway behind Armel's large form.

"Don't fuck with a real witch, boy," Armel said. "Now shut up and do whatever she tells you."

"Let's get this started." Isabel knelt on the braided rug.

"Hold hands," she told Drew and Noah, who already gripped each other tightly. Isabel looked at Grantham. "Step forward where I can see you. Don't want this magic landing on anyone but you."

Grantham looked at her with wide, terrified eyes, but did as she ordered. Armel took a step back but remained close enough to grab his prisoner.

"Light and life, cast out the stain of death," Isabel said in a clear, strong voice. Patrice and Megan had moved to stand next to each other, holding hands, focused intently on Isabel. The witches on the computer screen murmured supportive phrases Drew couldn't quite hear.

Drew felt his chest grow tight, and a burning sensation simmered beneath his skin.

Noah brought his left hand up to his own chest and looked at Drew with a fearful gaze. Drew squeezed Noah's hand in reassurance, although his own heart beat wildly. A glance at Grantham told him that their tormentor also felt the effects of the spell.

"Cursed tendrils unwind from these souls and burn away in purifying fire." Isabel held her hand over the chalice, and it burst into a smokeless violet flame that leaped inches above the silver rim.

Drew felt like his blood had turned to lava, and his chest

constricted so that he could barely draw breath. Noah wheezed, and his monitors squealed. Out of the corner of his eye, Drew saw Dr. Fisher start toward them, but Jeffries grabbed him by the shoulder and said something that halted the doctor, although he didn't look pleased.

"Malice, be gone. Forever remove the shadow from these spirits and trouble them no more." Isabel gestured over the black candle, and it melted in a slurry of wax to completely encase the mirror box.

Drew thought he might suffocate, starved for air, or that he would burn up from within. His wolf howled in his mind, angry, protective, and panicked. Noah's machines blared alarms, and he struggled to breathe.

Grantham tore at his chest with his hands and sank to his knees.

"So mote it be." All of the witches spoke in unison, and a rush of otherworldly power swept through the room, raising the hair on the back of Drew's neck and sending goosebumps across his skin.

The vise grip on his heart and the fire in his veins vanished as suddenly as they had begun. Drew curled in on himself, heaving for breath, and Noah drew deep, shuddering gasps as the monitors leveled out and stopped shrilling.

Armel knelt next to Grantham to ensure he was alive. The door to the room slammed open to admit worried nurses, and Dr. Fisher sprinted across the room to check on Noah while Russ rushed to Drew's side.

"Is Noah okay?" Drew gasped.

Dr. Fisher didn't answer until he had checked and rechecked Noah's readings and assured himself that the monitors functioned properly. He apologized to the treatment team for worrying them and blamed the malfunction on an energy surge. This being Fox Hollow, and with three witches and what was clearly an occult ritual set up in the room, the nurses gave Fisher the side-eye.

"Sure it is," one of them replied without heat. Drew heard her mutter "malfunction my ass" to her colleague as they left the room.

"Noah's fine," the doctor answered after a third round of checking. He moved around the bed to give Drew just as thorough a going-over and then nodded. "You seem to be unharmed as well."

"How about checking this one too, so I can get him back where he belongs unless the witches need him?" Sheriff Armel said.

Isabel shook her head. "We're done with him, and so is the curse. It's gone."

Dr. Fisher quickly examined Grantham and proclaimed him healthy. Armel manhandled the guide out the door.

"I'm still not quite sure what I saw, but it was impressive," Dr. Fisher said, sounding a little spooked.

"You saw magic done right," Isabel replied, dusting off her hands as she stood. "We'll clean up after ourselves, but I want to check these boys out for myself to be certain our work is finished."

Drew tried not to flinch when Isabel approached after that display of supernatural power. She gently smacked him up the side of the head.

"What's the matter, boy? Never seen a witch work before?" Isabel asked, chuckling.

"Nothing quite like that." Drew felt like he'd just been called on the carpet by his elementary school principal.

Drew wasn't sure what he expected, but Isabel skimmed her hand, palm down, an inch above his body from head to toe. She didn't say anything until she finished and gave a satisfied nod.

"It'll do." Isabel walked around the bed to do the same to Noah, and Drew held his breath. "Can't sense a bit of the curse now in either of you. Guess it worked."

Patrice and Megan gathered the magical items and tucked them back into the duffel, then signed off of the video call and put away the laptop. Isabel stood at the end of Noah's bed and regarded the two men.

"You should heal faster now, without heart problems. When you leave here, wash with Epsom salts and lavender. Cleanse your living space with the smoke of purifying herbs, and drink green tea with ginger every day for a week," Isabel told them.

"Sprinkle salt along the window sills and doorways. The curse is gone, but the wound is still tender, and you want to repel entities that would try to take advantage," she continued.

"Entities?" Drew echoed.

Isabel nodded. "There are all kinds of things in the shadows. Be glad you don't know more." She handed each of them a small velvet bag closed with a knotted drawstring and gave Noah a duplicate of the amulet Drew wore.

"Keep this with you at all times for the next week. And I do mean all times," she repeated, giving them a look. "Even in the shower. *Everywhere*. Don't open them. They are another layer of protection. In exactly one week, burn them under the moon and scatter the ashes in running water. Wear the amulets as long as you please—they are also protective."

Drew gripped Noah's hand tight and felt a shudder pass through both of them. "Thank you," he said, and Noah nodded.

"Are there really so many threats?" Noah asked.

Isabel's eyes held the memories of old horrors. "We who are guardians see terrible things so that others sleep soundly. It is an honor and a burden."

She turned her attention to Jeffries. "I'll make sure to send you notes for your files. Keep me posted." With that, she and the rest of her coven swept out of the room.

"I'll let you know if anything else important turns up," Jeffries told them before he followed them out.

"You okay?" Russ asked, giving Drew the kind of once-over he had when they were kids and Russ thought Drew was hiding being sick.

Drew gave a tired smile in return. "Yeah. I'm tired, but I feel fine. Better than fine, now that the curse is gone."

"Noah?" Russ gave him a look.

"What Drew said. I feel...lighter somehow."

Russ nodded. "Alright. I'll believe you. Liam texted me and wants to hear how this all went, and I need to go to the garage to finish some things."

"Do you need—?" Drew began, feeling guilty about not handling his share of the work.

"No. Absolutely not," Russ said, reminding Drew of their father. "Your job is to get better and help Noah. Don't worry—when Liam and I go on our honeymoon, you can cover for me."

"Deal," Drew replied, relieved.

"Don't forget to eat," Russ warned. "Both of you. The sooner you get better and leave here, the faster you can get to eat all the cookies Liam's been baking. We'll even stop by Bear Necessities and get Jack's special donuts."

"Bribery works," Drew said with a laugh. "Go see your fox. And… thanks for everything."

Russ left, and he was finally alone again with Noah. Drew folded Noah's hand between his own. "Tell me the truth—how are you?"

Noah paused as if taking an internal inventory. "Good. I never noticed a shadow dragging me down, but now that it's gone, I can tell the difference."

Drew nodded. "Me too. And now someday, I'll find out how you look with wrinkles."

Noah snorted. "Shifters don't age quickly. You'll have to wait a long time."

Drew nuzzled their joined hands. "That suits me just fine. Now hurry and get better so I can finally jump your bones." The contented growl he got from his wolf made their success all the sweeter.

EPILOGUE
NOAH

THREE WEEKS LATER

"I HOPE I never need to see another Tribunal trial," Noah said as he and Drew got into the truck where Russ was waiting to drive them home.

"Most people in the supernatural community never even see one trial. Hell, they don't know Tribunals exist unless something really fucked up happens." Drew closed the door and fastened his seat belt.

"You both did well." Russ pulled away from the curb, having appointed himself their chauffeur for the day.

"It's over," Noah said, letting his head fall back and closing his eyes. "Grantham is going to jail, the Rod and Gun Club has shut down their private hunts, and the clients discovered that cryptids bite back. All in all, a good day."

"Not to mention, you're off the de-wormer pills," Russ joked.

Noah grimaced. "Ha, ha, ha. My lynx kept me fed. Taking a few pills is better than starving."

Damn right, his lynx said, preening. *You tell him.*

"I don't know what was worse—the trial or all the lead up to the trial," Drew said, utterly exhausted. He held Noah's hand, and they sat wedged together hip-to-knee in the truck's cab.

"The lead-up," Noah replied. "I kept thinking of all the ways it could go wrong, or how Grantham could wiggle out of the charges. I didn't want him to come after us—or anyone else."

"I think Inspector Chatham was on a mission when he prosecuted this case," Russ said. "He can be scary. I'm glad he was on our side."

"The important thing is, it's over." Drew leaned against Noah, who wrapped an arm around his shoulders. Drew's hand fell to Noah's thigh, and Noah knew that only Russ's presence in the cab kept Drew from stroking the inseam to his crotch.

"Get a room, you two," Russ teased.

"We have one," Drew replied, grinning. "Planning to make use of it." He gave Noah's leg a squeeze.

"TMI, dude!" Russ protested.

Drew gave a wicked laugh. "Like I haven't had to bleach my brain with you and Liam carrying on."

"We are always circumspect," Russ said, managing to keep a straight face.

"That's what you call it? I remember your cowboy phase—"

"Alright, that's enough," Russ stopped him. "You've made your point."

"Cowboy?" Noah whispered.

"You don't want to know," Drew whispered back.

The truck pulled up to the cabin, and Liam bounded out on the porch to greet them. "Well, how did it go? Don't make me wait for an answer!"

Russ pulled Liam into his arms and a lingering kiss. "Drew and Noah were total bosses on the witness stand. Calm, cool, and collected. Grantham, the hunter who shot the Bigfoot, and the two survivors who hunted Noah, have been taken to a Tribunal facility where they'll remain in spelled stasis for the rest of their lives, and a cover story was concocted to explain their absence."

"Good. Serves them right," Liam replied. Noah had learned that the fox-shifter was deeply loyal and never forgot an injustice done to someone he loved.

"Is the food here? I'm starving." Russ changed the subject.

"I picked up wings and pizza on my way home," Liam said. "They're in the oven—warm and hopefully not burned to a crisp by now."

"We aren't that late," Russ protested.

"The proof is in the pizza," Liam replied airily with a toss of his head, and once again, Noah could almost imagine the swish of his fox tail.

Fortunately, nothing had overcooked. Drew and Noah ate more than usual, and Noah was sure that stress accounted for the hunger. As they ate, they took turns filling Liam in on the trial.

"Wow, you had all the excitement," Liam said, licking the grease off his lips. "Well, almost all," he added coyly. He wiped his hands, got up from the table, and went to the counter, where he held up a large envelope.

"Sheriff Armel delivered this personally," Liam added with a cat-that-ate-the-canary smile, waving the envelope back and forth. "He said it's your visa. Welcome to the US of A."

Drew grabbed Noah and pulled him into a kiss. "You get to stay!" he said breathlessly when they parted.

Noah grinned. "And thanks to the new photography contract I just landed, I can also pay my keep. Plus, Rob picked up the lease on my apartment, and he's going to rent it out to tourists by the week to make some extra cash." Rob had been relieved to know that Noah recovered from his injuries and was cheering for him and Drew. Noah made sure to let his friend know he was welcome to visit Fox Hollow any time.

Amid all the drama of recovering from his injuries, moving to a new country, and the Tribunal, Noah had finished the documentaries he owed the Ottawa station and submitted proposals on several posted opportunities. Three of those had hired him, meaning he could pay his share of expenses for the next several months.

"The library and Arts Festival got preliminary approval for next year's budget," Liam added, looking smug. "And that includes a grant for one of Noah's documentaries. Also, Adiel and Joel are interested in talking with you about collaborating on a paid project for the 'secret' history initiative."

A true history of Fox Hollow couldn't be disclosed outside of the supernatural community. Adiel, a historian with the Fox Institute, and Joel, a still photographer who was Adiel's personal and professional partner, were documenting that secret history.

"That sounds wonderful—and more than I imagined," Noah replied, grateful and a little overwhelmed.

After dinner, they watched the new superhero movie on streaming and celebrated with a good bottle of whiskey. Drew and Noah snuggled on one end of the couch while Liam and Russ sat close together at the other end.

All through the movie, Drew traced his finger just under Noah's waistband in the back or stroked the sensitive skin on his side beneath his shirt. Noah jiggled his leg so that it rubbed up against Drew's and let his thumb rub circles on Drew's palm. At one point, he wrapped one hand around Drew's index finger and thrust slowly in and out.

Noah saw how Drew's cock chubbed in his jeans, and his own was painfully hard. In the couple of days since his escape from Grantham and his hunter, Drew and Noah hadn't been together in private outside of time in their hospital room. There had been kisses, hugs, furtive hand jobs, and a couple of spectacular blow jobs, but between his recuperation and the Tribunal, the stress had thrown cold water on their plans for a hot sex reunion.

Now, with the trial over and everyone healthy, Noah had plans to change that.

He jolted when Drew slipped a hand behind him and traced his spine to slip a teasing finger down the cleft of his ass.

Noah shivered, growing even harder. He shifted, trying to give himself more room as his cock strained against the zipper of his fly.

He leaned toward Drew and pressed a kiss to his forehead as he slid two fingers up and down on Drew's wrist.

"Would you two get a room already?" Liam groaned theatrically. "Not only are you stinking up the room with pheromones, but the longer you're awake, the longer you're cockblocking me."

Russ elbowed his mate and rolled his eyes.

"What?" Liam demanded. "It's the truth."

"Well, when you put it that way, it's really our civic duty," Drew replied with a smirk. He rose and grabbed Noah's wrist, dragging him to his feet. Drew made a show of stretching and gave an exaggerated yawn.

"Oh, my! Look at the time. Who knew it was so late?" Drew mocked in a sing-song voice. Russ shot him the bird.

"Just go, already," Russ said, with a joking, put-upon tone. "And keep the noise down. We don't need sound effects."

Noah felt his cheeks color, but Drew just laughed shamelessly. "No promises," Drew told them with a smoldering look that went right to Noah's leaking cock.

Drew tugged Noah down the hall, and Noah didn't think he had ever been this turned on. When they reached their room, Drew shut the door behind them and pushed Noah against the wall.

"I want you; been waiting too long." Drew kissed Noah, licking into the seam of his mouth until his mate opened to him.

Noah let Drew plunder his mouth, tracing his lips and sucking on his tongue. Noah liked the fierce hunger in Drew's kiss. He brought his arms up to pull Drew closer.

Drew slotted his thigh between Noah's legs and Noah's hips jerked. Drew leaned closer, pressing their erections together, and set up delicious friction.

"Keep that up, and I'm going to cream my pants before we ever get to the main event," Noah gasped, arching.

"That's okay," Drew murmured. He kissed Noah, then mouthed along his jaw and down Noah's neck to the still-reddened mating bite. The drag of Drew's stubble and tongue over the sensitive just-healed mark made Noah shake with pure lust.

Noah pivoted and pushed Drew against the wall in his place. "I want to fuck you," Noah growled. "I want you to fuck me. I want it all."

Drew nipped at Noah's neck, tiny welts that didn't break the skin but would leave a mark. Noah thought his blood might boil.

"Want you too, but not up against the wall—at least, not the first time," Drew clarified.

Noah pushed Drew's leg between his own and rode his thigh as he kissed him hard and ran his hands up and down Drew's sides.

They had spent so much of their time apart, satisfying themselves with phone sex, jerking off to video chat cameras, and resigned to frustrating wet dreams. The fantasies they detailed when they talked each other through orgasms had been explicit about adding anal to the positions they tried.

But their visits had been short and too far apart. Each time, they had planned to expand their repertoire, but something always got in the way. Noah knew that what they had already done counted as sex, but he still longed to join himself completely with Drew and share that new intimacy.

"Too many clothes," Drew breathed. "We need to get naked. Now."

"I can help you with that." Noah took his time unbuttoning Drew's overshirt, then pushed his T-shirt off to expose Drew's toned chest and abs.

"My turn," Drew said, sliding his hands down Noah's shoulders and arms. He tugged Drew's shirt over his head, then pulled him into a tight hug, skin to skin.

They fumbled with each other's belts, buttons, and zippers. Noah pushed Drew's jeans and boxer briefs down over his ass, freeing his hard, blood-dark cock. Drew kicked the clothes away and slid his hands into Noah's pants, tugging them down until they pooled at his ankles. He took a long, appreciative look at Noah's dick, which made Noah even hornier.

"How do you want it?" Drew's voice dropped into a sexy growl.

"Watched a video where the guys switched in the middle, took turns fucking each other. Want that someday—looked hot as hell," Noah replied in a low rumble. "But the first time? Want you in me."

"First-first time?" Drew asked, surprised.

"*Our* first. And…first in a very long time. It's been a while," Noah admitted.

"Same here," Drew admitted, blushing. "I don't have a lot of experience."

Noah let his fingertips trace Drew's cheek and gently tipped his chin until their eyes met. "Even better reason to let you top. Do you have lube?"

Drew blushed harder. "I made sure I had a new bottle."

Noah leaned in and kissed him, sweet and hot. "Then we've got everything we need." Shifters couldn't get STDs, so condoms weren't necessary. Noah had packed his supply of lube, but it had gotten left behind with his luggage in the crash.

They tumbled into bed, tangled up with each other. Noah loved the feel of skin-on-skin, the friction of body hair, and the dark stubble on Drew's face. He could smell their arousal, mixed with the unmistakable scent of his *mate*.

"Want you to bite me when we come," Drew admitted. "That way, we're both marked. I know it's not strictly necessary, but—"

"But it's hot as hell," Noah replied and licked at the spot he had fantasized about biting. "God, Drew—Wanted this for so long."

Drew had landed on top of Noah when they fell onto the bed, his hips slotted between Noah's thighs, their cocks rubbing together just right. He kissed Noah's lips, then worked his way down his throat, pausing to lick and suck each nipple until they were hard.

"Love when you do that," Noah said, voice husky. "Do you have a fantasy about how we do this? Want my ass in the air, or us facing each other? Or do you want me to ride you?"

Drew bit back a moan. "Ride me. Want to watch you."

"This first time...not going to last real long. I promise I can do better with practice," Noah warned.

"I don't care. Just want to feel you."

Noah moved so that his knees bracketed Drew's hips and sat back on his heels. He took the lube and poured some into his palm, cupping his hands for a few seconds to warm the gel before he made a show of stroking both their cocks.

"Don't tease. I'm so ready," Drew said, breathless.

Noah added a little more lube to his palm and slicked the fingers of his right hand, then reached behind himself and turned just enough so Drew could see. He slid one finger between his ass cheeks and let himself enjoy the sensation of running it along the rim.

"Ever been rimmed?" he asked breathlessly as he worked the first finger into his too-tight hole.

"Read about it. Watched it on videos. Always thought it was hot. Haven't done it."

"We're gonna have so many firsts together." Noah met Drew's gaze and loved how his lover shivered at his look. "When it's your turn, I'm gonna feast on your ass." Noah eased his finger in deeper, letting his body adjust.

"You've got such a perfect butt. I'm going to hold those cheeks apart and run the tip of my tongue over your hole, then lick you, then back to that tip tracing all around the rim. Get you so wet, then I'm going to work my tongue inside and keep on licking and poking until you're begging for my cock," Noah fantasized out loud.

Dirty talk definitely got Drew wound up, as Noah had learned from their long-distance phone sex and video jerk-off sessions. He added a third finger to his ass, relishing the burn, letting his body open up after a long dry spell.

"I could rim you for an hour, tease you with my fingers until you're nice and open. Ever do it to yourself with your fingers?"

Drew's breath hitched. "Yeah. It was okay—"

"Oh, babe. When you do it right, it is much better than 'okay,'" Noah assured him, starting up a rhythm as he fucked himself on his fingers, spreading them apart to stretch his hole wider. He felt impatient, afraid he'd shoot before he even got settled on Drew's cock.

"And that little magic button that makes you see stars and go off like a rocket? Gonna make sure I stroke that sweet spot every time I pound into your sweet, tight ass," Noah promised. Between the visuals and Noah's porn-worthy narrative, Drew was panting, and a sheen of sweat glistened on his skin, eyes lust-blown. Noah thought he'd never seen anyone more beautiful.

"Ready to fuck me?" he asked, open enough to make the entry more burn than pain and impatient to wait longer. He removed his fingers, hating the sudden emptiness, and lubed Drew's cock, pleased to find him hard as steel from Noah's little show.

"God, yes!"

Noah met Drew's gaze as he aligned himself, holding the base while he let the head breech his hole. His breath caught at the intrusion. Drew's cock was longer and slimmer than his own. Noah let himself descend a couple more inches, allowing Drew to fill him, adjusting to the sensation. Then he sank the rest of the way and let his head fall back with pleasure.

Noah moved, rising and falling, circling his hips and giving Drew his own, very private lap dance.

"Like that?" he teased, although it was clear from Drew's expression that he was overwhelmed with sensation. "So many ways we can do this, make it a little different each time. I've got a few favorites I want to show you and some new ones to try out."

"Less talking, more fucking," Drew managed.

Noah quickened his pace, then wrapped his hand around his cock. It didn't take much to get himself hard again once his body opened to the shaft inside it, and Noah figured Drew was so overwhelmed he didn't have the presence of mind to stroke him through it this time.

"Getting close?" Noah breathed, knowing he wasn't going to last much longer. The pillow under Drew's head meant he had a good view, both of Noah jerking himself off and of their joined bodies. Drew's hand gripped his hips tightly enough Noah knew he'd have marks, although Noah controlled the pace.

He changed his angle enough so that Drew's cock slipped across his spot on each stroke.

"Come with me, Drew."

Drew arched to meet Noah's thrusts, then Noah felt his lover tense before his hips bucked as his orgasm claimed him. Noah bit down hard on the spot where Drew's shoulder and neck joined, sealing their union with a mating bite. He came seconds later, his release fountaining warm and sticky over his fist.

Finally, his lynx snarked, clearly happy about the bite.

They were both breathing heavy and covered with sweat. Drew reached up to pull Noah closer so he could kiss him, hard and claiming.

"I love you," Drew said, meeting Noah's gaze like a challenge.

"Love you too. That was amazing."

"Yeah?" Drew's self-conscious smile reminded Noah how inexperienced his lover was with some things.

"Oh, yeah. And the best part? Practice makes perfect," Noah added with a wink.

He pulled off gently, then reached for his discarded T-shirt to wipe them both clean. He tossed it toward the laundry basket before settling in beside Drew beneath the covers. In his mind, his lynx purred.

After a long day and a hard climax, Noah knew they weren't going to stay awake much longer. He reached up to push a lock of Drew's hair out of his eyes and smiled at the affection and contentment he saw there.

"Plenty of time for round two in the morning," he promised.

Drew smiled. "Then hurry up and go to sleep. That's definitely something worth waking up early for."

Six months *later*

Everyone cheered as Russ and Liam cut an elegant white wedding cake covered with fondant branches and pine cones in a glistening sugar "snow." Drew and Noah raised their Champagne glasses in salute.

While the hotel staff whisked the cake away to be plated and served, Russ and Liam headed onto the dance floor at the Fox Hollow Hotel's ballroom.

"They clean up surprisingly well," Noah said, looking at Russ and Liam in their tuxedos. The new husbands slow danced to a favorite song, so clearly in love it made Noah's heart squeeze. When the song finished, they walked away hand-in-hand, laughing.

"Yes, they do, amazing as it seems," Drew replied with a chuckle.

Noah knew that they were both thrilled to see Russ and Liam tie the knot. He slipped an arm around Drew and pulled him close. Drew rested his head on Noah's shoulder.

"We've got a couple of minutes before they bring the cake out," Noah said. "Come with me."

He grabbed Drew's hand and led him out of the warm ballroom to the balcony. The temperature change made them shiver, but the view was worth it—a full moon in a clear, starry sky over Fox Lake.

For a moment, they stood with Drew facing outward, wrapped in Noah's arms from behind, taking in a moment of quiet after a hectic day.

Drew looked perplexed when Noah let go, then came around to stand in front of him and suddenly went down on one knee.

"What—?" Drew's eyes went wide, and he caught his breath.

"Drew Lowe, fated mate and true pairing, would you and your wolf do my lynx and I the honor of being our husband? In this life, and all the others yet to come?" He held out an opened velvet box to reveal two matching gold rings.

Drew sank to his knees and wrapped Noah's hands and the box in his own. "Yes. Definitely yes—for all time."

Noah slipped a ring on Drew's right ring finger, and Drew nearly dropped its match since he was shaking with emotion.

You were mated with the bite. The ring does not make you mates. But... will there be cake if you have rings? his lynx asked, licking his lips.

Cake for everyone—including you, Noah promised.

They walked back inside, hands linked, having decided to keep their engagement a secret from everyone except Rob for tonight so as not to steal any of Russ and Liam's thunder.

After the cake, everyone went back to dance, and guests stopped by the head table to see the happy couple to wish them well. Rob had driven down for the event and seemed to be hitting it off with their Fox Hollow friends. Late in the evening, when the DJ announced the last song, Noah and Drew swayed together on the dance floor under dimmed lights. Noah kissed Drew and gave him a look that promised more once they were alone.

"You clean up pretty well too, Wolfie," Noah murmured.

"Not too shabby yourself, Catman. Now what do you say we go home, dance in the sheets, and howl at the moon?"

AFTERWORD

I love the Adirondacks. We went camping there for many summers when I was growing up, and it's still one of my happy places. The town of Fox Hollow is loosely based on Long Lake, NY, and if you ever visit, you'll see some of the landmarks that inspired the fictional version.

While *Again* is the direct sequel to *Huntsman* in the *Fox Hollow: Zodiac* series, there are several other titles in the Fox Hollow "neighborhood"—*Haven, Imaginary Lover, Gruff,* and *Trash and Treasure* are available on Kindle, KU, and paperback. *Romp* and *Nutty for You* are free on Prolific Works. Since characters have a habit of showing up over and over—including in *Again*—you'll want to read them all and meet the crew!

All my Morgan Brice books (and all the modern Gail Z. Martin books) cross over, so you're correct if you thought you picked up on some indirect references. Those hackers who helped find Grantham are Teag Logan (*Deadly Curiosities*) and Seth Tanner (*Witchbane*). The other private investigators who are helping Austin track down clues are Ben Nolan (*Treasure Trail*) and Brent Lawson (*Sons of Darkness*). I love leaving little bread crumb clues for readers to find!

ACKNOWLEDGMENTS

Thank you so much to my editor, Jean Rabe, to my husband and writing partner Larry N. Martin for all his behind-the-scenes hard work, and to my wonderful cover artist Adrijus Guscia and cover wrap artist Natania Barron. Thanks also to the Shadow Alliance and the Worlds of Morgan Brice street teams for their support and encouragement, and to my fantastic beta readers: Asher, Austin, Carole, Chris, Donald, Grace, Sandra, and Seth, plus my promotional crew and the ever-growing legion of ARC readers who help spread the word!

I couldn't do it without you! And of course, thanks and love to my "convention gang" of fellow authors for making road trips and virtual cons fun.

ABOUT THE AUTHOR

Morgan Brice is the romance pen name of bestselling author Gail Z. Martin. Morgan writes urban fantasy male/male paranormal romance, with plenty of action, adventure, and supernatural thrills to go with the happily ever after.

Gail writes epic fantasy and urban fantasy, and together with co-author hubby Larry N. Martin, steampunk and comedic horror, all of which have less romance and more explosions.

On the rare occasions Morgan isn't writing, she's either reading, cooking, or spoiling two very pampered dogs.

Watch for additional new series from Morgan Brice and more books in the Witchbane, Badlands, Treasure Trail, Kings of the Mountain, and Fox Hollow universes coming soon!

Where to find me, and how to stay in touch

Join my Worlds of Morgan Brice Facebook Group and get in on all the behind-the-scenes fun! My free reader group is the first to see cover reveals, learn tidbits about works-in-progress, have fun with exclusive contests and giveaways, find out about in-person get-togethers, and more! It's also where I find my beta readers, ARC readers, and launch team! Come join the party! https://www.Facebook.com/groups/WorldsOfMorganBrice

Find me on the web at https://morganbrice.com. Sign up for my newsletter and never miss a new release! http://eepurl.com/dy_8oL. You can also find me on Twitter: @MorganBriceBook, on Pinterest (for Morgan and Gail): pinterest.com/Gzmartin, on Instagram as Morgan-BriceAuthor, on YouTube at https://www.youtube.com/c/GailZ-

MartinAuthor/ on Bookbub https://www.bookbub.com/authors/morgan-brice and now on TikTok @MorganBriceAuthor

Enjoy two free short stories set in Fox Hollow: Nutty for You - https://claims.prolificworks.com/free/r54nldjv and Romp - https://claims.prolificworks.com/free/I4lCYKli

Check out the ongoing, online convention ConTinual www.facebook.com/groups/ConTinual

Support Indie Authors

When you support independent authors, you help influence what kind of books you'll see more of and what types of stories will be available, because the authors themselves decide which books to write, not a big publishing conglomerate. Independent authors are local creators, supporting their families with the books they produce. Thank you for supporting independent authors and small press fiction!

ALSO BY MORGAN BRICE

Badlands Series

Badlands

Restless Nights, a Badlands Short Story

Lucky Town, a Badlands Novella

The Rising

Cover Me, a Badlands Short Story

Loose Ends

Leap of Faith, a Badlands/Witchbane Novella

Night, a Badlands Short Story

No Surrender

Fox Hollow Zodiac Series

Huntsman

Again

Fox Hollow Universe

Romp, a Fox Hollow Novella

Nutty for You, a Fox Hollow Short Story

Imaginary Lover

Haven

Gruff

Trash and Treasure, a Fox Hollow Novella

Kings of the Mountain Series

Kings of the Mountain

The Christmas Spirit, a Kings of the Mountain Short Story

Sins of the Fathers

Treasure Trail Series

Treasure Trail

Blink

Light My Way Home, a Treasure Trail Novella

Witchbane Series

Witchbane

Burn, a Witchbane Novella

Dark Rivers

Flame and Ash

Unholy

The Devil You Know

The Christmas Crunch, a Witchbane Short Story

Sandwiched, Witchbane Short Story

www.ingramcontent.com/pod-product-compliance
Lightning Source LLC
Chambersburg PA
CBHW020628110726
47899CB00002B/693